AFTER THE WEEPING

AFTER THE WEEPING

David Mark

SEVERN
HOUSE

First world edition published in Great Britain and the USA in 2025
by Severn House, an imprint of Canongate Books Ltd,
14 High Street, Edinburgh EH1 1TE.

severnhouse.com

British Library Cataloguing-in-Publication Data
A CIP catalogue record for this title is available from the British Library.

ISBN-13: 978-1-4483-1534-5 (cased)
ISBN-13: 978-1-4483-1884-1 (paper)
ISBN-13: 978-1-4483-1535-2 (e-book)

All Severn House titles are printed on acid-free paper.

FSC
www.fsc.org
MIX
Paper | Supporting
responsible forestry
FSC® C013056

Typeset by Palimpsest Book Production Ltd., Falkirk, Stirlingshire, Scotland.
Printed and bound in Great Britain by TJ Books, Padstow, Cornwall.

The manufacturer's authorised representative in the EU for product safety is
Authorised Rep Compliance Ltd, 71 Lower Baggot Street, Dublin D02 P593
Ireland (arccompliance.com)

Praise for the DS Aector McAvoy Series

'A satisfyingly nuanced and complex procedural'
Kirkus Reviews on *Past Redemption*

'[A] dark, creepy, twisted mystery that will keep readers
awake far into the night'
Booklist Starred Review of *The Burning Time*

'An involving, nail-biting police procedural from
a masterful storyteller'
Kirkus Reviews on *Flesh and Blood*

'A fine police procedural . . . Ian Rankin fans
will be pleased'
Publishers Weekly on *Past Life*

'[Mark is] on the level of Scottish and English
contemporaries such as Denise Mina, Val McDermid,
and Peter Robinson'
Library Journal Starred Review of *Cruel Mercy*

'To call Mark's novels police procedurals is like calling
the Mona Lisa a pretty painting'
Kirkus Reviews Starred Review of *Cruel Mercy*

About the author

David Mark spent seven years as crime reporter for the *Yorkshire Post* and now writes full-time. A former Richard & Judy pick, and a *Sunday Times* bestseller, he is the author of the DS Aector McAvoy series, the Sal Delaney police procedurals and a number of standalone thrillers. He lives in Northumberland with his family.

www.davidmarkwriter.co.uk

'How blessed are some people, whose lives have no fears, no dreads; to whom sleep is a blessing that comes nightly, and brings nothing but sweet dreams.'

—Bram Stoker, *Dracula*

PROLOGUE

*Dreghet Orphanage, Carpathian Mountains, Romania
April, 1991*

'This is the Dying Room.'

A spilled yolk of sunlight bleeds through barred, barbed windows. It oozes into this rat-grey, bog-damp space; lends a pale, sulphurous sheen to the row upon row of cribs, cradles – cages.

He smells a deep foulness – gags on the reek of it. Feels the tiny particles of grime adhere to his skin, climb into his mouth, nose, eyes. He presses his hand to his mouth. Breathes in the grease and cigarettes of his own skin. Tugs at his beard as if trying to pull himself away. He becomes aware of the silence. Feels it creeping into and over him; a chill tide of empty air.

'Bad children. Bad blood.'

He feels her beside him. Smells her: all wet wool and hairspray, all rose water and spiced meat. She slaps, absently, at a chapped little fist that clutches the flaking metal bars. Glances into the cold corridor. A child is holding a mop between two half-formed hands: scabbed flippers clasped in prayer. Soundlessly, he smears the mop-head across the damp floor. Raises his head and sees her staring. Jerks as if electrocuted and scuttles away, one leg dragging like a tail.

She joins him at the bars. Follows his gaze.

'Days,' she says, shrugging. 'Perhaps more, perhaps less. Who can say?'

He peers down into the cage. Thinks of nature programmes. Thinks of subterranean burrows; pink shapes blindly mewling, suckling, crawling over one another in the blackness of the earth. He wishes he'd stayed in the truck with Paddy. Wishes he'd let his new mate come and deal with this. He doubts it would bother him. Hasn't seen anything shift the mad Irishman's unnerving little half-smile.

'Imbeciles,' she says, without judgement. 'Cripples. No good.'

He feels his gorge rise afresh. Glimpses a limb wriggle free from the tangle of sodden blankets. Sees a clubbed fist reach out for the upended bottle, its contents dripping, dripping: greying fluid from a plastic teat.

'Do not look. They will make you sad.'

He leans forwards. Moves to nudge the bottle towards the grasping hand. Jerks his head back as the flies buzz fatly upwards: swollen, blood-filled polka dots dancing in his vision, humming at his ear.

'These not for you. No good. No point.'

He forces himself to stay. Grips the rusting metal of the bars; paint flaking against his palms, knuckles bulging against the skin: chicks bursting from pale shells.

'We go. I show you better.'

He feels dizzy. Sick. His thoughts slosh in his skull. There's a static drone behind his eyes, across his brow: his joints all thrumming metal and grinding cartilage. He couldn't move if he wanted to.

'They're alive?' he asks.

The woman gives another shrug. 'Until the Lord calls them.' Crosses herself, half-heartedly. Turns away from the crib.

'I need to see,' he says, under his breath. He needs to touch the waxy, mottled skin. Needs to commune with this dying flesh.

She sighs, the sound theatrical, forced. He smells strong coffee. Smells decay. She pulls up the cuff of her jumper and licks her wrists. Reaches through the bars of the crib and angles her arm until the damp patch of skin is beneath the still, open mouth. The flies rise. Settle. Feed.

She straightens up. Shrugs again. He thinks of French waiters. Thinks of wine.

'We go, yes? Better children. Pretty children.'

He can't make himself let go of the bars. Can't bring himself to follow this stout, flat-footed woman deeper into hell. He'd thought he had seen the worst this country had to offer. Envies himself his ignorance. Knows that he will never again be who he was. Knows that nothing will ever be the same.

'You want? Why? For who?'

The thing in the crib begins to move. For an instant he sees twisted, distended limbs. Makes out a malformed foot; a twist of elbow, wrist; a turned-back ankle. Sees the curve of ribs cutting against mottled, fatless flesh.

'How many?' he asks, his voice a breath.

'In here? Three. That one – already dead. These two – they cling to each other. We pull them apart, they find one another again. Like tree roots. Like branches, yes?'

She plucks at his sleeve. Nods towards the doorway. She is busy, she says. He can do what he came here to do, or he can be on his way.

'You take picture, yes? For Mummy? Daddy? They not want these. These . . . no use. No good. Why cry for those who cannot be saved?'

He forces himself to let go of the bars. Staggers back as if the metal had contained an electrical charge. He steps in wetness; steps on meat. Looks down into dark eyes; clippered skull; a sheen of scabs and lesions.

'Fata rea!' she barks at the silent, twisted boy who stares up from the sodden cement floor. She raises a hand. The child at his feet flinches, stiffens. He feels curved fingers grasping at his calves; feels the greasy warmth of the trembling child as it huddles against him.

'Don't!' he says. 'Don't hurt him.'

'Him?' She laughs; an ugly sound that bounces back off the damp grey walls; multiplying, echoing, filling the half-dark space with hollow reverberations. 'This is girl. Maria. Do not touch. Unclean, yes? You understand?'

He puts his hand to his stomach, holding himself. Thinks of home. Of the way his wife cradled her belly in those last weeks of pregnancy; the feeling of those little fists and feet beneath his palm. Remembers singing against her swollen gut; the promises he had made – the life he had sworn to provide. Feels tears silvering the grime upon his cheeks. Feels his throat close as if his neck was being stepped on.

'You bring toys, yes? Money? Clothes? We make use – help children that can be helped. These no good. No mother. No father. Nobody to say yes to adoption. These . . . there is no point, yes? They serve no purpose.'

Through the bars, a bone-white hand, reaching out through the twist of rotting, sodden blankets. Fingers like lugworms, curling around the metal. Flies rising. Settling. He thinks of bats, pinned in glass cages. Thinks of butterflies twisting beneath the glare of the magnifying glass; wings smouldering, burning, erupting into flame.

'I can't . . .' he begins. 'Can't walk out. Not now I've seen . . .'

'You not take. You take, they ask questions. We lose money, yes. These children – they already dead. They just not know it yet.'

He realises he's panting. Realises that his mouth is hanging open, spit dripping from his lower lip. His skin seems to vibrate. His bones grind against one another. He wants, more than anything, to let her guide him away from this small, square room. Wants to go back into the flickering light of the corridor and into the dormitory, to find solace in the everyday ugliness to which he has immured himself. Wants to do what he came here for.

'We go now,' she says, her voice softening. She glances at her watch. It's a better brand than the one she was wearing last time they did business. She wears a Western perfume too. She has done well out of their arrangement. They have done some good.

'I can't,' he says, again. Means it, too. Not this time.

She tugs again at his sleeve. He shakes her off. Reaches down. Folds his big, grimy hands around the sodden, piss-reeking blankets. Lifts up the assemblage of fragile limbs and greasy skin. Wraps the parcel to his chest. Thinks of chips in news-paper. Thinks of drain rods in a carrier bag.

'No. Put back. Put down. These not for you . . . not what we agree . . .'

He shakes her off. Pushes her away. Unwraps the parcel and stares down. Two children; stick thin, twisted, wrapped around one another, mouths wetly sucking at the air.

'I shut,' she says. 'Stop all this. Stop you . . .'

He feels her tugging at his sleeve again. Feels her trying to pull the package from his grasp. She starts to raise her voice. Starts shouting, swearing; air filling with guttural vowels, angry consonants; rage pat in a language he cannot understand.

He pushes her away. Shakes her off. Feels her nails at his neck, fingers tugging at his hair. He shoves again, harder this time. Doesn't see her stumbling over the little girl who still clings to his leg. Just hears her sudden intake of breath and the dull thud; a sound like a teapot smashing against concrete.

He looks down. Watches her twitch. Watches the redness spread, ooze, spilling across the grey concrete like spilled paint.

'No,' he stutters. 'No no no . . .'

The parcel begins to move in his grasp. He feels bones twisting beneath the folds of wet fabric. Feels the shaved skull of one of the infants banging against his sternum, over, over. Thinks of caged bears. Thinks of lunatics. Thinks of home.

A noise from below; the child with the dark eyes, naked and twisted, reaching up with malformed, blood-stained hands. Her every gesture a prayer: *take me too. Please, take me too.*

Footsteps nearby; the sound of rubber soles on hard floors; the spit and sizzle of flickering light.

He holds his cargo of sticks and stones, pulling his jacket around them like the wings of a bird. Folds them in his embrace as he splashes, slips, through the spreading redness.

He doesn't run. Not at first.

He doesn't look back. Doesn't let himself see the children that lay, helpless, in the cradle. Who watch him leave. Who raise spindly, malformed arms and beg, like Maria, to be taken too.

Who sob, silently, as the darkness turns red.

ONE

Humber Bridge Country Park
2 January, 2026, 11.11 p.m.

Transcript
Yorkshire TV's *Daily Update* programme,
broadcast on 18 January, 2002

Voiceover: The aid worker arrested in Romania on a so-called 'mercy dash' has arrived back in Hull, promising to keep up the good work.

Trucking boss and self-styled 'Dark Angel' Rab Hawksmoor was held by Romanian authorities amid allegations he had helped in the illegal abduction of several starving and disabled orphans.

Hawksmoor, 56, claims he was the victim of a corrupt police force in Romania, determined to tarnish his legacy.

Speaking at Hull's Paragon Station, where he was met with a rapturous reception from his loyal family, friends and supporters, he made it clear he was just getting started.

Hawksmoor: You can't keep a bad man down, eh, love? Every time they think they've got me I find a way to outsmart them. I've been doing this long enough to know what's a real threat and what's somebody just playing silly beggars. They say I took children from orphanages all through the nineties – that I'm involved in some sort of smuggling outfit. It's repugnant. I do what anybody would do in a situation like that – I let my conscience guide my judgement. They hate me over there because I've exposed just what's going on, but for every corrupt copper and politician who's got my name on their hit list, there are hundreds of people who are alive because I've spent the best part of my adult life doing whatever is in my power to help these children. To

call me a people trafficker – that cuts right to the bone. But
if they think that a few more days in a prison is going to
change who I am, they can think again. I'm always half a
step ahead.

Presenter: This is by no means the first time Mr
Hawksmoor has been in trouble with Romanian authorities,
claiming to have been held at gunpoint on more than one
occasion.

Hawksmoor: You wouldn't believe the way they run that
country. It's a disgrace. Even now, all these years I've been
taking the aid and the presents and the supplies, they're still
shoving kids into orphanages and leaving them to rot. Those
that survive get booted out and left to fend for themselves.
If they're lucky they end up on the streets but I tell you,
there's worse places than that. You look under the sewers
down there, love – whole blasted cities of them, drug-addicts,
HIV-positive, dying in corners. People step over them in the
streets! I might not be welcome back there again any time
soon but I'll keep doing what I can from here and my lads
will keep doing the runs.'

Camera pans to Rab Hawksmoor in bike leathers: *Dark
Angel* painted on the back.

Trish Pharaoh holds smoke in her lungs. Holds it until it hurts.
Stars and fireworks collide in the darkness behind her eyelids.
Thoughts uncouple, her temples pounding. Only when she
feels death in her throat does she allow the grey air to trickle
out of her red, cracked lips. Watches the vapour slip through
the crack between window and door frame. Sees it shredded,
obliterated; a tiny white wedding gown ripped to shreds by the
ceaseless, merciless rain.

She flicks the cigarette butt out of the car window. Angles
her face so some of the hissing spray bounces off the ripped
leather upholstery and mists her cheek. Turns her head. Screws
up her face. Sits back and listens to the rain beating like so
many beaks upon the soft canopy roof of the old convertible.
She feels a sudden dribble down her face, glossing her damp,
dark hair to her cheek, looping through the silver hooped

earrings, trickling down her damp black jumper, her rain-glossed leather jacket.

'Fuck, not another one.'

She takes her gum from her mouth and sticks it, forcefully, against the inside of the sagging roof, plugging the hole where the offending droplet has oozed through. It is not the first such makeshift defence – the roof littered with Elastoplast, Blu Tack, glittery Sellotape clawed from Lilah McAvoy's school bag. Above the passenger seat, the tail from an applicator tampon dangles from a plugged hole like the tail of a dead mouse.

'That'll do it,' she mutters. Glances at the clock on the dashboard. It's well after 11 p.m. but given that the assignation had been arranged for 'around midnight', she isn't sure whether she's absurdly early or facing the kind of late night she no longer has the energy for. Like the little silver Mercedes, age and mileage are beginning to take their toll. She's having to stop for breath from time to time. Hangovers are staying until teatime. She's found herself waking up twice a night for a pee and there are pains in her limbs that make her wonder whether she mightn't be secretly working as a rodeo clown in her sleep. Being called Grandma doesn't help. She likes it even less than Detective Chief Superintendent – a title that, to her mind, may as well be replaced by a symbol, the way Prince did in the nineties. She spends long hours doodling on the backs of important documents, drawing turds in uniform, all wearing epaulettes.

'Come on, Vick,' she mutters, lighting another of her black cigarettes and staring, intently, at the glowing flame. She wants her bed. Wants to get under the covers wearing her best jogging trousers and baggy shirt; wants to watch *The Repair Shop* on the laptop, sipping a half decent malt from something more sophisticated than the toddler's tippee-cup which she currently grips between her thighs, and which she fills, absent-mindedly, from the bottle of supermarket red in the footwell.

She screws up her face, pissed off with herself. Glances again at the laptop on the passenger seat – the screen paused on Big Rab Hawksmoor's back, arms raised in victory. Looks, again, at the faces in the crowd of onlookers. Sees what Vicky Dexter

saw when she found the old broadcast on a DVD recording
and spotted somebody who shouldn't have been anywhere near
Hull in January 2002.

'Who are you, eh?' she mutters, glaring at the face of the
thin, scarred figure in the corner of the shot. She truly wants
Vicky to be wrong. 'What are the chances?' she asks herself.
Doubts she would be able to do the maths.

She slumps back in the chair, wafting a hand half-heartedly
at the smoke. She's spent most of the day playing grandma to
her eldest daughter's indefatigable toddler, an important task
interrupted only occasionally by press briefings, quarterly
accounts and the six active murder investigations she is
currently overseeing. She considers the day a relative success
– only two tantrums and a spillage, and Pharaoh had apolo-
gised for each. They'd made rock buns in the kitchen, Pharaoh
breaking off from spooning out flour and sugar to shout
discouraging things at junior officers ranked in portrait squares
on the screen of her phone. She can feel herself getting tired
and hates herself for it. The bad thoughts always attack her
when she's vulnerable. She hates falling asleep halfway sober
– her thoughts becoming predictably maudlin, self-destructive,
the more fuzzy-headed with fatigue she becomes. It's only the
drink that muffles the bellowing chorus of self-recrimination
and petty resentments that try and get her attention at bedtime.
Only the drink that allows her to exist, like this, to play this
role she slipped into in her mid-twenties: to be Trish-bloody-
Pharaoh for the remaining hours in each bastard day.

She looks up as a light appears to her right, a single shimmering glow, casting a hazy circle of illumination into the
teeming dark.

'About pissing time,' mutters Pharaoh, rearranging the items
on the passenger seat and stuffing her supplies deeper into the
footwell. She wafts another hand at the air. She's run out of
Issey Miyake. Can't see the point of wasting money on expensive perfumes when the nipper is so insistent she smell of Calpol
and crisps.

'Gosh, this is beastly!' announces Vicky, wrenching open the
door and levering herself into the seat. She's several inches

bigger than Pharaoh, but fits into the seat with considerably
more ease than Pharaoh's usual passenger. She hides a smile
with her hand as she pictures McAvoy, neck cricked, head out
of the window, hair and beard blowing like the ears of a big
ginger rottweiler.

'Nearly didn't come,' announces Vicky, her accent southern,
precise: every inch the newsreader. She pulls down the sun visor
and checks her reflection in the little mirror, switching off her
torch. She tastes the cigarette smoke and makes a face. She's
got her hair cut in a sensible bob with a feathered fringe:
brunette hair tastefully highlighted. A multi-coloured silk scarf
disappears into the neck of her sodden Barbour jacket: white
jeans tucked into stylish yard boots. She looks a good decade
younger than her age: could play the sexy stepmum in any
number of BBC dramas. If Pharaoh didn't think of her as a
friend, she'd hate her on sight.

'You were watching it again,' says Vicky, angling her head
to look at the image on the half-closed laptop. 'Still not
convinced?'

'I'm the queen of the open-mindedness, Vick,' says Pharaoh,
settling herself on the rubbed-bare upholstery of the head rest.
'I'll believe pretty much anything.'

'That's hardly true,' says Vicky, rummaging behind herself
and pulling out a hairbrush, taffled up with twists of black
hair. She considers it, finds it slightly too grim a proposition,
and deposits it in the footwell. 'You're a cynic at the same
time.'

Pharaoh decides not to contradict her. She wouldn't mind
having a proper catch-up with her old friend if there was decent
Amarone, a tray of olives and an attentive waiter, but here,
now, she just wants what she came for.

'You know how unlikely this is,' says Pharaoh, flatly. 'You
might have just seen what you wanted to see.'

Vicky wipes the outline of her lips with a plump finger, gold
and rubies providing glittering cummerbunds around the pink
skin. 'Coincidences happen all the time. One-in-a-million shots
do actually happen.'

Pharaoh knows she will have to say the same thing herself

if she were to even consider launching the investigation that will inevitably follow if she takes Vicky Dexter at her word. She knows her companion's character well enough – has seen her blossom from a timid young news reporter into a celebrated documentary maker during their twenty-year association. Seen her grow in confidence and reputation. Insofar as she can trust anybody with the word 'journalist' on their CV, she does think of her as possessing a vestige of integrity. And she's right. Coincidences do happen.

'It's not even that much of a coincidence,' says Vicky, looking a little put out. 'I mean, I see people at interesting times in their lives. Those sort of occasions tend to draw crowds so I see a lot of faces. And I've got a good memory.'

Pharaoh nods, begrudgingly. She doesn't want to hear it again. It's only a few days since they sat here beneath gathering clouds and Vicky told her of the links she had made between two seemingly unconnected stories on her showreel.

Vicky lives in one of the big, set-back houses in West Ella: all leylandii and high fences, remote control gates and person-alised plates. It's been home since she married the spry, bookish Benedict Robbins – thirty years her senior and a successful wine merchant. Pharaoh knows her friend has endured a torrent of jealous whispers and vile accusations about her motives for marrying the octogenarian millionaire and doesn't agree with any of them. She's always presumed Vicky just did it for the wine.

'Benny is so insistent that I don't let it all go to waste, you do understand,' says Vicky, a little flustered, and Pharaoh real-ises she has started retelling the story of how she found the link between a Hull murder and a Romanian criminal. 'Like I told you, he wants me to maintain my independence – to do what I love to do, but . . . I don't really love doing what I've always done, Trish. Being good at something doesn't mean you take any pleasure in it. And I'm feeling a bit weak in the knees to be climbing around war zones or filming some ghastly poverty porn about sink estates and orphans and people traf-fickers. I'd rather liked the idea of doing the garden, if I'm honest with you. But I thought that if I got the old showreel up to date, I might be able to get some corporate work here and there – keep the hand in. But you know how I get once I fall down a rabbit hole. Soon as I started diving back through all the old clips and highlights – I mean, gosh, doesn't uploading the contents of a floppy disc feel positively archaic . . .'

'You've told me this, Vick,' says Pharaoh, squinting as she begins to feel the hard thumbs of a migraine pressing at her temples. She realises that she wants Vicky to tell her that she hasn't been able to find what she was looking for – that everything will remain speculation and hyperbole. That she won't have to do anything at all. 'You couldn't find it?'

Vicky gives a bright smile. Opens her coat and pulls out an A4 envelope, folded at the top. Rectangular shapes bulge against its insides.

'Jesus, Vick, if we ever meet in a dark car park again, please don't hand me a brown envelope – doesn't look good.'

Vicky smiles, opening the envelope and reaching inside. She holds out a silver disk. 'Complete raw footage,' she says. 'Everything we ever shot. Same disk has the translation. The rest of this – I'm giving it to you with reservation, you understand. I'm doing my civic duty, I'm giving up the chance of a bloody Bafta, so you will . . . you will . . .'

Pharaoh softens her demeanour. Puts a hand on Vicky's damp forearm. 'I'll do everything I can to keep him from finding out. I swear.'

Vicky blinks back tears, expensive mascara beginning to smudge: inked spiders pressing against her pale cheeks. 'It was before him. Mostly. Almost all before him.'

'I get it,' says Pharaoh, and does. Vicky has a lot to lose.

'There's a printout of the article as well. Some footage. Everything we have from my *Calendar* days. That one didn't air – I told you that, didn't I? Editor on shift decided it struck the wrong note to celebrate the safe return of a people trafficker.'

Pharaoh shakes her head. 'Many would say he's a hero. He helps people nobody else gives a damn about. His sons too. Does something when other people are sitting around saying "gosh it's terrible" . . .'

'Don't play devil's avocado with me, Trish Pharaoh. You don't believe that.'

Pharaoh gives a fleeting smile. 'Devil's avocado?'

'Joke I have with Benny,' she says, staring out into the splintered dark. 'I do love him, Trish . . .'

Pharaoh doesn't doubt that Vicky believes herself to be in love with the man she met in the Beech Tree in Kirk Ella just weeks before her production company was threatened with liquidation over unpaid business rates. In her experience, people can convince themselves of anything that can balm their conscience. She starts counting down in her head. Reckons that before she gets from five to one, Vicky will begin explaining herself; her innocent motives; the pragmatic benevolence of still having her sexual needs met by her fuck buddy in Bucharest.

'I know people think I'm having my cake and eating it, but nobody knows the truth of us. Benny would give us his approval, I don't doubt it. I just don't want to have to put him in that position. He knows, I'm sure, just in a kind of opaque way. He doesn't ask, he respects my privacy, so I don't tell . . .'

Pharaoh makes a face. Draws a stick man in the condensation on the window. 'Rab's son,' she says, quietly. 'Davey. Still unsolved, Vick. We never got close. Nobody would tell us a thing. Plenty of rumour to play with but no witnesses, no forensics − just a big hard bugger dead in a cemetery and his little dog licking his face. Would have taken half a dozen lads to put him down, according to the lads at the fight club. Makes us look bloody daft that it's still unsolved.'

'Well . . . this may open a door or two, don't you think? Maybe put a bit of a squeeze on Big Rab. They're on the verge of the proper big time with that upcoming deal. Talking millions, Trish. You reckon he'll do what he says − put it all into building schools and care homes over there?'

Pharaoh gives her a withering look. Ignores the question and asks one of her own. 'You think he'll call?'

Vicky nods, earnest; sincere. 'We've been through things together. There's a bond that's forged when you've been through darkness together. It's something bigger than language. Something almost . . . timeless. Sublime.'

'Your arse is ringing,' says Pharaoh, trying not to gag. She nods at her companion's pocket. 'You ready for this?'

Vicky licks her lower lip, suddenly still, body rigid. Her fingers spasm into fists. 'God, what's wrong with me? I want this.' She closes her eyes. Takes a breath. Answers the call, just as Pharaoh starts to record on her own phone.

'Josef,' she says, breathy, warm. 'God, I've needed to hear your voice. Are you OK? After we spoke, I don't know, it felt like you weren't sure . . .'

Pharaoh watches as Vicky flaps at the air, decades falling away so she takes on the air of a flustered teenager trying to talk to a handsome boy. She smiles, despite herself. Doesn't begrudge her friend a little bit of the best of both worlds. Josef was her fixer on one of her production trips to Romania. Together they descended into a subterranean city: a network of sewers that housed countless hundreds of orphans and foundlings, runaways and street kids. The programme won an award. The experience left Vicky with post-traumatic stress disorder, a long-distance lover, and hours of extraordinary footage: dead-eyed, white-faced urchins, barefoot and sallow-skinned, sucking down black bags of lung-stripping solvent; huddled together around camping fires, candles; the flickering surfaces of TV screens running from tangles of wire. She had enough footage to make a whole new programme; perhaps to use the audio for her first dabble into the lucrative world of the half-decent podcaster. She even found a suitable pretext to make return trips to Bucharest, utilising her bedroom companion for more than just his obvious attractions. Over endlessly delicious long weekends and frantic overnighters, he translated hours of raw audio. Lost himself in testimonies of brutal poverty; neglect and abandonment; abuses and sufferings that bled into his mind like squid ink. Listened to the words of a Fagin-esque sewer king; the lord of the darkness: The Tinman. He had granted her an audience. Had spoken of his underworld empire; the new lives he had given his 'children'. He spoke of those who had found a new life beneath the teeming streets; the children and adolescents who found home, found family, in the stale-aired reek of the reclaimed tunnels. He spoke of the service he provided; the succour and warmth he gave his followers when the state offered nothing but contempt. It wouldn't have amounted to much more than the grandiose boasts of a bottom-feeding drug dealer, if not for the moment, midway through the recording, when he stopped to ask Vicky where she was from. When she replied that she lived near Hull he changed his manner. Spoken with a new urgency; paranoid; jittery. Asked her whether she knew Big Rab Hawksmoor. She'd been asked to leave moments later; a sudden rush of children urging Vicky and Josef back towards the shaft of light; the rusting ladder; a chorus of yapping dogs following them as they ascended the wet, grime-streaked rungs and out of the manhole cover in a quiet corner of a rain-lashed city park.

Vicky had emerged into the sunlight and set to work. Acquainted herself with the trucking boss that was Rab Hawksmoor; the charity campaigner; the devil-may-care anti-hero whose name she had uttered countless times when she worked in local news. Watched old footage, unaired recordings; his brushes with Romanian authorities; the death of his son Davey. Something began to take shape: the first whispered suspicions that there was a story here; something ripe for the plucking. Her notion was fanciful; the suspicions patently absurd. But she knew that the suggestion alone would make for good content. Could a Romanian crime boss be responsible for the death of a much-mourned family man from Hull? The answer would be 'no', but she could get five episodes out of existing audio alone if she strung it out. She'd have to get interviews with the Hawksmoors, maybe a few cops and another couple of tame ex-journalists, but she could make it work. She would need to see the Tinman again, too. Would need to make her accusations and record the resulting fallout. Josef would arrange it. Josef would do anything she asked.

Pharaoh becomes aware of a sudden silence at her side. Vicky's stopped gabbling. She's sitting perfectly still, phone to the side of her face. Her eyes gleam with unshed tears. The colour bleeds from her face as if her throat has been cut.

'Vicky?' whispers Pharaoh, leaning forwards. 'Vick, what's wrong . . .'

She lurches forwards, beckoning for the phone. Vicky grips it, fingers white. Pharaoh can hear a tinny voice, a half-strangled croak; low, precise.

'Vicky, is it Josef? What's wrong? Vick . . .'

Vicky snatches up the envelope from Pharaoh's knee. Scrabbles for the door handle.

Pharaoh reaches out, tries to grab her arm.

'Please,' begs Vicky, hissing into the phone. 'Please, whatever you're doing, stop. Please, he did it for me. For me! Please!'

Vicky drags her sleeve from Pharaoh's grip, yanks open the door and all but throws herself into the scything rain. Pharaoh grabs for the papers that swirl up in a maelstrom of flapping whiteness: cursing, dropping her cigarette into her cleavage and slapping at the embers.

'Vicky, what the fuck? Vick, hang on, what's happening . . .'

Pharaoh yanks open her own car door. Pulls herself out into the rain and the dark. Sees a sudden glaring headlight: thunderous rattle and hiss and a perfect circle of yellow light flaring in her vision. She throws herself back into the car. Cowers as she hears metal on metal; a blizzard of smashed glass; tiny jagged icicles puckering her hand, face, hair.

She raises her head. Hears the roar of an engine. Looks back through the smashed rear windscreen. Listens to the blood thump inside her own ears; fingers suddenly trembling as she brushes the glass from her hair.

Peers into the darkness; a silence turned to static by the ceaseless rain.

Vicky's disappeared into the night.

TWO

Heartless Detectives Should Let My Son Rest In Peace
Report by Lucy Bingham, *Hull Daily Mail* Crime
Reporter
Saturday, 10 January, 2026

Police have been slammed as 'incompetent' and 'heartless' by a Hull charity campaigner who believes her murdered son should be allowed to 'rest in peace'.

Humberside Police recently began a review of its own investigation into the death of popular Hull fight coach Davey Hawksmoor, who was found beaten to death at the city's Hedon Road cemetery in March 2012. He was 43.

Mum Susie Hawksmoor, 79, told the *Hull Daily Mail*: 'As far as the family is concerned, we've done our grieving. We carry the weight of our loss every day. Davey was larger than life – a person who did more good than harm. He never shrank from a fight and he made some mistakes in his life but he helped a lot of people. The work he's done with kids from this area is phenomenal. He got kids off the streets, off drugs, and into his gyms. A lot of people owe their lives to our Davey. Losing him hit so hard that I didn't think I would ever get up.

'Of course we want to see justice for him – what kind of mother wouldn't? But as far as we can tell, the police have got absolutely nothing new. All they're doing is stirring the pot to see what bubbles to the surface, and I find that kind of manipulation pretty deplorable. It's heartless at best. I've seen nothing to suggest they'll be any less incompetent than last time around.'

Davey was a haulier with Hawksmoor Freight and Logistics and was a well-known local figure, both for his bare-knuckle fighting exploits and his involvement in his

father 'Big' Rab Hawksmoor's charity work taking aid to
underprivileged children in Eastern Europe.

Davey's widow, 63-year-old Mae Lockhart, of Swine, near
Patrington, has been an outspoken critic of the initial
investigation and has long campaigned for Humberside
Police to re-open the investigation.

She said: 'I lost my soulmate. The man I loved went out
for a jog with our little dog and he never came home again.
Somebody jumped him, attacked him and left him to die.
The police barely found a suspect the first time around but
I've had some very productive meetings with the officer
leading the review and it's clear there were some missed
opportunities and a lot of people are going to have to think
very hard about whether they will sing the same song this
time around.

'I had to leave a job I loved because I couldn't be around
the things that reminded me of him. I walked away from
everything. His daughters lost their hero that night – the
man who made them feel safe. We deserve justice.'

Susie Hawksmoor, whose husband Rab founded the
charity to help Romanian orphans and has since overseen
the delivery of millions of pounds worth of aid, said: 'We've
met with the detective leading the review and it's clear the
whole thing is going to be a whitewash. It feels very
fag-packety, if I'm honest. Lacklustre from start to finish. I
don't believe they've got anything new so they're doing what
they always do – making a lot of noise and seeing if anybody
suddenly remembers something. Don't they think that they
would have come forward by now if they had? Davey
wouldn't have died quietly, I can tell you that. There must
have been a vanload of them. We've asked around, believe
me. If somebody had seen who did this, we would know. So
the whole thing's a farce, really. It's popped up out of nowhere
and is just another opportunity for them to cause this family
pain. They should let him rest in peace.'

Susie's husband, 'Big' Rab Hawksmoor, has been
imprisoned several times by Romanian authorities during
his thirty-plus years taking aid to disaffected children. He

was arrested on suspicion of child abduction in 2002 and has twice been held at gunpoint by bandits in the Carpathian Mountains, but has never considered calling time on his good works.

Rab is owner and operator of the family firm, which has been synonymous with Hull since his father founded it in the 1930s. The company now has a fleet of more than thirty vehicles and reported a turnover of £33 million last year. Business insiders recently reported that the company was about to be purchased by global freight giant Omnia, but the deal fell through at the eleventh hour.

Operations Manager Rafe Cadogan told the *Mail* that the deal has since been resurrected and fears that the police are deliberately sabotaging the proposed buyout.

He said: 'There are some people who just don't want the good guys to win.'

Humberside Police press office did not return requests for comment.

•

Transcript
In Deep: Behind the Scenes of the National Crime Agency
Episode 6 – The Celtic Cartel
First aired 13 June, 2019

Punam Gulhane: I'm Punam Gulhane, and this is *In Deep: Behind the Scenes of the National Crime Agency*. This podcast series unearths the murky world of dangerous criminals across the UK and the incredible work undertaken by the NCA to bring them to justice.

Scott Skewis, NCA Senior Investigating Officer: He's the real deal. You think of a villain with their finger in every pie, that's Quinlan. Before we got the cuffs on him he was one of the number-one criminals in Europe. I mean, they've compared him to El Chapo, for example, the El Chapo of Europe. They regarded him as the biggest drugs supplier on the continent. The war he provoked in Dublin . . . it turned the city into the Wild West. There are things we know he's been involved in that make you question whether you really know what human beings are capable of. The man is the devil incarnate.

Amanda Wye, Journalist: When I started writing about him, I had no idea what I was letting myself in for. He sent people over to threaten me that if I carried on writing, then I was going to get burnt. I don't doubt that if he gets the chance, he'll make good on his promise.

Scott Skewis: He's as dangerous as they come. We don't know how many bodies he's responsible for. Perhaps we'll never know. He's a nasty, violent, horrible man. And that is the man I'm looking at face-to-face that day. I know what that guy's done, and what he's ordered, essentially, over the years. This is a man who kept teenage boys in cages and made them fight for the chance to be one of his clan. He ran his outfit like it was the Dark Ages – spotted people with a darkness and a violence inside them and nurtured that until they were willing to kill; desperate to kill. They're still out there, doing his bidding.

Punam Gulhane: The man you're about to hear about was a notorious figure in the British criminal underworld, the head of a global organised crime group, a major player in the international drug trade and one of the most influential and feared organised criminals in Europe until he was captured at his Spanish villa in 2015. This is the story of how the NCA finally caught up with the man known simply as *The Irishman.*

PART ONE

PART ONE

THREE

R ain upon glass: steam rising, darkness, neon and darting streaks of light . . .

Here, now, in the damp, blue darkness, Lilah McAvoy is chuntering. She's expostulating. Her father might go as far as to accuse her of maundering, were he given to severe language.

'All I'm saying is that for £17.75, we should get a fish. Like at the fair. Just a little one. In a bag.'

She's holding her dad's hand, her little fingers folded into his huge palm. She's jabbering away at the level of his hip, and in the strange blue-black tunnel he can barely make out what she's saying. The sounds reverberate and echo: a chorus of disapproval.

'Megalodon,' she says, prompted by one of the information posters, presently being pored over by a soggy husband and wife; spectacles steaming, anoraks dripping grimily onto the sloping floor. 'I like saying that. It sounds like a Transformer. And ooh, no – that's not a real thing. Chocolate surgeonfish? Who would come up with that? It sounds like a pudding in a posh restaurant . . . . I think I need a fish again, Daddy. Or a lobster.'

From time to time she tugs him down to her level. Rubs his beard between her forefinger and thumb, soothing herself the way she has taken to. Each time he bends he glimpses his own distended reflection in one of the gaily coloured tanks. Sees himself making his way down the slanting floor in a sort of half-squat, the tails of his coat trailing on the floor.

'You had a fish, Lilah,' says McAvoy, gently. 'You got bored with it.'

She stops, mouth open in shock. She looks thoroughly aghast. She's been practising 'aghast' in front of the mirror, having read it in a Victorian fairy tale and been somewhat taken. Stares through her father as if betrayed by the person she trusts most.

'Mr Flappy was a particularly boring fish,' says Lilah, eyes hard. 'Honestly, if he was a person, he'd work in accounts.'

McAvoy gives her hand a squeeze. Nods down the slope to where a group of children are forming two haphazard horseshoes in front of a great wall of glass. There's going to be a talk soon; a youngster in a purple T-shirt will tell the assembled day trippers about coral reefs and zebra sharks, about whiptail rays and sawfish. McAvoy's listened to the presentation more times than he can count. Fancies he could lip-sync, if pushed. Wonders, idly, whether this mightn't be something he could do for a living. He rather likes the idea of spending his days telling people about marine conservation and why they shouldn't flush wet wipes down the toilet. Thinks it might be a job that serves some purpose. He can't say the same for his current line of work. Can't look himself in the face and say that he's serving much of a purpose as Detective Inspector at the helm of the Cold Case Unit at Humberside Police. Wonders when he last felt as if he was doing some good. Thinks again of the words in the article. *Incompetent. Lacklustre. Heartless.* Feels his cheeks burn.

'Can I ask him my question?' asks Lilah, excited. 'Can I? Please, Daddy, can I?'

McAvoy wonders why she still goes to the trouble of asking permission. He doesn't say 'no' to anything and she has long since decided that Daddy supplies only suggestions and guidelines rather than boundaries and rules.

'It's not a question, Lilah,' says McAvoy, apologising as a toddler cannons off his knees. He steps through a group of teens, seated on the floor in an obstacle course of hoodies and backpacks; wet clothes steaming in the warm dark air. 'Sorry, sorry, can I just . . . och, did I get you, I'm sorry . . .' He manages to carve out a space where he isn't liable to squash anybody. Gives his attention back to his daughter, flustered and hot. 'You just like making them squirm.'

'It's a sensible question,' says Lilah, giving a young lad with long blond hair a hard glare when their eyes meet in the glass of the shark tank. He looks away, daunted. She has her dark hair in space buns today, each tied with red lace. She's wearing her leather jacket over a leopard-print roll-neck and black jeans, bare feet stuffed into silver boots.

'They're the ones standing there pretending to be experts,' she says, raising her voice. 'And they don't know, do they? Last one didn't even offer an opinion.'

McAvoy finds a spot by the wall and leans back into the shadows. He's warm and wet and there's sweat running down into the small of his back. He should have left his coat in the car, but Roisin had warned him he would get soaked just crossing the car park and made him promise to stay wrapped up warm. She hadn't said whether he was allowed to take it off once indoors, though he seems to recall some old wisdom about not feeling the benefit of it once he gets outside.

'You're just frightened I'll embarrass you,' says Lilah, elbowing aside a pre-teen who's standing a little too close to her father for her liking. 'Auntie Trish would let me.'

'I'm not saying you can't,' says McAvoy, feeling picked on. 'It's just . . . can't we carry on to the shark tunnel? You love the shark tunnel. And the penguins? I like the penguins.'

Lilah looks at her father: her eyes dark and pitying. She only agreed to come with him because she couldn't face the prospect of standing in the torrential rain watching her brother be bad at football. She left that to Mammy, though she has little doubt that Mammy will have parked the car next to the pitch and will be watching through the windscreen, bare feet on the dashboard, hot chocolate in one hand and vape in the other.

'You're trying to cause mischief,' says McAvoy.

Lilah gives a grunt as somebody tries to push past her, stepping on her instep and knocking her with a rucksack. 'Ow,' she says, pointedly, flexing and shooting angry eyes at the intruder. 'Excuse me, you realise you're not a vapour, yes? You have a solid mass?'

McAvoy bites down on his lip and puts himself between his daughter and the damp, straggle-bearded man who's trying to make a space for himself among the tows of chattering children and parents.

'The answer is yes,' says McAvoy, trying to distract Lilah before violence can ensue. 'Mermaids can be any size. And they can be any way up. Fish head with human legs, human head with fish tails. They can be goldfish-sized or orca-sized. We thrashed this out on the drive home last time.'

'Ah yes, but if they bred with a centaur, would the child be a full human, or a weird horse-fish?'

The conversation around them falls away. Faces turn. McAvoy feels his cheeks begin to pinken as he hears the question being repeated in little groups of ones and twos. Lilah waves a hand in the direction of the gathering philosophical debate. 'See. It's an important point. And they don't address it. Not once . . .'

McAvoy leans back against the wall. Stares into the glass tank and lets the words become a background static. Thinks, briefly, of Davey Hawksmoor. Forces himself to stop.

'Let's make a break for it,' says Lilah, nudging him in the hip. 'If we go now there'll be nobody at the ice wall and you can press your head to it. I like watching you steam.'

She tugs him through the crowd amid a chorus of apologies and pardon-me's, trying not to crush anybody as he manoeuvres his colossal frame through tiny gaps. He feels like a monster in a Japanese movie, crushing skyscrapers beneath his feet. He realises too late that Lilah has timed their exit so that the theme from *Jaws* is playing over the sound speaker just as he cuts through the darkness. There are giggles among the protests.

'It's amazing to think that a shark can even learn to play the cello,' says Lilah, waiting for him by one of the smaller tanks. 'Am I old enough to watch it yet, do you think? Fin says it's too scary, but then, he's named after a bit of a fish so, y'know . . . he's emotionally invested.'

It's been a long time since McAvoy felt as though he were the intellectual superior in his conversations with his daughter. Since she hit nine, there's been no stopping her. Beside him, a young lad in a Hull City hoodie is asking his dad the name of the orange-striped fish in the tall glass tank. Lilah spots an opportunity and leans in.

'Sharon,' she says, unasked, then darts away to the mouth of the long, cold tunnel where the ice wall awaits. McAvoy finds her with her face pressed to the imitation snow, arms out to her sides. McAvoy joins her. Leans forwards and smushes his warm forehead to the deliciously cool installation.

'Are you having a good time?' asks Lilah, her voice muffled. 'You're not . . . not thinking too hard, are you?'

McAvoy closes his eyes. He knows that she worries about him. She doesn't like her Daddy to be upset. Doesn't like him being picked on by anybody other than her and Mammy and Auntie Trish. Had to be physically held back when she saw what the horrible woman had told the *Hull Daily Mail* about the Cold Case Unit. She'd looked up the words she hadn't been familiar with. Took particular umbrage at 'incompetent' and was willing to do bloody murder over 'lackadaisical'. It had been little comfort that the journalist had spelled it wrong.

'I'm having a lovely day, my darling,' he says, reaching out to squeeze her shoulder. 'Promise.'

Coming to The Deep had been Lilah's idea, though McAvoy fancies that Mammy and Auntie Trish might have had a hand in things. He is, they claim, working far too hard. He's getting too deep into himself; disappearing inside his own head again. Auntie Trish – or Detective Chief Superintendent Trish Pharaoh, to give her the title on her business cards – had only given him the Cold Case Unit to try and stop him getting into mischief. Lilah had been in favour of the promotion, not least because it decreased the likelihood of him ending up in hospital again. She's seen her daddy hooked up to too many tubes and bleeping machines to like the idea of him catching any more murderers. At least with cold cases, she fancies that he'll only have to catch really old people, and she can't see any of them being able to stick him with knives or hit him with hammers or shoot him with anything big enough to make a problematic hole. She hadn't been prepared for the fact that cold cases tend to come with a lot of publicity, and that her daddy would see his integrity – another word she had to look up – called into question. If he had his way, he'd be at work today; would be poring over dusty case files, grimy witness statements, sitting in the centre of a rapidly expanding land mass of paperwork, looking for a killer that has eluded his colleagues for the past fourteen years. Instead, he's here with Lilah. He's in one of his happy places with his little girl, trying to snatch a moment's peace as the din in his head threatens to drown out every coherent thought.

'She'll have to say sorry,' says Lilah, into the ice. 'When you catch him, she'll say sorry for all the horrible things she said.'

McAvoy presses his cheek to the ice. Hopes that none of his red-grey beard hairs detaches itself, clinging to the exhibit like a pubic hair on a bar of soap. These days, such an action could be mistaken for an act of social disobedience, or the work of Just Stop Oil.

'She's grieving,' says McAvoy. 'People need to direct their anger somewhere. That's what I'm here for.'

'Auntie Trish says you like being people's punching bag,' says Lilah, looking up at him. There's real worry in her eyes. 'She says you're like those monks that wrap ropes around their legs and pull them so tight they cut into the skin.'

'I don't think that's very fair,' says McAvoy, under his breath.

'And Mammy says that she knows where the lady in the paper lives, and that it wouldn't take more than a phone call for her to really have something to whinge about.'

McAvoy looks away, unsure whether his smile is good parenting. He'd thought that having two women pushing and pulling him through life had been a lot to contend with. Now that Lilah also knows what's best for him, he can't help visualising a blasted heath; three witches stirring the cauldron and nudging him in whatever direction they see fit. He suffers a flash of memory; his dad at the kitchen table in the family croft, raising his head from the book in his lap to tell him that aye, there was some truth to the rumour that there was a link to Macbeth in the family tree. He hadn't believed it then. Doesn't doubt it now.

'Are we going to see the nice lady after?' asks Lilah, nuzzling her dad's hand with her head. 'The one who makes the nice lemonade? I won't tell. I promise.'

McAvoy chews the inside of his cheek. He knows at once who she's referring to. Mae Lockhart still believes that DI McAvoy will find out who killed her husband on that dismal, rain-lashed morning in 2012. Thinks the big, awkward, diffident highlander will find the men who ambushed her husband on his regular run; who lay in wait for him at the columbarium at the cemetery on Hedon Road then set about him with an efficient brutality. He was found with fractured eye sockets, broken jawbone; a subdural haematoma that would have killed him even if his killers hadn't gone to the trouble of strangling him to death. He had dislocated shoulders, both arms broken at the elbow. There were minimal signs that Davey had got in much offence; the battle-scarred knuckles showing no signs of punches thrown. The downpour washed away anything of forensic value. No witnesses came forward. No suspect was ever identified. The investigation had little to go on, save vague suggestions that Hawksmoor might have won a fight he was supposed to lose and that the resulting punishment beating had gotten out of hand. For all that the dead man's family have painted him as a local hero, he's been told by numerous sources about his thuggish side – deliberately hurting the young-sters at his gym to see whether they have the guts and gumption to come back for more. He served time in a couple of Romanian prisons alongside his father and brother – took part in numerous aid convoys across the Carpathian Mountains where he routinely ran into criminals and corrupt officials. To die a hero did seem somehow perverse.

From his own rereading of the case, McAvoy isn't sure that the beleaguered DI at the time could have done very much more – not least because at the time of the enquiry, Humberside Police was a force in decline; the Criminal Investigation Department rocked by scandals and Trish Pharaoh only just beginning to undo the damage caused by her corrupt prede-cessor. McAvoy can't argue with the contention that he's on little more than a fishing expedition. He's got nothing new to work with. No new witnesses. One of Trish's informants has given her a nudge in the direction of Big Rab's controversial charity work, but so far, people at Dark Angels aren't returning his calls. Neither are the police in Romania, to whom he has already sent a dozen emails asking for clarity on their previous involvements with the freight boss and his crew. He'd even gone to the trouble of having it translated. So far, he's got nowhere. The Hawksmoors had made that plain as soon as he was seated in an uncomfortable chair at the long, gleaming mahogany table in the centre of the green-walled blue-carpeted board-room; the walls hung with oil paintings showing whiskered, pocket-watched, pinstriped patricians staring out from thick, gold-edged frames. The men in the frames had made him more welcome than Wayne Hawksmoor, the murdered man's brother: dark eyes glittering blackly as he processed what McAvoy was trying to tell him. So too his mum, Susie: sneering from her Queen Anne chair, blanketed in front of the fire at the family compound, jaw working in furious circles as she told him that she couldn't go through it again; couldn't handle the questions and the poking around and the bad memories. He'd tried to reassure her. Told her that it was only the very first step towards a full reinvestigation and that he believed there was hope a new witness might be willing to come forward. She'd all but laughed in his face. The article in the *Hull Daily Mail* was almost polite when compared to the vitriol that has been spat in his face and sprayed like manure across his inbox in the days since. They don't want the police digging up painful memories – nor digging too deep into the paperwork of the family haulage and logistics business. Susie, the family matriarch, has been quite clear when she told him that, as far as they were concerned, the matter had been 'dealt with'. She had resisted all efforts to persuade her to elaborate. She won't even take his calls now. Has informed him that all future communication must be through the company lawyers, or the Operations Manager. Rafe Cadogan. McAvoy doesn't dislike many people on first meeting, but there had been something about the young executive that had made him think back to boarding school – to picture the cocksure, arrogant bullies who had mocked his Highlands accent; his work-scarred hands; his fondness for poetry and high grades. He's sure Cadogan thinks of himself as a tease; a master of rapier-sharp takedowns and collegiate banter. McAvoy wonders whether he's ever considered the alternative. Whether he might just be a bastard.

'Daddy, can we?'

'Mae? I mean, we could. We've got to pop to Gordon Street help move some of the boxes, of course. We can't leave it all to Andy.'

'Hull won't flood again,' says Lilah, shaking her head. 'No way.'

McAvoy wishes he shared her confidence. The rain has been falling like an upturned sea since New Year's Day. The rivers have burst their banks and the sewers are glugging and gurgling beneath the streets. There are impassable roads to the east of the city. Across East Yorkshire, householders and businesses are moving their treasured possessions to higher ground. McAvoy's unit, housed in the spectacularly unfit-for-purpose police station off Hessle Road, is far from exempt from the danger. McAvoy can't help wondering if whoever decided to move the archive to Gordon Street mightn't have been a little hard-of-thinking. He pictures his number two, Detective Sergeant Andy Daniells, red-faced and wet-legged, struggling up the crumbling stairs with crate upon crate of yellowing files, and feels a stab of guilt that he isn't there to lend a hand. It was gone midnight when he left the scene, having lugged over a hundred case files to the upper floors, but he still feels as though he's shirking. Not that he has much to worry about from on high. Trish has barely spoken to him since dropping the Davey Hawksmoor cold case in his lap and telling him to ruffle some feathers. She won't tell him what it is that's occupying her time. She's overseeing six active murder investigations but according to the Detective Chief Inspectors, she's providing little more than thumbs-up emojis and the occasional promise to check in for a full briefing when time allows. Last time he'd bumped into her in the corridor at Clough Road HQ, she'd barely looked up from her phone as she barrelled past him; eyes dark, hair still wet from her run across the car park, lips set in the grim line he always associates with an impending explosion. He finds it mildly unfair that his daughter gets to speak to her more than he does.

'You planned this, didn't you?' he asks, with a slight smile. 'She's a witness in a murder investigation, Lilah. We don't just drop in and see her because you like the lemonade and she's got a funny-looking dog that loves you.'

Lilah turns spaniel eyes on her father. 'I'll let you see the penguins on the way out,' she says. 'The keeper fancies you – she might even let you feed them.'

'She doesn't fancy me,' begins McAvoy. 'And you shouldn't talk like that. Who said she fancies me?'

'Mammy,' says Lilah, as if it were obvious. 'Told me to keep you away from the pink-haired trollop.' She winces, as if she's betrayed a confidence. 'What's a trollop?'

'A type of fish,' says McAvoy, his face neutral. 'You sure? You don't mind?'

Lilah gives him a grin. Presses her palms to the icy wall and makes jazz hands in the chill wetness.

'You have to walk like a penguin the rest of the way, yes? I mean, that's the rules.'

McAvoy winces. Turns it into a smile. Turns his big arms into wings and follows his daughter, flat-footed and flapping, down the long corridor. He doesn't look at his reflection. Can't stand the sight of himself.

FOUR

Big Rab Hawksmoor. Shrunken now. Diminished. Grey hair and straggly beard, scrawny chicken-skin and a lank ponytail hanging whitely from his otherwise bald head. He leans himself against the door of the red-brick outbuilding – the pain in his left hip so hot and searing that it is all he can do not to cry out. He doesn't like showing weakness. Can still remember his dad's ham-hock fist smashing into the side of his head whenever he dared to complain of discomfort, of pain. He's grateful for the lessons. Hopes he's passed them on to the boys.

He watches the rain fall. He's seen worse, of course. The people on the radio, on the telly, down the pub – they're getting themselves in a tizzy over it all. Worst flood in a generation, record rainfall, rising tides – he's heard Susie whittering on about changing climates and islands of plastic. Can't work out how everybody is going to put things right by paying twenty-five pence for a carrier bag and using a different type of straw in their plastic bottles.

'What's it all about, eh, my pretty? What's it all about?'

He holds one of his homing pigeons in his left hand, its coral claws pricking at his palm, heart pulsing rapidly against his wrist. He turns it. Raises it to his face. Lets it nuzzle his craggy features and peck amiably at the grey, straggly moustache and beard.

He looks up into the dovecote. He built this collection of wood and wire from scratch. Could have afforded to have it done properly but Big Rab likes to spend his money wisely. Likes to do things himself if he can. Hates it when he's not capable.

'Capable,' he scoffs, a snort of hot air ruffling the pigeon's

iridescent throat. He turns his head and gazes at the wall above
the cooing, humming birds. There was a doorway up there,
once upon a time – a hatch that opened onto a conveyor belt,
connecting up to the grain silo at the far end of the compound.
Plastered over now, of course. No use for what lies beyond
since they buried Davey. Wayne said he had plans for the place
but he has no doubt they've come to nothing. Talks a good
game, does Wayne. Thinks a lot of himself. Truth be told, he
was never Rab's favourite. Neither was Davey.

The wind seems to change direction as he stares out across
the pitted, oil-puddled yard. Slaps of cold rain against his face.
He doesn't move. Just stares out, eyes like cherry pits, face
unreadable. This is his kingdom: a large farmhouse and a
smattering of outbuildings, empty stables, workers' cottages;
a couple of acres of muddy nothingness, all bound up in electric
and barbed wire and only accessible down a video-monitored,
tree-snarled private road. It may only be a ten-minute walk
from the local pub in Sutton, but nobody comes here uninvited.
Nobody comes here without an appointment.

A muscle twitches by his left eye as a memory demands
attention. The big copper. The Scotsman. Eyes like a poet
and a body like a berserker in a smart suit. He'd knocked on
the door bold as brass. Hadn't looked more than slightly
embarrassed as the dogs went halfway rabid and three of Big
Rab's boys ran across the muddy yard wielding the first things
they'd laid their hands on. Detective Inspector, he said, a
little embarrassed at the fuss. Cold Case Unit. Wanted to talk
about Davey . . .

He'd known it was coming, of course. Known all his life
that he was only ever a few steps ahead of what was coming
after him. All he asked was time. He's so damn close to making
amends. So close to retribution, redemption, revenge. He'd
been spared a meeting with the copper. Too ill, they told him.
Too old. Doesn't know up from down and can't be trusted
with anything sharper than a wooden spoon. Gone ga-ga. Sits
in his bed in the big house and drools into his pyjamas. Wayne
had laid it on thick. Susie had backed him up. There'd be no
talking to Big Rab any time soon. His doctor had been called

upon to provide a diagnosis of vascular dementia. He hadn't made a fuss. Just pocketed the envelope and asked Rab just how sick he wanted to seem. He's warned him not to push it too far. He needs to be ill enough not to talk to the police, but still considered compos mentis enough for the deal to go through without fear of being called into question further down the line.

He shivers. Hates himself for it. Pulls his leather jacket closed around himself. It used to be tight on him. Used to cling to big muscles and show off his thick, inked neck. Hangs on him now. Makes him look like a kid wearing his dad's clothes.

He raises the pigeon again. Goes slightly cross-eyed as he stares into the dark circles of its eyes and rubs one lined, dirty finger through the soft feathers at its throat.

'What else could I do, eh?' he whispers to the bird, feeling its head against his cheek and nuzzling it with a softness, a gentleness, that few see. He loves his birds. Always has. Treats them softer than the books recommend. He was a good scrapper, back in the day. He never really enjoyed fighting but he was good at it. Capable. Kept his head when all those about him were losing theirs. Fought steady, letting his opponents tire themselves out with ill-disciplined storms of adrenaline and rage. Weathered the storms and put them down once they were too tired to stay standing. He remembers the feeling of peeling the bandages off his hands; blood staining them red, his limbs trembling, every inch of his body feeling bruised, used. Remembers the feeling of having his hand raised. Remembers the feeling of looking down upon whichever man he has beaten bloody. The feeling of conquest. Of victory. He'd hate to admit it but there are times he has fancied himself as some sort of modern gladiator – a warrior engaged in brutal, winner-takes-all combat. Rather likes the idea that he is a link in a chain of warriors going back to the first men. Wonders, sometimes, how he would fare against different warriors from other ages. Makes-believe he is stripped to the waist and going one-on-one against martial artists; ultimate fighters; tries to decide whether he could take down a Viking, a samurai, a Native American.

'Daft sod,' he mutters to himself, turning away from the teeming rain. He reaches up and puts the bird back into its box. Listens to the other pigeons emit their chorus of warm coos in the adjacent boxes and sings a chorus of some half-remembered sea shanty to calm them – his voice barely audible over the sound of the rain on the mossy slate of the outbuilding. For a moment he feels lost. The instant he turns his back upon the familiar view he suffers a sensation of falling; of coming loose, un-tethered. His balance seems to go. Suffers a vision of a porthole in high seas – the landscape seeming to shift and slosh. He lets out a gasp and has to reach out to steady himself, his hand not quite closing around the greasy wood of the supporting wall. He feels drunk. Feels like he's fallen asleep in the sun. Feels the way he did when little Den Jarvie headbutted him under the chin and caused both legs to render themselves unconscious – the top half of his body continuing to swing punches even as his lower extremities gave in to unconsciousness.

He manages to get himself to the paint-splattered wooden stool by his workbench. Through the smashed glass of his vision, he sees his father's tools scattered across the old, rain-speckled wood. Feels a sudden anger at himself for not putting them away properly – for letting his weakness win. He presses the heel of one hand to his eye and starts picking up hammers, chisels, an awl with a wooden handle that still carries his father's faded yellow thumbprint on the worn wood. The effort of movement seems to drain him and he sinks onto the wooden stool, head pounding, sweat breaking out across his forehead; a musky scent of talc and baby formular, wood shaving and sweat, bird shit and Golden Virginia tobacco. Closes his jacket around his loose, sagging gut. Feels shame.

'All right, Dad?'

Big Rab pulls his nose with forefinger and thumb. Hocks back snot and tears and spits into the dirty water and pigeon droppings. Wipes his eyes and gives his attention to his son. Middle-aged, now. Middle-aged and doing grand, thank you. Nice house, decent family, a wife who doesn't make a fuss; nice little sideline teaching waifs and strays how to solve their problems without picking up a knife. Taken his brother's idea and made it real – his fight club and training school now something of a local institution, and a useful place for Rab to identify the lads who are worth keeping an eye on; sponsoring, making loyal; bringing in to the fold.

'Miles away,' grunts Rab, rummaging in his pocket for his tobacco tin. He starts trying to roll a cigarette. Feels his hands start to tremble and forces himself not to give in.

'Here, have one of these,' says Wayne, offering him a cigarette from a white packet with a circle of gold beyond the tip. Rab takes it. Lets his son light it for him then place it between his dry lips. Breathes in and pushes out a long plume of smoke with a grisly, rattly noise. Makes a face.

'You suffering, Dad?'

Rab shrugs. 'In my prime. Don't I look it?'

Wayne smiles. Finds a plastic school chair under a pile of discarded boxes and sits himself down. He's trying to keep his expression warm but Rab can see there's a worry gripping his features beneath the surface.

'You want a tea or owt? There's some of that cherry brandy if you want a tot. I can make you something to eat if . . .'

'Don't fuss, Wayne. I'll eat as and when.' He looks at his son until he meets his gaze. 'You'll give yourself an ulcer worrying the way you do.'

Wayne changes his position. He opens his mouth as if trying to find the right selection of words. Stops himself. Puts his head in his palm. Closes his eyes before he speaks. 'He's coming, Dad,' he says, quietly. 'You know that, don't you? One in Braşov. Another in Sibiu. Took down a Krav Maga teacher on the Austrian border. Rafe hears everything. Says he's coming . . .'

'Let him fucking come,' grunts Rab, glaring at his boy. He shakes his head. 'One mistake – I make one bloody mistake and it turns into a life sentence.'

He thinks for a moment of that day, decades ago, when his compassion got the best of him: when he took something he shouldn't have. When he made a deal with a bad man in exchange for the chance to do some good.

'That copper,' protests Wayne, miming a stranglehold. 'You think he's got the first idea?'

'Least of our troubles, son,' says Rab, spitting foully onto the damp floor. 'We just need to hold firm. Get the deal over the line. Then nothing else matters. We can do what we always said we would do. He'll honour the deal. What have we got if not our word?'

Even as he says it, Rab knows he's lying. Every good deed he's ever carried out has been tainted by association. He wants something pure. Decent. And he won't have that until he's paid off his debts.

'I can warn him off,' says Wayne, without enthusiasm. 'Or Rafe could send the lads . . .'

'This is where you get yourself in trouble, lad,' snaps Rab, his voice catching. 'This is how you think yourself into drama.'

'What do you expect?' asks Wayne, volume rising. 'We could lose everything, Dad. All your plans, everything you've worked for, the people you've helped . . . and the gym. I mean, that's my lifeline, Dad. They're my boys. Ryan – if you'd seen him when he first came, three stone wet through, eyes like yoghurt pits, all cat bites and ticks and hadn't eaten more than dry noodles for months. You see him now – he's got a future, Dad. A bit of sponsorship, a couple of big name victories and I swear he could be in the octagon within five years. But not if . . . not if it all comes out . . .'

Rab holds up a hand. Looks at his son with the same gentleness he tends to his pigeons. When he speaks, his voice is soothing, soporific.

'Knuckle down, son,' says Rab. 'Keep a hold of yourself. Whatever happens down the line, we can't affect that and I doubt I'll be here to deal with it. All we have to do is hold our nerve until the deal goes through. Owt comes out after that, pin it on me. What are they going to do? I'm ga-ga. I'm nigh-on eighty. Hero of the parish. You think they're going to pursue it? Let 'em. A few months inside? Holiday camp, lad.'

Both men are silent for a moment, their memories the same. They have shared cells together. Shed blood together. Huddled up for warmth in the corner of an overcrowded concrete cell, taking it in turns to stay awake in case any of the other prisoners decided to go and make a name for themselves against the Englishmen. Rab closes his eyes, his head flooding with memories. A gallery of faces swims in his imagination; dark-eyed, pale-limbed children staring out silently through rusted bars. Hears the thud of the matron as her head smacked against the floor. Feels again the pressure against his chest as he runs, quickly, down an unlit corridor – two children clinging against him, half wrapped up in blankets, his coat; the blood rushing in his ears as he realises what he's doing, what he's becoming; the crimes he has just committed.

He stops the train of thought. Breathes out, raggedly.

'Look at this, lad,' he says, wheezily. Pulls himself up and reaches up to the workbench, fingers searching for the groove behind the vice. He feels the little bump with the pad of his index finger and pushes it, letting the whole top panel of the workbench slide free on well-oiled casters. He puts his weight on his forearms and pushes himself up. He feels Wayne at his side. Together, they look down at the blueprint. Rab feels a warm blush of pride in his chest. This will be his legacy, he tells himself. It's all for this. Tell the lies, keep the secrets, do what needs to be done but the deal must go through. He's already paid out more than he could afford to get the builders sinking shafts and digging out foundations. If Rafe lets the deal slip through, he's ruined. Not that Rafe seems worried. The cocky bastard never looks anything other than in perfect control, even when he was little more than a teenager who found himself locked up in a Romanian jail with Rab and his boys. Seemed in his element, truth be told. Made friends quickly. Made alliances. Learned how the place worked and how to make the most of it. Came out of that hellish place smelling sweeter than when he went in, having made the contacts that could, God willing, make them all rich.

Rab looks at the blueprint. At the succession of little passport photographs that frame them, each stuck down with a blob of glue; dozens of children. Some smile, others stare into the camera as if it were a gun.

'We've changed lives, lad. Made a difference. But this – this is legacy. This is keeping up the good fight even after I'm gone. This is what it's all for.'

Wayne puts a hand on his dad's shoulder. Squeezes it. 'They could still fuck it for us, Dad. That copper – he's not like the last one. Doesn't seem like a copper at all. You know he can fight, yeah? Puttock sent me a clip – him and this mad gypsy bastard and the copper got the better of him, and . . .'

'Stop,' says Rab, flicking his cigarette. It tastes wrong. He pulls out his own tin again, trying to open the lid with his painful, twisted hands.

'Mae should know better,' mutters Wayne. 'Talking to the papers. I mean . . . how does that look?'

'Your mam's on that, son. Playing a blinder. Rafe knows what he's doing. It's in the blood.'

'Rafe, Rafe, fucking Rafe,' spits Wayne, a sudden flash of temper. He slams the tin down on the blueprint of the lavish building. 'You'd forgive him anything if it meant you got a statue when you're gone, Dad. Everything we've lost – it doesn't get put right just because you've built a fucking orphanage . . .'

Rab thinks about slapping his son. Thinks again. Doesn't reckon he could even be relied upon to connect, let alone put him down. He isn't angry with the lad. God knows he's paid a high price for being a Hawksmoor. Never got a chance to decide who he wanted to be. Got it easier than others, of course. Got it easier than the children that Rab pulled out of hell. He has to cling to that certainty. Can't ever allow himself to think he may have done the wrong thing. Doing the right thing has cost him dear enough.

'Has he called?' asks Wayne, lowering his voice. 'I know he thinks he's being recorded, but . . . he must want some reassurance?'

Rab doesn't answer. Chews his cheek. Thinks of the boy. Thinks of the kid with the twisted limbs and the dark eyes and the look of desperate pleading. Remembers the feeling of his knitted limbs about his torso. Remembers the perfect feeling of the two infants slumbering against his chest. Remembers the feeling of having done something from which there was no coming back – something that would define his life. He swallows bile as his mind folds in on him. Shows him again the pit beneath the railway bridge. The wet, gritty floor. The two semicircles of supporters, enthusiasts, gamblers. Remembers the moment the fighter walked out from between the two ranks; the birthmark on his cheek now incorporated into a great whirling mass of tattoos and scars. He closes his eyes. Remembers grief more bitter, more delicious, than he felt the night he learned about his son's execution. He reaches for his cigarettes. Manages to open the tin.

He takes a pinch of fluffy, coppery tobacco. Lets his fingers dwell upon the hard, yellow-white objects that nestle in the base of the tin like toppled headstones. He feels the electrical charge as they touch his skin. Stirs them with his finger. Counts them. Presses his fingertip against the sharpness of point and root. Closes the tin before Wayne can help. Isn't sure he's ready to explain the tin of cracked, scraped adult incisors that he carries in his pocket like rosary beads. Thinks: Davey, and feels the fist of grief and loss in his gut.

'Dad, is he coming? Is he on his way? If we lost everything now . . .'

Rab puts his hand on his son's cheek. Makes him hold his gaze. 'Play your part, lad. Do things my way and we all get what we want. Even the journalist. Even that copper with the big eyes.'

'McAvoy?'

Rab makes a face. Shrugs. 'No,' he concedes. 'No, I think he's going to be disappointed.'

'And if he gets too close?' asks Wayne.

Rab lights his roll-up. Looks out through the smoke and into the tumbling rain. Accepts that he can only part the seas so many times. He can't save everybody. Feels a moment's compassion for the big, lumbering Jock. Poor sod doesn't know what he's up against. Doesn't even know the name *Strigoi*. By the time he does, he'll already be halfway dead.

'We'll send flowers to the funeral.'

FIVE

Irish Examiner Special Investigation: How Ireland's Most
Dangerous Gangsters Still Rule The Roost Behind Bars
By Padraig O'Connell
12 September, 2022

Quinlan cartel-linked gangsters are now the undisputed
controlling force within the criminal population of Mountjoy
Prison. Official figures claim there are currently 166 inmates
from 14 criminal gangs jailed in prisons across the Republic
of Ireland.

However, prison sources say the reality is the lines between
the different gangs have become so blurred, with the influence
of the Quinlan cartel all pervasive, the traditional divides
can no longer be said to apply.

Five prisons, in particular, house the majority of the
country's most notorious gangland criminals. These are
Mountjoy, Portlaoise, Wheatfield, Castlerea and Limerick.

Castlerea Prison is currently home to the criminal dubbed
by prison officers as 'The West's Mr Big'. This man cannot
currently be named as he is before the courts on serious
charges relating to gangland crime.

Sources said the criminal who is on the prison's A-Wing
controls the drug trade in Sligo and the surrounding
counties . . .

SIX

The rain beats angrily at the dirty glass, hammering on the roof of the battered SUV with a sound like static and burning leaves. The wipers screech and thunk their way through a transparent lacquer of rainwater, carving little viewing holes into the flood. Beyond the glass, the trees thrash madly, bare black branches twisting as the gale rushes in across the flat, bare farmland; a mosaic of flooded fields, drowned earth.

'Coming down, isn't it?' says Lilah, again. She's in the passenger seat of the tatty SUV, legs drawn up, squinting through the gap she has smeared in the condensation. 'It's weird we only have one word, isn't it? I mean . . . rain. It's more than that, isn't it? This is . . . mental.'

McAvoy shoots her a glance. She's been told about using the same words as Mammy and Auntie Trish.

'Sorry,' mutters Lilah, into her knees. 'I mean rain with a particular set of problems that it's working through.'

McAvoy gives a nod, satisfied that he's done something that qualifies as parenting. Checks the speedometer and realises he's only ten mph below the speed limit. Slows down, lest anybody think him a maniac. He isn't sure who might make such an accusation. They've barely seen another car since leaving the city boundary. Here, five miles north, they have the dead roads to themselves, the road shimmering where the raindrops smash into the pitted tarmac, the flooded dykes; black water seeming to boil beneath the onslaught.

'Torrential,' says McAvoy. 'That's a good word. You should try and work that into one of your stories.'

Lilah gives him a look. 'That isn't how it works, Daddy. You don't pick the words first and then the story after. I thought you'd know that.'

McAvoy can't help himself. He takes a hand off the steering

wheel and gives his daughter's head a little rub. Scratches her behind the ear. She puts her tongue out. Rolls her eyes in ecstasy. Kicks one leg like a dog.

'Funny, isn't it,' says Lilah, sighting the street sign through the teeming rain. 'A place called Swine. And it's a *ham*let. I mean, that's funny.'

McAvoy made the joke last time they came to see Mae. He doesn't mind her repeating it back to him.

'It's an old word for "creek",' says McAvoy, slowing down as they pass the red-brick houses and pull in at the shingled drive of the tall, ivy-clad property at the end of the lane. 'It's probably unpopular with the real hardcore vegans.'

Lilah flaps a hand, shushing him. She turns in the seat and gives him what she likes to think of as her hard stare. 'You're proper sure it wasn't Mae, aren't you? I mean, what if she killed her husband? Everybody's a suspect, and this story about being at the hairdresser's sounds proper suspect to me.'

McAvoy chokes on a cough, sucking in a quick, gasping breath as his mind sprints ahead to the inevitable decades of psychiatric therapy that his daughter is going to need. Wonders, with a familiarity of thought, whether it might be impossible to undo some of the damage that his profession has inflicted upon his family.

'We can't talk about the investigation, Lilah. You're still too . . . little.'

Lilah hardens her stare. 'I'm going to pretend you didn't say that, Daddy. Anyway, Mammy says she thinks that it's that Susie woman, the one who said the mean things in the paper. She reckons she's a dark horse and a sly one and that we shouldn't believe all that butter-wouldn't-melt nonsense. I think I've remembered that right. She said "fecking" a lot, if that helps.'

McAvoy imagines his wife in full flow, eyes flashing, silken black hair tangled in her necklaces and earrings, letting out her full Pavee temper. He wishes he could dismiss her theory. Doesn't trust Susie Hawksmoor an inch. He just hopes he's right about Mae Lockhart. If it turns out she battered her own husband to death at the columbarium, he fancies he'll regret introducing her to his daughter.

'She's very grateful we're looking into it,' says McAvoy, in his best politician voice. 'Mae was the one who pushed and pushed for this. To be honest, I don't think Trish really had many plans to do anything with it, but then suddenly her reporter friend starts making noises and then . . . well, here we are.'

'Her reporter friend?' asks Lilah, pressing her lips together. 'I don't know this bit.'

'Auntie Trish has an old friend who makes documentaries. I'm probably being cynical, but I think it might be about getting ahead of the problem. Auntie Trish is being a bit . . . a bit evasive.'

'Cynical,' muses Lilah. 'That's different to sinful, yes?'

A gap in the hedgerow permits McAvoy the chance to change the subject. He turns in through the big gates, stomach in his throat, trying once more to reconcile himself to the selfishness of making a living by helping people.

McAvoy kills the engine. Listens to the rain. Reaches out and takes Lilah's hand in his. Looks into eyes that are so much like her mother's that he sometimes finds it unnerving.

'If Mae talks about anything grown-up, you know what to do, don't you? I can trust you to go to the toilet? Not to listen?'

Lilah gives an audible tut. 'It's not my first rodeo, Daddio,' she says, in an accent he hadn't heard before. 'No grown-up stuff. Promise.'

McAvoy looks up as the light comes on over the front door. Watches through the smeared glass as the little shape appears in the doorway: a damp impressionist painting, blobs of pinks and cream and browns.

'Come on,' says McAvoy, opening his long dark coat and gesturing for her to climb inside. 'Cling on tight.'

He tries not to wince as she clambers onto him, arms around his neck, face in his beard, trying to wrap her legs around his middle. He opens the door and feels the storm rush inside – half stumbles as he extricates himself from the vehicle and dashes to the safety of the front porch, Lilah laughing against his neck, coat wrapped around her and one hand protecting her scalp.

'Blowing a hoolie!' says Mae, stepping back inside the house

and pulling a face. McAvoy wipes his feet on the rug. Shakes
the rain from his hair. Puts Lilah down and tries to straighten
his clothes. There are footprints on his dark blue jeans and the
stitching has come unfastened at the pocket of his waistcoat.

'Well, you've got Daddy trained up well, haven't you, little
miss,' says Mae, indulgently. She's wearing a cream cardigan
pulled tight over a bony frame; woollen tights disappearing
into a pair of plum-coloured slippers; a roll-neck jumper with
a heart-shaped necklace; greying hair cut short, mid-range
spectacles adding definition to a pinched, mousy face. She
always looks cold. Always looks like she should be sitting in
front of an electric heater and reading *The People's Friend*.

'It's boiling in here,' says Lilah, tugging at the neck of her
top. She shrugs herself out of her leather jacket. Looks at her
father. 'Daddy, you can't come in here. You'll melt.'

Mae pulls her cardigan around herself. A tissue falls from
her sleeve but she doesn't bother to pick it up. Mae hasn't got
very much energy. Saves it up for when it's needed.

'It is rather warm, Mae,' says McAvoy, feeling the raindrops
evaporate and a sheen of sweat take their place. 'Is it the
warfarin, do you think? They thin the blood something fierce.'

Mae looks up. Licks pale lips. 'You don't have to come,
Aector. That's five visits in two weeks. People will talk! I don't
need checking up on. Not if there's nothing new to say.'

McAvoy takes off his coat. Hangs it on the hook behind the
door. Unfastens his waistcoat and lets out a breath of relief.
'Not my call, Mae. Her majesty here – wouldn't let me go
home without seeing you.'

'Seeing Kenny, you mean,' says Mae, with a tired smile.
She plucks at the material of her jumper. Looks around. 'He
was here. Go look, if you like. The biscuits are where they
should be.'

'No they're not,' says Lilah. 'But they will be when I've eaten
them.'

She pulls off her mucky boots and speeds down the hall,
leaving little wet footprints on the polished wood. McAvoy
hears a sudden round of bronchial barking; a sound like somebody inflating an airbed with a foot pump full of custard.

'He's sounding well,' says McAvoy, impressed. Kenny is the Methuselah of the canine world, a dog old enough to remember the last time East Yorkshire was assaulted by a Biblical flood. McAvoy has stopped reminding Lilah to be careful with him. He may look like the end of a sweep's brush and have no control over any of his bodily functions, but there's a toughness about him that suggests he'll outlast his owner.

'I see Susie was giving you hell,' says Mae, sitting down on the second step and pulling her cuffs over her sleeves. 'That woman. Thinks she's only got to snap her fingers and people will do what they're told. Not that she's got that much snap in them. Arthritis. Going a bit dotty, too, though you didn't hear that from me.'

'Where did you hear that?' asks McAvoy, running his gaze over the pictures on the staircase.

'I've still got friends there, Aector,' she says, as if this should be self-explanatory. 'I worked for that family, that woman . . . that *clan!* . . . for nigh-on twenty years. The drivers keep their ears to the ground but their mouths open and they say she keeps having funny turns and repeating herself and talking like she's got her head stuck in the wrong year. Wouldn't be surprised if it's all an act. Deceitful to the bone. Mean, too, if you read between the lines. You didn't take any notice, I hope. Didn't let it get to you.'

McAvoy leans back against the door. Considers the slight, frail figure at the foot of the stairs. Gives her the truth.

'She wasn't wrong, was she? I've done nothing. Got nothing. Dug things up and made a lot of people unhappy and I haven't moved an inch closer to a conclusion. She's within her rights to have a go.'

Mae reaches up and straightens a watercolour that hangs askew on the gallery wall by the stairs. It's a church; big yew trees and bright summer flowers, pretty headstones, popcorn clouds. 'If I thought that was true I wouldn't have let you in the house,' says Mae, quietly. 'Certainly wouldn't have the little princess eating my Jammie Dodgers and upsetting Kenny's digestion. You know you're a good man, don't you?' She stops herself. Tilts her head and looks up at the giant scarred

Scotsman in her hallway. 'Maybe you don't, eh? Maybe you've no idea.'

'The piece in the *Mail* . . .'

She shakes her head. 'Didn't tell me, of course. Didn't know the *Mail* was running it until I was in the newsagent and his face was staring up at me. You can imagine, can't you? Felt like I'd turned to water.'

McAvoy closes his eyes. Curses himself afresh. He hadn't had time to warn her. Didn't know the *Mail* was running the article until it was already on newsstands and lighting up phone screens.

'She's hurting too,' says McAvoy, gently. 'We all grieve in our own way.'

Mae plucks at her sleeve. Scrunches up her handkerchief. 'Never seen much in the way of sadness from her, Aector. Just temper. You're seeing that now. Bet she was sweet as lemon meringue the first time you met, eh?'

McAvoy spins his wedding ring. Sucks his cheek. Mae's a good judge of character. Wonders what she really thinks of him – what she tells her handful of friends and acquaintances about the big lumbering copper who's promised the earth and delivered only more disappointments.

There's a peal of laughter from the kitchen followed by a clatter. McAvoy winces. Mae smiles.

'Everything all right?'

The pause speaks volumes. Mae pulls herself up. She pauses, briefly, as she makes her way down the hall. Looks up at McAvoy with a sad, tight smile. 'Sometimes we don't get answers, you do know that, don't you? Sometimes bad things happen and we just have to live with them.'

She doesn't let him answer. Carries on down the hall, trailing a scent that makes him think of home: of biscuits, soap, furniture polish. He takes a moment to collect himself. Wishes he'd been able to bring Roisin. She's good at making people feel better. Saves his life every day that she loves him.

He lingers for a while in the doorway. Lets his gaze rest on the gallery of old photos and bland watercolours. Spots Mae, curly haired and bright-eyed, grinning from a rococo frame:

ivory wedding dress and a posie of pink and purple flowers. He'd like to know what they are. Pulls out his phone and takes a picture of the snap. Examines it on the screen, forcing himself to zoom in on the groom. On Davey Hawksmoor: solid and meaty and big across the chest: silvery-grey suit straining across a great slab of torso. It's a mandarin collar worn over a fuchsia shirt and gaudy purple tie – neck bulging over the hard line of material like batter. He's managing a half-smile for the camera, one eye closed, cigarette held in a round, ape-like fist. He's got ink on his knuckles: the symbols from playing cards, a spider-web; a pale blue sparrow curling around his thumb.

'Bit of a spillage here, Aector – would you mind?'

McAvoy makes his way into the kitchen. It's a warm, cosy space, terracotta flagstones and a red Aga, pans hanging from a stainless steel range and a bunch of fresh flowers haphazardly stuffed in a tall vase on the wooden table. Lilah is on her hands and knees, mopping at a spreading pool of water with her hoodie. Kenny is shivering by the washing machine, looking guilty.

'It's not a bother, my love,' says Mae, fussing, rummaging in drawers. 'Honestly, your lovely leggings . . . your mother will have my guts for garters. Little sod's forever thinking he's still a puppy.'

McAvoy crouches down beside his daughter. 'You OK, my love?'

She looks up, hair falling in front of her eyes. Pulls a face that offers a heartfelt apology. 'He got a bit overexcited . . .'

'Here, use this,' says Mae, throwing a yellow hand towel to McAvoy. He helps Lilah up and starts blotting the spillage. Glances up and out through the big double glass doors and into the garden – rain falling in great diagonal blasts onto the neatly landscaped rectangle of green; trees bent at the waist, ripples on the ornamental pond.

'We'll be losing the koi if the water doesn't stop rising,' says Mae, absently, following his gaze.

'Could that happen?' asks Lilah, crossing to the windows. Kenny trots beside her.

'Happened last time,' says Mae, rearranging the flowers in

the vase. 'Course, we were in the other house then. He dug that, y'know. My Davey. Did it all himself. Dab hand at anything practical. Could wield a hammer better than Thor.'

McAvoy stands, knees wet. He notices the little square of card on the table beside the vase. Angles his head and reads the message. *Thinking of you at a difficult time, R x.*

He wonders if he should ask. Whether he could find a way, this late in the game, to get good at small talk.

'Rafe,' says Mae. 'Cadogan. You'll have met, I shouldn't wonder.'

McAvoy moves to the sink and wrings out Lilah's sodden hoodie, dislodging a handful of diamanté crystals from the sleeve. He fancies Roisin isn't going to be pleased. Opens a drawer at random, hunting out a carrier bag. Pauses, for just a moment, as he spies the collection of pictures stuffed away among the tea towels and Tupperware. Sees Big Rab Hawksmoor, open-necked shirt and straggly beard, big silver cross and mutton-chop sideburns. He's standing in the back of a wagon loaded with gaily coloured shoeboxes and bulging pallets, hands on his hips. He's wearing a Santa hat on his head. There's a red cross painted onto the side of the wagon, the paint barely dry. Davey lingers in the back of the shot, leaning against a stack of pallets, drinking from a lager bottle. His gold belcher chain dangles at his tattooed chest, disappearing into a greasy white vest that shows off lean, athletic muscles. McAvoy finds himself thinking of the postmortem report; of the pattern of bruises around his neck; his chain pushed deep enough into his own flesh to break the skin. He stops himself before he lets the full horror of the report flood him. Has spent long enough dwelling on the horrific injuries; the snapped limbs, torn tendons, dislocated joints. Whoever had killed Davey Hawksmoor, the one thing he knows for certain is that they must have taken him unawares. Davey was the real deal, an old-school hard man who'd started fighting on the cobbles before finding his way into kickboxing, Krav Maga and jeet kune do. He helped out at his brother's mixed martial arts academy and McAvoy has read first-hand accounts of the dead man's grapples with a litany of bare-knuckle fighters; his unblemished record; the people he hospitalised in bouts conducted in front of only a handful of attendees and an occasional camcorder.

McAvoy looks again at the crimson paint. Gives a little smile, remembering the incident from the file. Big Rab got into a lot of bother with the Red Cross for using their symbol without permission. He'd told the authorities he'd had no choice – used it as a deterrent to the snipers who preyed upon wagon drivers in the snow-filled, dark-forested wilderness of the Carpathian Mountains. He wonders why Mae put the picture in the drawer – whether she did so when she heard him pull into the drive, or if he's being paranoid. He'll ask Roisin. She knows him better than he does.

'Thoughtful lad Rafe, but a bit smooth for my taste,' says Mae, appearing at his side and closing the drawer with her hip.

McAvoy gives a little nod. Pictures the smooth, briskly efficient executive: crisp blue suit, brown brogues, hair gel and neat moustache. He fancies that his eye-glasses are an affectation, an accessory worn to project an air of bookish intellectualism. He'll admit to not having warmed to him, though he fancies he may have caught him at a bad time.

'Did you hear that, Daddy? We might get carp if they swim to Hessle. If we leave buckets out, we could get anything. A cod. A squid.'

'A mermaid,' says McAvoy, smiling. He arches his back. 'It's getting mad out there. Darkening over too. I think we'll get out of your hair, Mae. Now we've made a mess of the kitchen I think we've achieved everything we set out to. Lilah, what do you say to Mae?'

Mae crosses back to the window. Bends down and strokes her dog. Loses herself in her thoughts. 'Did you get your biscuits?' asks Mae, suddenly, looking at Lilah. 'I think I made flapjacks. Rafe didn't touch them. He's on some fancy diet. No carbs or sugars, or some such. Training regime, I think. More Davey's business than mine, all that. Never did like violence.'

McAvoy feels the questions lining up like bullets. Knows

he's mishandled things. Shouldn't even be here, making nice and playing house with the grieving widow. He suddenly feels uncomfortable – hot inside his skin.

'Kenny showed me where they are,' says Lilah, grinning. 'Nearly as good as Mammy's.'

Mae grins, happy with what she knows to be a genuine compliment. 'You get on home, then. Keep an eye out for dolphins. Sharks too. You don't want a conga eel coming up the toilet, do you?'

Lilah smiles, her mind awash with delightfully naughty images. She runs to her dad and folds her hand into his. He gives it a squeeze. Stands for a moment. Sees himself, all hopeless and guileless, pitifully inert. Lilah pulls him towards the door.

'We'll see you next week,' shouts Lilah, over her shoulder. Then, to Kenny: 'Don't die in the meantime!'

McAvoy spots the *Hull Daily Mail* on top of the recycling bin as he leaves. It's folded to the page that slates him; lays his inadequacies bare. Sees the picture of Susie Hawksmoor: devil horns and evil eyes scrawled on her likeness in black pen. Allows himself the slightest smile.

Mae doesn't see them out. Just sits and stares at the pond her husband dug, stroking the dog who watched him die.

SEVEN

Pharaoh winces. Shudders. Gives in to the beginnings of a swoon. Acts like she's not entirely familiar with how easily a limb breaks and how far blood can shoot from a broken nose. If she had a fan, she'd waft it and ask for her petticoats to be loosened: perhaps call for smelling salts and sweet tea.

'Go on . . . look, love. Easier than explaining, innit? This is Agi. Asian lad. Nice lad. Davey did it for his own good, I swear. Not that he was grateful at the time.'

Pharaoh snatches a look at the screen. Sweaty bodies, muscle shirts and jeans, white-trainered lads bouncing on their toes and yelling death-cries as their sensei goes to work on a small, pot-bellied teenager; face all but ripping open as he screams with the enormity of his pain.

'Snaps it there, see,' says Daz, a little unnecessarily. He jabs at the screen with his finger. Pauses it just as the arm bends the wrong way; wrist contorted at a grotesque angle, forefingers wrenched and twisted inwards to touch its tip against a tattooed, blue-veined pulse.

'It's a customised half-kimura,' says Daz, his mouth full of pickled egg. 'I can do it nearly as well but I've never gone past the breaking point. Makes me feel all dizzy just thinking about it.' He swallows. Takes another bite. He looks to Trish as if he's biting a golf ball in two. 'An arm lock, basically. Snaps the wrist like a stick. So painful I can't even find the words. Like, nothing else in the world matters to you in the moment – all you want is for them to let go. You can put it on from any position. Standing, mount, side control, closed guard, open guard. Here, watch.'

He presses play on the paused phone. 'Look at the poor sod's face. That's not healing for months. Some initiation, eh? Came back, though. Anybody worth a shit came back.'

Pharaoh looks at the man in the booth beside her. They're uncomfortably close together, her damp black dress touching his sodden tracksuit bottoms. She can see the spots at his hairline where he's shaved with a blunt razor. Can smell the diesel and sawdust fug that rises from his denim jacket.

'He did this to you?'

Daz sniffs. Tugs at his nose with his forefinger and thumb. Looks at his empty whiskey glass and seems to be about to suggest another. He's already eaten three eggs and two packets of chicken-flavour crisps. Deciding which to eat first hadn't proven a philosophical conundrum, opting to stuff great fistfuls into his sloppy mouth without pause.

'I appreciate this, Daz,' she says, putting her hand on his forearm, preening as if the scent of vinegary Sunday roasts were a potent aphrodisiac. 'It's brave, what you're doing. It matters.'

Daz huffs out a little snort of laughter. 'Don't give me any of that flannel,' he says, taking a tobacco tin from his jacket pocket and starting to roll himself a thin cigarette. Pharaoh spots a little bud of green herb nestling within the chocolate-coloured strands. She's being tested. He wants to know if she can turn a blind eye to the little things in pursuit of something important.

'He was a fucking bully,' says Daz, moistening the rollie with the tip of his tongue. He picks a piece of stray tobacco from the stubble at his chin. Places the finished cigarette on the top of the closed tin and stares at it, trying to smoke through osmosis.

'We can go outside if you'd rather,' says Pharaoh, keeping her manner light, helpful, eager-to-please. Daz Nolan wouldn't be her usual choice of company on a wet Sunday evening in January, but right now she's willing to keep supplying him with smiles, words of encouragement, Jameson's whiskey and any number of pickled eggs. It's a small price to pay for what he knows. She's not even asking the barman for receipts.

'Pissing down, innit? Feel like I've been wearing wet clothes for a month. I'll leave it for a bit.'

Pharaoh sips her fresh orange juice. Sees her own reflection in the darkened windows of the country pub; eyes dark, grey at her roots, boobs squashed together in the bra she wears when she fears that appealing to somebody else's good nature isn't going to work. She disgusts herself, sometimes. Wonders whether she'll ever have time to reconcile pragmatism with her ideals.

'He always said that fighters had to know what they were letting themselves in for,' says Daz, twisting his glass on the beery tabletop. 'Reckoned he was doing people a favour. Snap a wrist or dislocate a shoulder; fracture an ankle – he said that if you came back for more once you knew what's at stake, then he would give you everything he had. Would make you a fucking killing machine.'

Pharaoh cocks her head. Repeats the phrase.

'Oh aye, he spoke like that,' says Daz, grinning to show gleaming white prison-issue dental implants. 'No embarrassment in him. Called himself the Alpha. The Big Dog. Wanted us to start using "the General" one month 'cause he'd heard it in a film and reckoned he liked it. Thing is, it didn't feel daft at the time. Like, he was a warrior, you know? Stepped up against proper hard bastards and fought for his life. Put his body on the line for bragging rights. Had the right to crow about it, didn't he? And he did do us all some good. Him and Wayne both. I was in a fucked-up place when they found me. Plenty of us were. Don't get me wrong, my life's turned to shit anyways, but they spared me a few years. They're good people, the Hawksmoors. I read that the company is worth millions now, is that right? I mean, they were always pretty well off for money but the truth is, Big Rab would have given his last bloody penny to anybody who needed it – bet he's giving away his dividends and living on his pension, eh? Remember me to him, would you?' His face falls, a happy memory giving way to sad. 'Half broke him, losing Davey. And like that, too? I mean, he was hard as nails, love. If he'd been stabbed or shot or something . . . to die like that, in that place . . .'

Pharaoh drains her glass. Nods softly, eyes gentle. Wonders if he will be forthcoming, or whether a little visual aid of her own mightn't steer him towards making the disclosure she's come here for. She pulls out her own phone. Daz puts his away. She hadn't really wanted to see the compilation of locks, holds and strikes that he'd insisted would help her better understand what he was talking about. But she'd been glad she acquiesced – noting his passcode as he opened the home screen.

'This is you, isn't it?' says Pharaoh, gently, showing him a still from the footage recorded at Paragon Station. 'Welcoming back the conquering hero?'

Daz sticks his tongue inside his lower lip. Sucks his teeth. He looks at the screen and then at Pharaoh. Hardens his gaze.

'This a set-up, is it? Fuck, I said I would talk to you, that I'd try and remember something useful – same old coppers, always got a fucking truncheon behind their backs . . .'

Pharaoh smiles. Readjusts herself. 'No truncheon, Mr Nolan. Not so much as an unkind look, I promise you. It's not you I'm interested in. It's him.'

She zooms in. Angles the screen. Shows Daz the grainy image. 'Friend of Rab's?'

Daz sniffs again. Looks down at the table. Makes a face. 'Rab helps people. People want to repay him, y'know? That bloke was some friend of his. Fucked up, isn't he? Face like a chopping block. Scared the shit out of Wayne and me when we first saw him. We were clearing out some knackered old farm building up in the arse end of the mountains. Turned up with a pack of dogs and two dozen kids all milling after him like he was Jesus or Rocky or something. Wanted to come and say a personal thank you to us for all we'd done for the poor people of Romania. I think he was taking the piss a bit but it was all done through an interpreter, so I don't know. Wouldn't want to fight him, though. Chains on his wrists and ankles. Not jewellery, I mean proper chains, with padlocks and keys dangling off. Sucked silver paint out of a bag like it was sherbet. Could have been twenty-five or fifty, no clue.'

'He doesn't look like that here,' says Pharaoh, cautiously.

She doesn't want to put words in his mouth, much as she needs him to confirm her suspicions.

'Tarted himself up, didn't he?' says Daz, dismissively. He peers at the screen. 'This wasn't on the telly, was it? I'd have seen it. I remember the day, like. Long couple of weeks without much news of how they were doing. All we knew was he'd been banged up over there and that people were trying to get it sorted. Next thing one of the drivers who did a bit of work on the side for Rab – he's getting a call to say he's in the UK, getting on a train, that he's been through the wars but he's beaten the bastards at their own game. Susie's dancing a jig, Davey's feeling good, Wayne decides to get all the lads down there to welcome him back. Loves the cameras, does Rab.'

'And this is the same man you saw in Romania?'

'Different hair,' shrugs Daz, laughing at a memory. 'Reckon he'd have stood out, eh? I know Wayne had some good scraps with him. Training fights they called it but the fists fair flew. Said it was like fighting his reflection – bloke was as mad as he was. Wayne made a joke about it once – said that in a different world they could have been kin. Smart bloke, Wayne, under the bluster. Knew how to get people to do what he wanted. We heard all the stories, like. Him and those Irish nutters; the fights he had when he was still nowt but a boy, all gangstered up . . .' he stops himself, suddenly remembering who he's talking to. 'Fee for information, ain't there? Usually, like?'

'Do you remember the name, Daz?'

'Not worth your bother. He'll be dead now, love. Amount of track marks and scars and diseases that were running through that body. Why are you bothered about him anyway? You're not thinking he did in Davey, are you?'

Pharaoh doesn't reply. She'd love nothing more than to blurt out what she suspects. Would love to unburden herself to somebody, anybody, even if she fears she'd probably have to kill them afterwards. These past days have been lonely; isolating. She's given McAvoy what she can. Has created a passable cover story for the questions she's suddenly asking. Only feels slightly uncomfortable with the fact that she's had to order the re-opening of a murder investigation so she has a cover story for a larger, deeper investigation. Truth be told, she isn't sure she gives a damn who murdered Davey Hawksmoor. But she cares about Vicky. And Vicky hasn't so much as answered a phone call, a text or her own front door since she darted from Pharaoh's car on the third night of the tempest. Benedict told her she'd gone away for a few days when he allowed her as far as the inner door of the mansion in West Ella. Had looked a little put out. Pharaoh had only been able to see as far as the porch but she'd clocked that Vicky's coat and travel bag were missing from their hooks. He wouldn't be drawn on where she'd gone. Just said that she'd been given a last-minute job and had to dash. Wouldn't be in a signal zone. Had been good enough to stock the fridge before she'd gone.

'They call him Tinman, don't they?' asks Pharaoh, quietly.

Daz pauses, mouth pressed tightly shut. Eventually he gives a nod. 'I don't know why he was there, love. I don't know much. Nobody ever asked me 'owt when Davey died, like. I know some of the lads from the club got a knock on the door but I wasn't really . . . well, I wasn't in their good graces by then. Not that I had a grudge or anything.'

Pharaoh nods, understanding the unspoken dialogue. By the time of Davey Hawksmoor's murder, Daz Nolan had already slipped into the bad habits that the Hawksmoor brothers had tried to steer him away from. He was midway through a stretch in a young offender institute at that time – his gift for violence being put to use by a Preston Road drug dealer. His transgression meant he was no longer welcome at the fight club; the apprenticeship with the family firm yanked away from him the moment he felt the cuffs on his wrists.

'You could be forgiven for baring a grudge,' muses Pharaoh. 'You might have met some very helpful people on the inside, Daz. People who wouldn't think twice about taking somebody out for a few quid or bit of protection from a big lad like you.'

Daz closes an eye, all but tasting the air as he tries to detect the traps. 'I've had nowt to do with them for years, love. Have problems of my own, haven't I? More ups and downs than a Toblerone, that's my life. Every time I think I'm doing things right, I find a way to fuck it up. But I'm hanging on, love. Got a lass. Stepkid. Even working out a bit – keeping my hand in with a bit of coaching now and again – not that I can do much of that with my record. I don't think about the Hawksmoors.'

'And yet you responded to a TV producer when she called you, didn't you? Straight on the phone, wanting to talk numbers.'

Daz sits back against the cracked leather, his face illuminated by the flashing neon lights of the fruit machine; gaudy against the darkened windows, frosted with the diagonal rain.

'They make money on those things, don't they?' he asks, petulantly. 'All that true crime stuff. I'm no grass but nobody blames a fella for making a few quid for telling a few stories, do they? Anyway, she never got back in touch, did she? I didn't give it another thought until you called. Next thing there's a piece in the *Mail* with Susie saying you lot are a bunch of morons. Fierce, isn't she? We were more scared of her than Big Rab.'

Pharaoh straightens her dress. Steeples her fingers. Tries not to think of McAvoy. She's thrown him to the wolves, she knows that. Has put him in an impossible situation. Can already picture how reasonable and obliging he'll be when he realises she's used him as little more than a distraction so she can pursue her missing friend. She wonders how much more her conscience can take. Whether she mightn't just find the answers at the bottom of her next glass of wine.

'You were one of the last people she called,' says Pharaoh, evenly. 'Forty-three seconds. Six fourteen p.m., 2nd January.'

'Must have gone to voicemail, love,' he shrugs. 'She still keen, is she? 'Cause I can say what she likes if the price is right.' He picks up his cigarette. Rolls it under his nose. 'Mad start to the year, this. Biblical weather, TV reporter wanting to talk about the old days – now I'm sitting in a pub with a copper talking about Brazilian jiu-jitsu. My fucking life, eh?'

Pharaoh slides out of the booth to let him pass. Feels the bulk of his muscles under his coat. Hopes he doesn't ask her. Hopes he doesn't want to know why she's referring to the reporter as if she's missing or dead. If he doesn't ask, it's suspicious. And by Christ, she'd like to suspect somebody other

than the spectre she's putting together in her own mind and
whom she is rapidly coming to fear.

'She all right, is she?' asks Daz, looking back. 'Like, you
said it as if she's in bother.'

Pharaoh manages a grateful smile, even as her heart sinks.
'I can't discuss active investigations, Mr Nolan, I'm sorry.'

Daz shrugs. Mooches towards the door, rummaging in his
jacket for a lighter. Pharaoh watches him lumber out into the
dark: a chorus of 'shut the door' emanating from the group
of hardcore drinkers by the bar. As soon as he's gone she opens
his tobacco tin and takes out the cannabis bud. Wraps it in a
napkin and tucks it in her pocket. His phone is underneath
the tin. She doesn't even hesitate. Keys in the passcode and
scrolls nimbly to his recent text conversations. Finds a message
from a contact named RC. She reads the most recent, received
moments before Daz had returned her call. It's a strict instruction, written in capitals: MEET HER. TELL HER ENOUGH.
THEY'VE GOT NOTHING UNLESS YOU GIVE IT TO THEM.

Pharaoh starts reading the panicked, badly spelled message
that had prompted the response. Sees herself referred to as
'some copper' and a 'fucking bitch' in the space of the same
sentence and feels mildly gratified that she's lost none of her
touch.

She picks up her phone. Starts to take pictures. Almost drops
it when it starts to vibrate in her hand.

She looks at the screen, a message from an unknown number,
the area code unfamiliar; somewhere overseas.

Be by your phone at 8.

Moments later, the phone buzzes again. It's a photograph
– a grainy shot of an abandoned grey building; roof ripped
and torn, glassless windows like black eyes and gap teeth in a
leering Hallowe'en mask.

In her hand, the phone buzzes again.

I'm scared, Trish.

Pharaoh looks up as Daz returns, rubbing his hands, face
gleaming with a varnish of rain. He gives her a funny look.

'You all right, love? Pale as milk, you look. You want a glass
of water or something . . .'

Pharaoh snatches up her bag. Half drops her phone and catches it just before it hits the ground.

'Belting reflexes, love,' says Daz, approvingly. 'You off, are you? That all you want? I've been reading that there's people who get aid for providing a bit of help to the police, like. I mean, maybe we could formalise this a bit, eh? Take a look at the budget, see what you might—'

Pharaoh pushes past him, plucking a fiver from her bra and dropping it on the table.

'Don't spend it all on eggs,' she mutters, and stomps towards the door. She pulls her sunglasses on as she steps into the rain and the dark. Drives home too fast, three fresh tears in the fabric of the roof, rain cascading in. She opens the windows too. Takes the rain full in the face. Feels parts of herself revive. Feels her mind unspooling.

Screams into the teeth of the gale, throat half-scorched as untold secrets and bitter lies tumble into the storm in an unintelligible rush.

In time, the scream becomes a prayer.

Please, let me be wrong.

EIGHT

'This is flipping ridiculous. I mean, seriously. Look at flipping this! Flipped. All of it, soggy as a flipping flip.'

Detective Sergeant Andy Daniells isn't given to strong language but would presently be turning the air blue if not for the presence of Lilah McAvoy, sitting on the staircase and watching him waddle, watered to the waist, snatching at box files and folders and trying to push the filing cabinets back against the walls, even as the filthy water inches its way up the brick.

'It's still swearing,' says Lilah, disapproving. 'It just means I have to spend a moment working out what you really mean.'

Daniells splashes his way towards the brick staircase. Lilah is under instructions to hold the torch but has instead busied herself casting spotlights onto the dark, cracked ceiling. She's fascinated by the water that surges down through the gaps in the hanging plaster; that rises from the gaps between the bricks from underneath.

'This was a cell, wasn't it?' asks Lilah, again. 'Like, people would be handcuffed here and just left to rot?'

Daniells plods back to the shallow end of the repurposed holding cell. There'll be hell to pay when the waters recede. McAvoy had been warning that the storage system at the crumbling old red-brick station was vulnerable to this kind of meteorological event. The powers-that-be had told him that millions had been spent on flood defences across the city, and that Hull had already endured its fair share of Biblical deluge. Finding better storage for Trish Pharaoh's pet hadn't figured in any future budget plans. McAvoy hadn't even looked cross when Andy informed him that the storage room had been flooded from both above and below. Just shook his head for a moment, then asked what he could do to help. In the event, most of the clear-up had fallen to Andy and the two detective constables serving under him. They've managed to save perhaps half of the case files that were stored within. The other is reduced to so much papier mâché.

Daniells looks up as McAvoy appears at the top of the stairs, blocking out the light that spills in from the single bulb in the cold, wet corridor. Wonders again at the wisdom of having the cells downstairs; how many prisoners lost their footing thanks to a push in the back from a custody sergeant.

'Come on out, Andy, you've done your bit. Get yourself warm. Anything still bobbing around is going to be next to useless.'

'Flipping useless,' says Lilah, smiling. 'Wasn't that what you said, Andy?'

Daniells sticks out his tongue. He's known Lilah McAvoy since she was a few months old. Has watched her grow into the spitting image of her mother and equally able to wrap her father around her little finger. He decided long ago not to have children but does sometimes think how proud he would be of the precocious little girl and her quiet, lumbering big brother. Both have been through so much. Both have seen their father bleed; have looked into the eyes of evil men and women and known that they were only in harm's way because of who their father is. He admires them both. Even so, she's going to get a hard flipping stare for dropping him in it.

'Permission to come aboard,' says Andy, pulling himself up beside Lilah and shaking himself like a damp dog. Lilah squeals and McAvoy grins at the pair of them.

'It's been quite good fun, actually. Never been one for fishing but I'm a flipping wizard at hook-a-duck.'

McAvoy hands his junior officer a hot chocolate. Watches him shiver. Fights the urge to strip out of his nice warm coat and wrap it around him. Has to fight the urge not to leap into the waters like Tarzan going mano-a-repto with a crocodile.

'Mae's dog still won't spill the beans,' says Lilah, wrinkling her nose. 'Tried playing Bad Cop but he's just not going to crack.'

'Sausage dogs are never going to help the pigs, Lilah,' says Daniells, sagely. He gives his attention to McAvoy. 'Sam emailed last night. Wanted to know whether the boss was happy with the report on the chemical samples. I played dumb, which isn't difficult. Do you know what he's talking about?'

McAvoy frowns, unsure how to respond. Sam works for one of the many private forensics companies used by Humberside Police. He's been infatuated with Pharaoh since he was a youngster and always goes the extra mile to get her what she needs. He presumes Trish simply made the request because she knew it would be cheaper and quicker if he thought it was for her rather than for him. Still, he feels an unpleasant sensation in his throat, all acid and iron. He feels left out. Sidelined.

'The silver substance on Davey's necklace,' continues Daniells. 'Wasn't identified first time around but he says Trish pointed him towards a database of chemical paints and gave him the name of a substance to test our samples again. Got a match. Give me a tic and I'll remember the name. Oreo? Orthodontist?'

'Aurolac,' says McAvoy, surprising himself. Words have a tendency to stick in his mind, though he can't recall precisely where he heard it. 'It's a solvent, isn't it?' he asks, losing one eye in concentration. 'People sniff it like glue.'

'I'm sure it'll make sense when the boss forwards the report.'

'Hmph,' says Lilah, pointedly. 'Would be nice to be kept in the loop, don't you think?'

'Oh, your Romanian chap called,' says Daniells, teeth chattering. He blows out steam as if making smoke rings. Slicks back the few remaining strands of hair across his bald head and slumps back against the wall. 'Gheorge somebody-or-other. I was up to my elbows as it were but there's a Post-it note on your desk with a mobile number. I'd have talked to him myself but I knew you had some things you wanted to ask directly, so . . .'

McAvoy steps back into the corridor and makes room for Daniells and his daughter to pass. He strokes her head as she passes him and she turns, wrinkling her nose like a rabbit. He wonders how much longer she'll be like this. How long it

will be before it's all phones and social media, make-up and
boys. Wonders who he'll talk to once he's the only child in
the family.

'You'd think we'd take the hint, wouldn't you,' laughs
Daniells, splashing his way down the corridor as the light
flickers above. Lilah's got her wellies on and splashes through
the dark water like a toddler. McAvoy had decided not to put
on his wellington boots before descending into the dark alongside his number two. Had wanted to show solidarity by being
equally damp and miserable.

'Helen sends her best, by the way,' says Daniells, conversa-
tionally, as he reaches something like dry land, pushing open
another door and stepping into the main body of the oldest
part of the station. It was condemned once. Scheduled for
closure and advertised on the open market. When nobody
bought it, Humberside Police decided to make the most of the
opportunity, isolating Pharaoh's sometimes troublesome little
team within its damp, dismal embrace. The Cold Case Unit
isn't popular, despite its successes. No officer likes having their
investigations pored over by disapproving eyes.

'See her at Christmas, did you?' asks McAvoy, trying not to
wince as his trouser legs cling to his shins. 'How's her dad?
Did Penelope get on OK with that ointment, do you know?'

Daniells laughs, his round head splitting into his usual
amiable smile. 'Only had a moment with her, sarge. Was
looking for the boss.'

McAvoy decides not to remind Daniells that he is now an
inspector and that it is Daniells who should revel in the honor-
ific title of sarge. He hasn't got the energy.

'Boss going to be at the briefing tomorrow?' asks Daniells,
leading them down another corridor and towards the tiled,
wood-panelled elegance of what used to pass for the reception
area. It looks almost Gothic in its gloom: cracked tiles and
sagging beams; the grille in front of the old custody suites
hanging rustily askew.

'I'm hoping so,' says McAvoy, checking his phone. There's
a message from Roisin. She's home, fecked and filthy, and going
to go and lay in the bath until she can feel her bones again.

Fin's team won, but by the time the winner went in, the car was so misted up she couldn't see more than a few damp blobs. She misses him. Hopes he'll be home to watch her paint her toes. 'Did Helen mention what it was regarding?'

Daniells opens the door to his office. Grabs a towel off the top of a fan heater and begins sponging, ineffectually, at his sodden chinos. Lilah plonks herself down cross-legged in front of the filing system. Bored in moments, she crosses to the white-board. Starts drawing faces with the coloured markers. McAvoy alters his position so he's standing in the blast of hot air from the fan heater. Shudders as the two opposing feelings confuse his nerve endings. Twitches inside his own skin: a cat being stroked against the grain.

'Couldn't say,' mutters Daniells. 'Doing well, isn't she? How high up is she now? National Crime Agency? It just sounds cool, doesn't it? Does she still call Trish "boss" or is it all a bit complicated?'

McAvoy decides not to answer. The fact that his boss is also his closest friend remains one of the many sources of his perennial embarrassment.

'I've got that Post-it somewhere,' says Daniells, rummaging around under the junk food wrappers and paperwork on his cluttered desk. 'I'd maybe leave it until the morning. No doubt the boss will have made his evening more difficult.'

McAvoy looks up from his phone. 'The boss?'

'Your chap. Gheorge whatever-his-name. When you weren't around he asked for her.'

'Trish?'

'Yes.' Daniells looks a little put out. 'Have I missed something?'

McAvoy chews at the inside of his cheek. Looks at his daughter, busy drawing devil-eyes on an eerily accurate depiction of a bunny. Feels the familiar tingle in his cheeks; the suggestion that a blush is beginning to burn beneath his beard. God, now she's checking up on him. It must have been the article, he thinks. Must have got the brass talking about him for all the wrong reasons again. Wonders how long it will be before the axe falls; back to sergeant, back to uniform:

probably working security within the year. He keeps his face impassive. Makes fists with his hands.

'If you're seeing her, tell her that the bank are playing silly beggars but I should have something for her by close of play tomorrow. Old financial records are always a bugger, aren't they?'

'Whose bank?' asks McAvoy, feeling lost.

Daniells looks up from wringing out the hem of his trousers into the waste paper basket. 'Sorry, sarge, I think I may have got the wrong end of the stick. If it's not something you're involved in . . .' he stumbles over his words. Looks awkwardly at his boss. At Lilah. Makes a face. 'I'd best not say. Sorry, it's just, the way you two are . . . I assumed.' He drops his head, looking positively miserable. Looks as if he'd like to be back in the holding cell, bobbing for witness statements.

'I'm sure I've missed an email,' says McAvoy, looking down at his own steaming clothes. He looks smaller, somehow. Looks like a child after a humbling pass-the-parcel defeat. Puts out his hand for his daughter. He wants to go home. Wants to stroke his wife's hair and be told that he is loved. Wants to centre himself the way he only can when she is close; quickening his pulse even as she stills his racing thoughts. She'll tell him to trust her. Tell him that, much as she can't stand her, Trish has only ever lied to him to protect him from himself. He wonders if he'll listen. Whether he'll let the words make the slightest bit of difference to the feeling that he's being kept in the dark by the person he admires most.

'Definitely same guy?' asks McAvoy, quietly. 'Gheorge Cel Tradat?'

'Asked for you first if that helps.'

McAvoy feels his daughter squeeze his hand. It helps. But only a little.

NINE

I'm what people call 'slow'. I don't always understand and I don't remember things. I have fits sometimes. I'm supposed to have tablets but the facility often runs out of them and if I don't have any for months then I have to see the doctor, but when he gives my tablets to the women, they sell them to people in the village.

I don't have parents. I don't have proper arms or legs. I've lived in the cămin for as long as I can remember. I don't really want very much. When I was smaller I just wanted enough food to eat and shoes that would fit my stumps. Anghela from France said my deformities reminded her of some kids born in her country a long time ago. Their mothers had taken drugs the doctor gave them and they had children without arms or legs. I don't know what my mother took as I don't remember her but I've got no proper hands or feet. I have a single finger on each arm that sticks out where my elbow should be. But they work just fine. I'm not a dwarf, I've just got bits missing. The first time I saw my reflection I realised I was handsome. Maybe one day I will have a wife and children. I would not leave them in a cămin, even if I had to go without food every day to feed them. Cămin is our word for what Westerners call an orphanage, though we are not orphans.

I have friends in the cămin. Things have been better since the French lady arrived. They've tried very hard. The first thing they did was untie the children who were tied to their beds. They didn't know those children had devils inside them and that they would try and kill themselves and other people if they were able.

The first foreign faces I saw were a few months after Romania's leader was shot. I remember hearing about it on Bogdan's transistor radio. Everybody was happy but scared. What would happen now? Who would lead us now? The men in the truck came in the spring. The crops were starting to rise and the flies were hovering over the dung. I remember seeing through the window. The staff used to sit outside and enjoy the sunshine but we were always inside. I had horrible jobs like cleaning the shit out of the beds and doing the laundry. It used to make my skin sting like I was on fire.

I remember a man with a beard and a ponytail like a lady. He spoke to Anna – one of the staff who was sometimes kind to us but usually beat us for being stupid. He had brought toys and clothes from England. There was another man with him. He just stayed outside smoking cigarettes and speaking to Bogdan. I think they might have been old friends. Bogdan was the gardener and he hated us. He said Ceauşescu should just have shot us and had done with it. When he said that I felt real fear as he seemed to say it from right in his bones. He meant it.

I didn't see what happened when the Englishman and Maria went into the salon where the sickest children were kept. Afterwards there were people asking questions and some men I thought were soldiers came to talk to the director but nobody ever told us where Maria went or what happened to the two children the Englishman had been to visit. I know he never came back but I saw the other man again many times.

Sometimes the lorries would bring toys and clothes for us and we would pose for photographs. We were told to smile at first but we look scary when we do because we are small but have grown-up teeth, which are all black. We have got good at smiling with just our lips.

I hope the two children who went away with the Englishman are having a nice life. I am still at the cămin but they let me work in the barn now. I like it when the sheep have lambs. They're soft and cuddly and I like stroking them.

I heard stories from the other staff that Maria was killed but I don't know if that's true. Her family lived in the village but they moved away not long after the Englishman came and the other women were jealous because they had more money and a new car. I think I would have swapped Maria for a car, but I can't drive it. She used to call Dorin a Strigoi because he looked even stranger than me. He had a big birthmark on his face that looked like he'd had hot fat poured on his cheek. Maybe he did. I know he used to have nightmares. I remember he liked me to sing.

Anghela says I can do anything I set my mind to, but that isn't true. When I walk in snow I disappear. It makes the staff laugh to see me sinking into the snowdrifts so I'm just a head sticking out.

I hope when I am older I will be allowed to go to France. I do not want to go to England. I do not want to be in a place where the people think they can steal children, although I think it would be better to be anywhere than in the Dying Room.

•

I'm Innocent, Says Aid Worker Accused Of Baby Snatch
Yorkshire Post, 14 May, 1999
By Stella Hamilton-Booth

A British aid worker accused of smuggling an infant out of a Romanian orphanage claimed last night he was the victim of a corrupt political and legal system.

Robert Hawksmoor appeared before a Romanian court to admit he had taken the 15-month-old child from a hospital orphanage but denied he had hidden her in his lorry or brought her to Britain for adoption. The 53-year-old father of two, from Sutton near Hull also denied he had been the middleman who handed the child to a British family at a motorway service station as part of a baby-smuggling racket.

The child, who can only be identified as Baby L because she has been made a ward of court, has been legally adopted by a family in Yorkshire. Mr Hawksmoor admits he believes it was in the child's best interests to be taken out of Romania.

He said yesterday: 'It doesn't matter what I say in the court; they've already decided to find me guilty, to make an example of me. I am a victim of a judicial and political system which is completely upside down. By punishing me they are in reality punishing the children that I have been helping since 1990.'

Outside the court Mr Hawksmoor denied he had been running a baby-smuggling ring for profit. 'I came out here because I was touched by the plight of the orphans.'

Mr Hawksmoor yesterday appeared in court in the north Romanian city of Oradea for the first time formally to plead not guilty to a charge of conspiring to transport the child out of the country. If found guilty he faces five years in jail.

The prosecution case was outlined to an examining judge, who adjourned the hearing for a month to allow Mr Hawksmoor to 'prove his innocence'. The court heard how he had been on more than forty aid trips to Romania with his lorry since 1990.

TEN

Pharaoh winces, readjusting her position against the stacked, yellowing pillows. She hurts across her back. Can feel a cold throb between her knuckles. She's got her legs drawn up, laptop on her knees and knows that she'll feel the twinges in her calves and thighs as soon as she attempts something as audacious as straightening them. She's getting used to having to add a few minutes to her morning routine; a five-minute window where she can take stock of the day's discomforts and prepare the appropriate pharmacological reinforcements. She feels like she's falling apart. Sees herself briefly as an ancient church, held up by scaffolding and prayers.

'Come on, come on . . .'

On her bedside table, one of her black cigarettes is slowly burning down to the filter, a long turd of ash clinging to the handle of her World's Best Mum mug. It contains her false tooth, which smiles up from an inch of grey water. Her earrings and bangles catch the light of the anglepoise lamp, glinting from atop a dog-eared paperback.

'Be by your phone, be by your phone . . . what sort of thing is that to tell a person in this day and age? Who isn't by their bloody phone?'

She's muttering to herself, grinding her teeth, looking up to watch the clock by the window inch its way further and further past the allotted time. She isn't sure if she should ring the number. Whether to do so could make things worse. She swears as she remembers she's got a fag on the go. Extricates the butt and manages two deep breaths before it burns down to her thumb. She grinds it out on the dresser. Catches a glimpse of herself in the bulbous reflection of the lamp. Sees herself in her baggy hoodie, her leggings and bedsocks, wrapped up in a tangle of quilt and blankets, sheets of A4 printouts sliding from the little hillock of fabrics to lie like stepping stones upon the mess of clothes, shoes, food wrappers, wine bottles. In her lap, her phone buzzes. She jerks her head, banging it on the wall and calling herself a silly twat as she scrabbles to answer the call.

'Pharaoh,' she says, a cough building in her throat, stars in her eyes. 'Who is this?'

'This is Detective Chief Superintendent, yes? Patricia Pharaoh?'

Pharaoh narrows her eyes and glances at the screen. It's a call from the same area code as the message but a different number. The caller's voice is accented. Pleasant.

'This is my personal number,' says Pharaoh, sucking her teeth. 'Who's speaking please?'

'Inspector Gheorge Cel Tradat,' he says, and Pharaoh makes out the sound of chatter in the background; polite conversation; the occasional murmured laugh. Recognises the sound of a copper in trouble for leaving the dinner table.

'Ah, Gheorge, sorry for sounding brusque there – waiting for a call and thought you were playing silly beggars.'

'Silly beggars?'

Pharaoh rummages in the bedsheets. Finds her notes. Takes her cigarillo tin from under her pillow and lights another of her thin, black tubes. Rearranges her hair as she breathes out a long plume of grey.

'I'm going to say a few things that probably make no sense, Gheorge – only butt in if they're important, OK? And thanks so much for the call. The thing is, I really need some . . .'

'I tried the other one but he wasn't available. I can't say his name. What is it with you foreigners and your weird names?' He laughs as he says it. Pharaoh lets a little smile enter her voice.

'The other one?'

'OK, I'll try. McAvoy,' he says, enunciating each syllable. 'A-E-C-T . . . No, I'm not even trying his first name. You're on the same investigation, I presume? I mean, two emails from the same British police department in the same week? Did your colleague do wrong? I can call back tomorrow in office hours . . .'

'No, Andy was under instruction to give you this number if you called,' says Pharaoh, idly. She picks at a loose thread on her cuff. Watches as it starts to unravel. Tries to snap it and makes it worse. 'It's fine.'

'Robert Hawksmoor,' says Gheorge, precise with his words. 'He is, as you might say, a bit of a character.'

'I'm impressed, Gheorge. You said that so deadpan you could almost be a Yorkshireman.'

'Deadpan?'

'Don't spoil it.'

Pharaoh rummages through her notes. Looks at the dates. Arrests, detainments, remandings into custody – but nothing has ever stuck to the Hull freight boss.

'He's not as popular in Romania as he is in Hull, then?'

Gheorge makes a noise. 'It's not aid that Romania needs, Detective Chief Superintendent, it's investment. Those news reports you all seem to mention whenever you visit my country – they are a time of great shame for us. We do not wish to be reminded of the way things were before Ceaușescu paid for his crimes. Do you think we knew? You think we knew what the state was doing with the children that parents couldn't afford to keep? Shame . . .' he tails off, and she can hear the weariness as he sighs. 'A time of shame.'

'So you don't raise a glass to Rab and his charity? You're not waving flags every time he drives by with his shoeboxes full of toys for the kids? I'd heard he rebuilt orphanages, did up abandoned houses – he and his lads, playing Good Samaritan for the past thirty-odd years.'

'I do not doubt his intentions are noble,' says Gheorge, ruefully. 'And he is tenacious. That is the word, yes? Tenacious? Too old to cause us trouble now, perhaps.'

'I presume you googled the shit out of me, McAvoy and the Hawksmoors before you called, yes?'

She hears Gheorge give a spluttered laugh. Hears the sound of a child laughing somewhere in the background. 'What is it you need from me?' he asks. 'Your colleague, he said in his email that he is investigating the death of David Hawksmoor? You have his record there? Twice detained by police in

Carpathians – whole convoy of aid trucks impounded.' She hears a flash of temper enter his voice. 'People helping themselves – picking up our children like old toys from a box.'

'You believe what it says here? That he snatched a child?'

'In Romania, we try not to look back. At that time, who can say who did what and what was right?'

'Odd thing for a police officer to say, Gheorge. Come on, be honest – did he do it?'

Gheorge makes a low, tired sort of sound. 'He did many good things. Brought food and toys and care for the children the state let down. I have no doubt he thought he was doing the right thing. Perhaps he was. A prosecutor tried to make a case against him but he had . . . powerful allies.'

'In Sibiu,' she says, scanning the document on the screen. 'In 1993? Stopped by police on suspicion of taking a child from a state institution . . .?'

'I've read the report from the child's mother,' he says, softly. 'She was her seventh child. These families, they could barely afford to feed themselves and Ceauşescu was telling them to have more and more children, to raise the national population – all these promises that the nation would look after their young. The girl, Trina – she had a bad reaction to an inoculation. Didn't develop properly. The family doctor said there was a place where she could go to be looked after – she would be fed, clothed, kept warm. What could her mother do but say yes? As soon as Ceauşescu's body hit the floor and the world saw the orphanages she began trying to find her daughter. When she tracked her down to the facility at Sibiu, the administrator told her that the child had gone. Taken, they said, by one of the foreign aid workers.'

'And the Hawksmoors had visited that orphanage? Did you have a witness? A date?'

'This was not my investigation, Detective Chief Superintendent,' says Gheorge, a little ruefully. 'Things then . . . they were not as things are now, you understand, yes? His name was in the file so police acted upon it when he returned to Romania.'

'Arrested and interviewed?'

'Yes. So too his sons. There are no records of the interviews.'

'Rab's told the papers here that he was beaten up. Threatened.'

Gheorge gives a grunt of laughter. 'He does not seem the kind of man who would permit such a thing,' says Gheorge, carefully. 'He is a fighting man, I believe. His sons too.'

'So you have been googling,' says Pharaoh, grinding out her cigarette. She looks again at the clock. Closes her eyes. 'Did you get Trina back?' she asks, already knowing the answer.

'A family came forward. Southampton, I believe. Associates of Mr Hawksmoor senior. Surname of Albert. Trina was alive, safe and well. They had "adopted" her, though the adoption in question seems to have involved handing over a grand to a third party they met at a service station near Salisbury and pretending she was their niece. Questions were asked by the family GP. She had difficulties, you see. Didn't develop as a child should. And her time in that place . . .'

Pharaoh wonders what she would have done. Thinks back to that terrible footage she remembers so vividly. She was still in uniform, then. Wasn't married. No kids. She'd watched the reports with her nan, crying angry tears as the camera panned over those silent, fetid chambers: malnourished, malformed; hands clutching at rusting bars and half-dead eyes looking up without hope. If she could have reached into the TV screen and rescued those children, she knows she would have done.

'Trina was sent home?'

'Back to her mother and father,' says Gheorge. 'As is right. She was Roma. How you say . . . a gypsy.'

'And Hawksmoor? What did he have to say for himself?'

'Denied everything. The Alberts didn't name him. Wouldn't even confirm they knew him, though his wife had done some of the admin for Rab's charity.'

'You couldn't make it stick?'

'It is possible that the officers who arrested him were doing so for their own reasons. Corruption was rife. If they asked him for a payment to take a certain path with his aid convoy and he declined, well, they chose to make life difficult for him. I read that they got lucky, yes? His sons – they are fighters?'

'How did they fare in prison?' asks Pharaoh, ignoring the question. 'Even for hard men, that must have been a shock.'

'They were not there long,' says Gheorge. 'I do have a report into a visit to the infirmary hospital for one of their number. The young man. Treated for a broken hand and lacerations to the scalp. I imagine he said the wrong thing to somebody.'

'And you've cross-referenced the dates with other hospitalisations, have you?' asks Pharaoh, scribbling on her pad.

'No,' says Gheorge, with a touch of regret. 'You think there might have been a reprisal?'

'Always worth a look, Gheorge.' She realises she's drifted away a little, that Gheorge's voice sounds tinny, far away. She needs to end the call. Needs the damn phone to ring.

'OK, well . . .'

'Aurolac,' she says, suddenly, deciding to make the most of the opportunity to talk to somebody who might be able to explain the forensic anomaly on Davey's body. Sam's report has confirmed her suspicions. Now she just needs to find an explanation that makes any kind of sense.

'Aurolac?' he says again, surprised. 'A curse,' he says, moodily. 'A blight. That is the word, yes?'

'It's a solvent? Kids sniff it?'

'They do now. Originally it was designed to repair terracotta stoves. Contains ethers, ketones, acetates, methanol . . . toluene. Aurolac means gold paint, though it appears more silver to me. A couple of scrapings in a bag, take a nice deep lungful and suddenly the world is a bit softer. It makes you feel drunk, dizzy. Take too much and you lose your mind. The children beneath the streets – they use it to survive, to deaden the day. Why are you asking? If you have found traces of it in your country, I would bet my life they've been to Bucharest.'

Pharaoh doesn't answer. Screws up her face, trying to fit the information into the picture that's beginning to emerge.

'I need to talk to you further, Gheorge. There's a name I want to run by you. Fixer for a friend of mine. Translator, general Mr Fix-It. Josef Ionescu. And I might need a favour.'

Gheorge laughs good-naturedly. 'My wife is already mad at

me,' he says, with an audible shrug. 'Tell me what you need and I'll . . .'

Pharaoh jerks as the phone starts to jingle in her hand. Sees the familiar number. Knows this is what she's been waiting for.

'I'm so sorry, Gheorge, can I . . .?'

She ends the call without another word. Slides her finger across her phone and silences the persistent ringing. Watches the screen come to life.

Says a single word, under her breath.

'Vicky.'

ELEVEN

Blind Justice For Romania's Trafficked Roma Children
11 December, 2019
Extract taken from *The Truth*, online edition

Romanian prosecutors thought they had an open-and-shut case against the alleged leaders of one of Europe's largest child-trafficking rings. After almost a decade, why has no one been convicted? Deborah Brown reports.

A squat, round-shouldered man enters Room 42 of the court of appeal, shoes click-clacking on the parquet floor. The room falls silent. Reporters stop scribbling as police, politicians and press turn to look at the man accused of making a fortune from the trade in lost and vulnerable children.

Wearing a blue blazer with ink corduroy trousers, with a pig-leather flat cap in hand, he chooses an empty bench at the back. He could be sat on a park bench, feeding pigeons. He looks at ease with his world.

The man is Razvan Botezatu, 60 – but everyone calls him Ursu, a nickname for his bear-like build.

Along with twenty-five other men, Ursu is accused of trafficking scores of Roma minority children to Western Europe for a life of forced criminality. Two of the other accused are his sons.

The defendants and their lawyers start to fill the courtroom. They sit next to Ursu only after the other seats are taken.

Ursu meanwhile scans a handful of crumpled papers, though he knows them well. They have been his main line of defence for the past nine years.

'He's the top dog,' said Simon Riches, a former superintendent with the Greater Manchester Police who led the investigation that put the men in court. 'Top of the pyramid.'

Prosecutors say Ursu, a Roma person himself, is the kingpin of a notorious gang in southeastern Romania where grandiose mansions scream of wealth next to beat-up shacks.

'It's like a military operation,' said Riches, describing the group's alleged deployment of an army of children to panhandle and steal. Even an 8-week-old baby was trafficked into service as a prop for begging, drugged to keep quiet.

Investigators say Ursu's empire spanned far corners of the EU: Spain, Italy, France, even Norway – and especially Britain.

Officers arrested dozens of Romanians in Britain and Romania after an unprecedented joint investigation that took four years.

But justice played out differently in the two countries.

In Britain, around one hundred were convicted of crimes ranging from trafficking and money laundering to benefit fraud, forging documents and child neglect.

In Romania, all of the twenty-six accused were acquitted in a shock verdict in February – after a nine-year, stop-start trial.

While prosecutors appealed and the men are back in the dock, many saw the verdict as proof that Romania's judiciary is too weak – or too dysfunctional – to stand up to mobsters and the corruption that lets them flourish.

In a country where politicians convicted of corruption are known for trying to bend justice to their favour, the case touched a nerve. It also resonated with Romanians fed up with the state's dismal record of protecting the vulnerable.

Ursu is said to have links to the Quinlan organised crime gang, based in Dublin, which is responsible for a vicious turf war that has claimed dozens of lives.

TWELVE

'She's dicking you around again, my love.'

'I've probably just got the wrong end of the stick . . .'

'Aector, you know that's not true. This is what she does! Keeps you dangling at the end of her fecking line!'

'She's got a lot on her plate, Ro . . .'

Roisin McAvoy throws her arms up, and pulls at her wet hair. 'Sometimes, Aector . . .' she tails off. Screws her eyes up. 'Not your fault, is it? Just the way you're made.'

McAvoy stares immobile, unable to function, rendered inert by the merest suggestion she may have had enough of him. He feels his insides turn to water. Feels fresh agonies in his every wound and scar.

'Come here,' she says, gently, and pats the bed beside her. Picks up her towel and dries her hair in swift, vigorous strokes.

McAvoy manages to get himself to the bed. Lowers himself down lest he fall.

'I didn't mean to make you angry . . .'

'You don't make me angry, my darling. She does. But if I shout at her I'll probably end up smashing her skull in with a brick, so I shout at you instead. And to be fair, you are a fecking hopeless case sometimes.'

McAvoy lowers his great shaggy head to his wife's slim, tanned shoulder. She leans back. Moves his head to her stomach. He has a memory of talking to his children through the thin membrane of her skin: raising his huge hand for tiny high-fives from his unborn children. Finds himself smiling. Feels tears prick his eyes.

'Daddy's going to call you,' says Roisin, suddenly impish, running her fingers through his thick, damp hair. 'Got something that'll make you happy, so he says.'

McAvoy doesn't let himself react. Doesn't want to spoil the moment by worrying about Papa Teague. He breathes her in:

expensive body lotion, cheap perfume, laundry powder; her cherry menthol vape. Paws at her tummy as if trying to tunnel inside. He almost doesn't hear her.

'You got a hold of him?' he asks, as he realises she's awaiting a response.

'Just you wait and see,' she says, sounding pleased with herself. There's a little glee in her voice: a secret she wants to share.

He lowers his head again. Shuts down the part of himself that wants to ask her questions. Her father is a feared and respected Traveller whose opinion of the law has changed little since his favourite daughter fell in love with the copper who saved her from horrors that he did not. He tolerates McAvoy. Owes him, should anybody be keeping score.

'I mentioned the Hawksmoors and he started cursing like he was at the football, so I reckon it's safe to say he knows them.'

'He's near?'

He feels Roisin shrug. She either doesn't know, or doesn't want to say.

'I can call Helen, if you like,' she says. 'Find out if she's here for business or pleasure. Of course, you could do it yourself, but we both know you'd rather give yourself an ulcer worrying about it, so it's no bother . . .'

McAvoy kisses the soft warmth of her stomach. Wraps his arms around her. Lets her stroke his hair. Feels himself relax. Unspool. Melt.

'Tell me what you're thinking,' she whispers. 'Do you have any ideas? I mean, really?'

McAvoy sighs. Shakes his head against her tummy. 'The initial investigation . . . it maybe wasn't perfect but it was relatively thorough. All we're really supposed to do is see if there are some areas that might be worth a closer look – to see whether or not there mightn't be some forensic advancement that gives us a fighting chance. Doesn't help that the files are half-drowned. I read this case study in the night . . . I don't even know how it ended up in the box. Thing is, it was supposed to be softly-softly. That's what Trish said. Just thrust it at me and said this was priority, that I wasn't to make waves. I've barely had a word from her since. But she's hovering there at the edges, that's how it feels. I mean, why does she need to speak to this police officer in Bucharest? It makes me look feeble to have my boss hurry people up for me . . .' he lets the words become a long, slow exhalation. Gets a hold of himself. Realises that Roisin has stopped stroking his hair.

'I just want to know what it is I'm supposed to be seeing. Davey Hawksmoor had a lot of enemies. The original investigation got so bogged down in trying to untangle whether or not the Hawksmoors were crooked they lost sight of the fact that a man was killed. You can see it in the case files – the DI directing all resources into trying to prove the Hawksmoors were involved in illegal activity. Smuggling, drugs, people trafficking – all based on a few whispers and some audio from a CI.'

'CI?'

'Criminal informant.'

'A grass? How can you trust what a grass says?'

McAvoy raises himself up on one elbow. Looks down into his wife's eyes.

'It's the injuries,' he says, making a face. 'I could show you . . .'

With a groan of regret, he hoists himself to his feet. Stands in his pyjama bottoms in front of the mirror on the back of the wardrobe door. 'Would you mind?'

Roisin gives a little squeal of delight. 'Ooh, we haven't done this in years,' she says, standing in front of him. The top of her head reaches his sternum. 'Tell me what to do, my good man.'

McAvoy positions her in front of himself. Grabs his phone from her bedside table and opens the document on his phone. Acquaints himself with the injury pattern and then returns to his wife.

'Right . . . try and hit me . . . ow!'

McAvoy raises his hand to his cheek while Roisin screeches with laughter and apology. 'Oh, darling, I thought you were ready . . .'

Lilah appears at the door, bed-headed and lovely in her gingham pyjamas. Fin appears behind her, tall and broad and uncomfortable: an adolescent poured into the body of a Celtic warrior. He's holding a book open in his hand and pulling the face that his father employs when he has to regretfully request a diminishment of volume – a phrase still often mimicked by the officers with whom he served in uniform.

'Ah, Fin,' says McAvoy, beckoning his son forwards. 'Would you mind?'

Roisin pouts but returns to the bed. Lilah comes and lays beside her.

'Sorry about this.'

'Nae bother,' says Fin, good-naturedly. He's not as tall as his father yet but McAvoy fancies he'll be a proper whopper by the time he's fully grown up. Wonders if he'll outstrip McAvoy's older brother, Duncan, who at six foot eight makes for an unlikely crofter. He's banged his head on the low beams roughly every twenty minutes for nigh-on fifty years.

'Try and hit me,' he says. 'Slow-mo, if you like.'

Fin does as he's asked. Swings with a half-speed right hand. McAvoy catches it at the wrist. Winces, then brings his right hand, palm up, against his son's elbow.

'Ooh, that would be horrible,' says Fin, reddening.

McAvoy kicks him in the back of the left knee, as gently as he can. Puts his palm on his son's chest. Smells deodorant, grass, talcum powder. Has a sudden memory of the two of them, years ago, sitting eating chocolate cake on a cold day in Trinity Square. That was the first time Fin saw what his father did for a living. He's seen it too many times since. Has bled for his father. Paid a high price.

'It's OK,' says McAvoy, straightening up. He looks again at the image on the phone. Nods to himself. 'Must have been breathing hard after his run,' says McAvoy, crossing to the window and looking out at the shifting blackness; the rain, the puddles, the sand, the sea. He can make out the lights of the bridge overhead; the edge of the forest; the black windmill by the deserted pub. 'Although with Kenny, I mean, how fast can you really go?'

'With a dachshund? How fast can you run with a dachshund, is that what you're asking me?' Lilah and her mum look at each other and begin to laugh. 'I could ask Alexa?'

'It's just, the man was a fighter. A professional fighter. And these injuries . . . they're not random. It's not a load of baseball bats and boots. They've deliberately targeted every extremity. Who's hurt him . . . hurt him horribly . . . left him vulnerable, helpless . . . finished him off as if he wanted to watch . . . watch the lights go out . . .'

'Can I go now?' asks Fin, looking a little awkward. '*Of Mice and Men*,' he says, raising the paperback for inspection. 'Essay.' He makes a face. 'They call me Lenny at school,' he confides, colouring. 'You know. Big, stupid, clumsy . . .'

'Tell me about the rabbits, George,' says Lilah, from the bed, and then appears to regret it immediately. She makes a face. 'Anybody who says anything like that to you is getting taken down, bro. We are talking scorched earth.'

McAvoy tunes out of the conversation. Looks again through the rain-spattered glass. Watches the water ripple and swirl atop the parked cars. His eyes are caught by a sudden movement on the far side of the road. He narrows his eyes, glaring across the flooded road to the stretch of grass that runs as far as the little wall leading down to the mud and stones of the water's edge. He'd been sure that for just a moment a figure had appeared through the rain. For an instant he had been sure he had glimpsed the outline of a dark, hooded figure.

'Are you OK, my love? Your daughter is feeling left out. She demands to be power-bombed at once. And I'll let you put me in the full nelson if you're good . . .'

McAvoy turns back to the room. He can choose fear, or choose this: to allow himself to exist for just a little time in the perfect safety of his family and his home.

Later, he will wish he had chosen fear.

THIRTEEN

Sunday, 8.55 p.m.

Wayne Hawksmoor. Tall, when he stands upright. Skin like rhino hide. Lilo-lips where his shaven head meets his muscled shoulders. Hands clutched in fists where they punch through the stained, tatty cuffs of his sodden black hoodie. Cart-horse legs straining against wet denim. Piggy eyes, hidden behind thick glasses, half hooded beneath a Neanderthal skull.

He's pacing. Shouting. Getting himself all in a lather as he strides back and forth across the maroon-coloured carpet. He knows he's saying things he shouldn't. Knows he's dropping seeds for a future orchard of regrets. Can't seem to stop himself. He wants to put his boot through the gormless ceramic poodles at the side of the electric fire. Wants to smash his hand along the mantelpiece – scatter shards of the precious Lladró dolls; buttery figurines in a bland mélange of pastel hues. Wants to thump his broad forehead into the mirror that mocks him from the aubergine- and tangerine-coloured walls.

'You're going to give yourself an aneurism,' says Susie, from her tatty throne. It's as old as she is. High-backed, faded; antimacassar'd at the headrest and arms, *People's Friend* open at the crossword on her lap. She looks like a once-mighty queen subjected to dark magic in a fairy tale. She looks ancient; long white hair loosely plaited and tied at her heart; face so lined that she seems somehow drained; juiced. There's a dryness to her – something of the crypt. He sometimes wonders what would happen if he cracked open her fragile skull; whether secrets would spill out as if from the split belly of a fish.

'Fuck your aneurism,' spits Wayne, breathing hard. 'Fuck it good and proper.'

Susie puts her head to one side. Regards him with a tired

affection. 'I don't think that sentence has ever been said aloud before, my boy. Another famous first, eh?'

Wayne scowls at her. Tries to maintain his righteous fury. Doesn't want her to calm him down the way she always seems to. Likes this feeling. Likes showing his mam how he really feels. Likes talking to her the way he'd talk to Dad if he wasn't still shit-scared of the old bastard.

'Sit yourself down,' says Susie, gently. 'There's cherry brandy in the globe. Campari too, I think. You don't like crème de menthe, do you?'

Wayne feels his face twitch. Realises he's about to let go of his temper and allow his mam to make everything better. Realises that's what he came for.

'Here, you'll know this one,' says Susie, reaching out for her magazine.

Wayne makes a face. Waves his hands. It hurts to think when his blood's up. There are times when he wonders whether he mightn't have done himself a mischief; whether there mightn't have been some wisdom in those warnings about the impact of steroids and testosterone injections. Only took them because Davey did. Did every bloody thing his brother told him to, even when he knew it wasn't right.

'He makes me feel this fucking big,' says Wayne, holding up his forefinger and thumb an inch apart. 'It's my name, Mum. My name on every wagon . . .'

'The family name,' says Susie, carefully. 'Your father. Your grandfather.'

'Doesn't say Cadogan, does it? Can't even admit who he really bloody is. Shouldn't be making these decisions without my say-so.'

Susie looks at him with kind, tired eyes. 'He's made us rich, son. All of us. Will make us richer if we hold firm.'

Wayne waves a hand. Massages his knuckles. There are patches of white skin across the backs of his hands: an off-colour mottling left by the laser. He misses his tattoos. He and Davey had the same inkings; the same scrappy iodine squiggles and sigils. He doesn't recognise his own appendages. Doesn't know the backs of his own hands.

Susie scratches at the back of her neck. Makes the strange little moue that she adopts whenever she is sucking on a thought. 'He knows how to play this game, son,' she says, at last. 'Learned from the best. Hasn't steered us wrong yet, has he? No skin off my nose, is it? I don't mind upsetting a copper if that's what boy wonder says will get the deal over the line. Then we're out, Wayne. No more arrivals. No more watching our backs.'

Wayne rubs at his hands. Feels the strange smoothness beneath the skin. Remembers breaking his right hand for the first time – the icy pain shooting up to the elbow; the pretty nurse telling him that his knuckles wouldn't ever look the same; that they were buried under the flesh like fallen soldiers.

'It makes us look . . .' he waves his hands again, trying to find the right word. 'Makes us look callous. Like we don't want justice.'

'No, son. It makes us look like we've already dished it out.'

Wayne holds his mum's gaze. Listens to the creaks and squeals of the old house; the floorboards stretching, settling, contracting. She could move back to the big house any time she chooses. Could sit there elegant and comfortable within the warmth and luxury of the converted barn at the end of the family compound. Won't hear of it. Won't live there again, she says. Likes it here, in the little gatehouse that faces onto the road. She can see the comings and goings from here. Can see the drunks tottering out of the pub across the way. Can keep her eye on visitors. Sees herself as a sentry, watching out for unwelcome guests.

'We did, Mam,' says Wayne, plucking at the damp material of his trousers. 'We did what was best for everybody.'

'Wasn't best for him, was it?' says Susie, a flash of anger in her tone. 'What we did . . . what we had to do . . .'

Wayne holds up a hand, silencing her. Neither of them feel safe to speak openly. They know the tricks that coppers like to pull. Wouldn't be surprised to find listening devices beneath the porcelain dogs. They've trained themselves to switch the sim cards in their mobile phones every few days. Have got into the habit of covering their mouths when they talk.

'This McAvoy,' says Wayne, cautiously. 'He's known, Mam. I've asked around. Puttock's got some copies of a fight he got caught up in. Took down a pikey fighter a few years ago; right savage bastard and this McAvoy put him on his arse like he was made of straw. Put down a bare-knuckle bloke in America not long since, if you believe the rumours.'

'I never believe rumours, son.' She sticks out her lower lip. Teases him, lightly. 'Scared, are you, son? Big lad like you? Thought you were undefeated.'

Wayne kicks out at nothing. 'I'm not scared of anybody, Mam. There isn't a man alive who can take me down. Ask Dad. Ask Davey.'

Susie closes her eyes. 'Can't, can I? Can't ask your brother. Can't ask my firstborn because somebody let him go jogging without anybody there to protect him. Somebody was too busy getting his jollies to watch his back.'

Wayne doesn't respond. Just stares at the floor. Remembers the girl he'd been helping himself to while his brother was gasping for life. No meat on her bones and barely a light on in her eyes but by Christ she'd fascinated him. It was a true obsession; a compulsion; a hunger that pushed every other thought from his head. He'd been willing to leave Paula for her. Been on the verge of telling the girls that daddy didn't want to be around them anymore – that he wanted to spend his days and his nights in the cab of his wagon; bound and bandaged in the bony limbs of a woman who liked him no more than any of the other men who pawed over her each day. He still doesn't believe she had any part of it. Doesn't believe what Rafe has told them all time and again. Doesn't let himself wonder where she is now. What price she paid for what happened to Davey. Whether she admitted to luring Wayne away or went into the sea maintaining her innocence. Wonders when they stopped pretending what they were.

'Is he . . . OK?' asks Wayne, cautiously. 'Looked frail when I saw him. Looked . . . old.'

'Your father? Strong as an ox, son – strong as an ox. Don't go thinking anything to the contrary. Your father runs this company. We're good people. We help people. We make life better for people who've had it hard. Rab gives Rafe plenty of rope but he can still make it a noose if needs be. Your dad's not going to let anything tarnish his legacy. What he's got planned – it's his own private knighthood; recognition for all his good work. You know you did a silly thing, boy. Don't go making yourself look foolish by fighting it.'

Wayne feels the last of the fight go out of him. He's known Rafe Cadogan for years: seen him grow from a skinny little street thug into the driving force behind a multi-million-pound merger and all manner of side projects and off-the-books deals. He hasn't steered them wrong yet – not on the financial front. They could all retire now, if not for the debt that they owe and which they can never pay off. This sale, this merger – it'll give them a freedom they've only dreamed about. He grinds his teeth, thinking briefly of his brother. He misses him most days, but he doesn't ever let himself look at his grief. Just pushes it down. Davey's death was too . . . too complicated to allow him to simply mourn. Never could back down, that was his problem. Couldn't stand to show weakness. And by God he was a vicious bastard. Loved to hear bones break and teeth shatter. Bright as a button, too. Always knew who to make alliances with; how best to manipulate the minds of the malleable. That was one of his phrases, wasn't it. Had a way with words, too. Made the friendships that kept them alive and ensured they prospered. He'd be at the head of the table now if he hadn't gotten himself killed. Would be doing everything Rafe has achieved and more. Instead, he's interred in Northern Cemetery; his headstone proclaiming the lie that he was just a husband and father.

'You're not even listening, are you? Off thinking about some fancy piece, eh? All you men, all the blasted same.'

Wayne focuses on his mum. Lowers his eyes. His voice. 'The reporter. The one who called . . .'

'She's gone,' says Susie, quietly. 'Hasn't been seen since that night when you . . . well, when you decided to start acting the silly goose.'

Silly goose, thinks Wayne, rubbing at his jaw. Seriously? Is that what he had been acting when he did what needed to be done? He remembers the jarring impact as the van skidded on the greasy road surface and clipped the little convertible. Remembers the copper pulling herself out of the dirty water

and glaring after him as he sped away. Remembers the feeling
of elation; the adrenaline high. He'd done something real.
Done something to protect his family. He'd thought they would
all clap him on the back and tell him he was their knight in
grubby armour. Instead, Rafe had sent him on a long haul.
Thrown him the keys to the wagon he hadn't driven since he
took his seat on the board, and told him to get the fuck out
of Hull until he'd taken care of things. Ha! Like they could
order him around like an errand boy. They were getting their
knickers in a knot over the wrong person. Trish Pharaoh wasn't
the problem. Neither was Aector McAvoy. It was that bitch
with the microphone who could ruin everything: that snooping
cunt who didn't even know what she had stumbled upon in
that dark, putrid place beneath the streets of Bucharest.

'Hold on a little longer, love,' says Susie, softly. 'We've held
it together this long. Once the deal is signed, maybe we'll have
time to indulge ourselves. For now, do as you're told. If Rafe
oversteps, your dad will clip his wings.' She alters her pose.
Smiles at him indulgently, the way she used to when he came
home from school with a letter praising his spelling, his
colouring-in. 'Win, did you? While you were there?'

Wayne can't keep the smile from his face. Touches the sore
point beneath his left eye and gives a shrug. 'Barely got started.
Nutted me before the bell so that got me steaming. Took three
of them to haul me off.'

Susie makes a face. 'That's not true, Wayne. Don't tell fibs.
From what your father showed me, it could have gone either
way. Worked you hard.'

Wayne can't meet her eyes. He's feeling his age. Knows that
it's only a matter of time before one of the tattooed, steroided-
up bodybuilders puts him down. Wonders if he should retire
with his record intact. What he'll do then? What he'll tell
himself he's for when he's not meeting Eastern European thugs
in barns and car parks and abandoned buildings, grappling
bloodily with men who would be willing to kill him for bragging rights, and the winner's purse.

'Won, didn't I?' he says, sulkily. 'He'd have had Davey, I tell
you that much.'

Susie shakes her head, sadly. 'You boys. Dead for an age and you're still fighting one another.'

'He'd never take this shit off Rafe,' says Wayne, still petulant. 'He'd have put him on his backside for talking to me like he did. Just 'cause he's wearing a tailored suit, doesn't change what he was. What he is.'

'We're all of us more than one thing, Wayne,' says Susie, and lets out a tired sigh. From somewhere in the folds of her clothes an alarm buzzes. She reaches into a concealed pocket and pulls out a blue bottle. It pains her to open it and she looks at her son beseechingly. Wayne does as he's asked. Opens the vial and tries not to shudder as his mother opens her mouth and sticks out a tongue. He's supposed to give her three drops. Gives her nearly the full pipette. She swallows. Smacks her lips. Seems to sink into herself as the medicine floods her.

'Don't remind me about this, Wayne,' she says, a little dreamily. 'When I go . . . when it all fades. Don't tell me what we did, eh? Let me keep the memories I want.'

Wayne presses his mum's head gently into his gut. Strokes her dry hair. Wonders how long she has. How long any of them have. Whether Rafe's sense of gratitude to the man who gave him a chance, will preclude him from taking over everything once he's gone. Wonders, for a moment, whether the thing that is coming for them – the thing they have spent a decade trying not to admit – mightn't just deserve to take their vengeance.

'We gave him a chance,' says Susie, and her breathing changes as she begins to tumble towards sleep. 'He was better here than there. Better in this place than where we found him. It wasn't our fault, son. Not yours. Not even Davey's. It just happened. We picked a bad apple, that's all. What choice did we have?'

Wayne doesn't answer. His head is full of violence. That night. The sound of breaking bones. The drip of blood upon stone. The wordless pleas . . .

'He's gone, Mam. He isn't coming back.'

His mother whispers a word before sleep takes her; a word that grips his guts like a fist. A word he wishes he had never heard.

'Strigoi . . .'

FOURTEEN

Pharaoh watches the screen, clutching her phone like the hilt of a dagger. Stares as the darkness fills with jerky movement, the air with echoing sounds. Watches as the image jumps and bounces, offering glimpses of breeze blocks, corrugated iron; a row of tatty, wind-blown trees. She hears the running water of overlapping chatter. Hears the whoops and woofs of excited dogs echoing inside a cramped space.

Pharaoh fumbles with the keys. Starts to record. Sits back on the bed and pulls her laptop close.

From the screen, a rush of excited noise: bright voices, young voices, the sudden peal of laughter.

'This way, yes? You're certain?'

Pharaoh lets out a gasp. Recognises Vicky's voice. Enjoys a single moment of relief before the fears begin to flood her afresh.

'You're taking me to him, yes? Like you promised? Like we agreed?'

Pharaoh feels sick as she watches the live feed bounce around. Hears the scrape of boots upon concrete; watches crackling lights reflect from some deep, tar-like depth at the bottom of the screen. Pharaoh tries to get her bearings. Realises, as the angle lurches drastically to the left, that whoever is holding the camera cannot see where they are going. She watches as a face appears in the screen: a gaunt, dark-eyed teenager: black hair slicked down to a face pocked with sores. He peers into the lens, his pinched features illuminated by the flickering red corona somewhere above. She watches as he reaches forwards. In his hand, a black polythene bag, inflated. He beckons with his head.

'Is the blindfold really necessary? He knows me. He said yes . . .'

Pharaoh hears the note of rising panic in her friend's voice.

Knows suddenly where she is. What the silly sod has gone and done.

The face disappears. The image begins to blur. Pharaoh watches it flicker, fade. For a moment she can only hear the crunch and slop of footsteps through mud and stones. Glimpses great gaudy tags painted upon breeze-block walls.

Light now. Sudden, bright, as if a switch has been flicked. A sudden jerking motion, and the screen is filled with darkness. From nearby, laughter, high, echoing.

'Fuck sake, Vick . . .' whispers Pharaoh, teeth locked. She knows she needs to call this in at once – to alert authorities in Bucharest that her friend is deep beneath the city streets, crawling towards the man who, just two weeks ago, forced her to flee Pharaoh's car in fear for her life.

A sudden gasp erupts from the phone – a half-strangled cry. The camera angle lurches rapidly upwards and Pharaoh watches, open-mouthed, as the screen fills with the battered, swollen features of a man she almost recognises. Sees bloodied lips; a gap-tooth smile. Sees lacerations across his cheek and neck. He's naked. Filthy. Hangs with his hands above his head, bound at the wrists.

Vicky cries out. Lurches forwards, crying her lover's name. There's a thud and a line appears across the screen. Pharaoh hears her friend begging. Hears raised voices, sudden shouts.

Pharaoh readjusts herself. Makes fists. Wonders for a moment if she shouldn't just scream – tell whoever has the silly cow that the police are on their way. She can't understand where the image is coming from. Whether her friend is concealing her phone somehow or whether she is here as a witness to what is to come.

From the screen, a voice. It's low. Gravelly, as if the speaker has gargled pennies and nails. It's heavily accented, but she recognises the words when they are spoken.

'You are here to listen, and not to speak. Josef here, he will speak for me. If he pleases me . . . perhaps this cockroach will scuttle away.'

The phone seems to shake in her hand. Watches as the screen fills again with the image of Josef's bloodied features. For an instant the camera angles right, but a barked order stills the movement.

'Just at him, Florin. Not at me.'

From the phone, the sound of retching. Of snivels and snot and apologies, in English, in Romanian. She thinks of the big, brave figure who has journeyed into danger time and again without ever really risking anything of herself. She wants to reach into the phone and wrap her arms around her, then shake her until her bones rattle. 'You speak, Josef. You say what I say. And then, perhaps . . . we'll see.'

Pharaoh sees Josef's mouth working in circles. Sees spit froth at his lip. Realises, as the camera angle changes, that the strange patterns upon his skin seem to catch the light. Recognises the flecks of silver paint. Watches, horrified, as Vicky turns towards the dangling figure. Sees a slight figure, shaven-headed, bare-chested, hold a black bag to the sobbing translator's face. Sees him gag, eyes rolling back. Hears laughter from nearby.

'Do your job, Josef. Wakey-wakey, yes? My words . . . they let me down.'

Josef coughs. Spits. Starts to speak, softly at first, as a stream of low, indecipherable syllables that jar with angry consonants are delivered by a voice that seems to rise from the darkness like fog.

'I remember you . . . you came here what, eight years, ten . . . the time, it gets mixed up. You . . . you asked me about . . . them. Those people. Those *things*.'

'I don't understand,' stammers Vicky, sobs in her voice. 'Let him stop. Let him stop . . .'

'They shut this all down not long after you came. All you film people. Journalists. Filmmakers. Too many cameras, too many clips on YouTube. It made them look bad. So they destroyed it all.'

'Destroyed what?' asks Vicky. 'What are you talking about?'

'My kingdom,' splutters Josef translating the words muttered from nearby. 'I was King of the Sewers. Lord and master of the city under the city. I was father to a hundred sons and daughters. I kept them safe. Protected them. Fed and sheltered them. Gave them a place when nobody else would.

And they took that from me. Stormed down here with their masks and their sticks and their handcuffs. Six years. Heroin, so they claim. I hate heroin. Hate what it does to people. Any child under my protection who uses a needle . . . they are no longer my child. I give them the aurolac. It is a medicine for them.'

'A medicine? You get them hooked on something that will kill them!'

The screen tilts, and for a moment Pharaoh sees the figure who sits in the darkness. It is all she can do not to gasp. He shimmers with brilliant silver – plastered across his head like Brylcreem, smeared into his beard and neck. He sits bare-chested, his broad chest an ugly mass of tattoos and scars. He wears chains at his wrist, at his neck and around the cuffs of his filthy jeans. He's barefoot. Sits atop an upturned bucket, back to the crumbling wall. Behind him a gas canister, a camping stove, a portable DVD player surrounded by empty tins. She glimpses movement beside him. Sees a young girl, dark-eyed and filthy, laying her head upon his shoulder. He pats her cheek, a shepherd attending his flock.

'Why have you done this to him?' asks Vicky, unable to hold back. The screen fills with movement and suddenly Pharaoh is watching as Vicky begins tugging at Josef's bonds, telling him it will be OK, that they're leaving.

'You are a brave woman,' comes the voice – Josef no longer a mouthpiece for the man who sits in the shadows. Pharaoh sees the image shift. Sees Vicky turn and face him.

'Tell me why you're doing this,' she says. 'He's a translator. Somebody who helps me . . .'

'Helps you take your knickers off,' he replies, with a snort of laughter. From nearby comes a chorus of giggles; childish titters of approval.

'Don't,' she pleads. 'Don't make it . . . dirty.'

The man shakes his head, the low light illuminating his eyes – the silver contact lenses that make his gaze shimmer like the skin of a sun-kissed lizard.

'You asked him to listen to something. I know that already. I know, because he came back – let himself into my kingdom as if invited. Scared my children. Asked questions that he did not have the right to ask.'

'So what, you think you can just . . . *kidnap* somebody? He was doing his job. Helping me!'

Pharaoh admires her friend's courage. Admires, while willing her to shut the fuck up.

'He wanted to be your hero, I think. Wanted to hand it all to you on a plate. That's the phrase, yes? *Strigoi* told me how you people speak. About the words you use. I tried them in England – people still called me Boris. Or Vlad. All the same, yes? All the same to you. I do not want to go back there. It would have pained me to come and find you myself.'

Josef jerks his head up at the mention of the name. 'This is what he wants,' he hisses. 'The attention. The publicity. All this, just so you would come back and witness him rebuild his kingdom . . .'

'I brought you here because we have friends in common,' continues the man with the silver hair, unphased by the interruption.

'Rab Hawksmoor,' says Vicky, and the image creases and folds in on itself with a sudden rustling sound. The angle changes. Pharaoh realises Vicky has taken off her coat and laid it down – that the hidden camera is transmitting from somewhere within its folds. She can barely make out the shapes in the sudden darkness. Curses, willing her friend to improve the view or get the hell out.

'The Dark Angel,' comes the reply, each syllable elongated; tasted. 'He is a hero, yes? Good man. Noble man. An outlaw, doing what he must – doing the things nobody else has the balls to do? That's the story, yes? That's the story he tells so well. The man who saw the plight of our poor motherless children and couldn't help but come to our aid.'

'You don't see him that way?'

There's a moment's silence before the man speaks again, as if choosing his words carefully. 'Six years,' he says, and his voice takes on a tired, almost sluggish quality. 'Six years away from my children. Away from my kingdom. Away from my home. Six years.'

'You blame the Hawksmoors for that? How do you even know them?'

'The first time he came to Romania, the first time he tried to do good, he knew nobody, had no friends here, spoke no Romanian. He came anyway. Him and the lads in their wagon full of shoeboxes. Toys for the children. Clothes. Games. Picked the first orphanage he could find on a map and set off like he was leading a wagon train. Did something that made him feel good. Got the taste for it and kept coming back. Made some friends along the way.'

'You were one of the orphans?'

'I'm no orphan!' he shouts, anger in his voice. 'None of us were orphans! We had mothers, fathers, brothers, sisters. We were in those places because our parents couldn't afford us! Because doctors signed pieces of paper that said we were imbeciles and cripples and should be shut away from the world! Because the state said it could raise Romania's children better than our parents.'

'I'm sorry,' whispers Vicky, and the sorrow in her voice sounds real. So too the fear.

In the safety of her bedroom, Pharaoh feels a cold chill upon her skin; icy spider-legs tickling her pulse points, her neck, her lungs. Again, she thinks of calling the officer who had been on the phone just minutes ago. But what to tell him? That an award-winning TV journalist is being held against her will somewhere in the catacombs beneath Bucharest?

'They won't get me again,' says the seated figure. He clinks one of his padlocked chains against the gas canister at his side. 'They come again, I turn this on, light a cigarette, blow them all away. My children too. My dogs. Myself. Blessed oblivion, yes? Better that than leave them fatherless. The things they endured in my absence. The things Strigoi made them do.'

'Strigoi?'

A slow smile creeps across the man with the silver hair. 'They call me Tinman,' says the figure, confirming Pharaoh's suspicions. 'I had another name once. I was another man. I became somebody else when I found my home beneath the earth. Strigoi . . . he was not born. He was manifested.

Summoned. The darkness made flesh.' He pauses. Lets out a low sigh. 'He was my child.'

'I don't understand,' says Vicky, desperation in her voice. 'I don't care about any of this anymore. There's no story. I'm retired. I'm only here because I was afraid for Josef. Afraid for what might come knocking on my door.'

'You don't even know what he translated, do you? Don't know what he heard on that recording. You don't even know what you're doing here, do you?'

Vicky takes a breath before her reply comes out in a low, staggered sob. 'Just let us go.'

'You came here of your own free will. Asked your questions, paid your bribes, got yourself an audience. That took courage. I admire courage. I foster it in all of my children. To use courage, one must conquer fear. I am sorry I made you fearful. But I needed you to come here. To look into your eyes and tell you what is to come.'

Vicky whispers something to Josef. An instant later, the image on the screen changes. She realises the Tinman is holding the coat.

'No,' whispers Pharaoh. 'Don't you . . .'

She has a perfect view of his face. Of the scars that run along his jawline and neck, disappearing into the shimmering silver unguent. At his throat, a tattoo: faded blue ink spelling out unintelligible letters.

'We shared a cell once,' says Tinman, quietly. 'The Dark Angel and his sons. Their friends. The man I had known from the institute. The man who had brought us presents. Food. Who . . .' he shakes his head, as if the memory pains him. 'They could fight, those men. Those boys. Stood their ground in a prison where every inmate wished them harm.'

'Why?'

'They were accused of stealing our sons and daughters,' shrugs Tinman. 'Of taking our children to England, Holland, Italy. Of giving our infants to the Roma.'

'And were they?'

'That didn't matter. And they fought their ground. Impressed me.'

'And who were you.'

'I was becoming the man you see today. I was a man who saw how things could be.'

'You became friends?' asks Vicky, her voice breaking. 'Look, I would have come if you'd just called me. None of this is necessary. You don't need to . . .'

Tinman looks down. Peers closer. Stares into the screen. In her bedroom, Pharaoh finds herself leaning backwards, the intensity of the gaze unsettling. She glares into eyes that seem to burn with something timeless; something primal and unyielding. She sees the slow smile. Watches as the filthy finger and thumb close around the little pin on the coat lapel. Sees him hold it to one silvery eye for inspection.

'I'm sorry,' she hears Vicky cry. 'I needed insurance . . . I was scared . . .'

Tinman stares into the screen.

For a moment, he says nothing. He mutters one line in his own language. Says it with something like fear.

The screen goes dark.

The last thing she hears is a scream.

PART TWO

PART TWO

FIFTEEN

' I don't need it!'

'You do, Lilah. You can't go to school with just one sock on.'

'Tell me where it says that. Tell me where that rule is written down.'

'Do you want me to lift the sofa?'

'No, I want her majesty to get off the sofa and help you look.'

'She can have mine.'

'Then *you* would only have one sock . . .'

McAvoy stands at the living-room window and lets the sounds form a polyphonic symphony. Listens to his son doing his best; his daughter sounding for all the world as if she should be laying on silken cushions and being fanned with a palm frond. He can hear Roisin in the kitchen, shouting instructions, making sandwiches, taking care of the laundry with her foot while making herself a fancy coffee with the frighteningly complex machine that had arrived one morning shortly before Christmas. McAvoy has so far resisted the urge to google it. Doesn't want to know how much or whether any local coffee shops have recently reported one missing.

'Got it! It was inside my tights! Can you believe that, Daddy? I thought I had a growth!'

McAvoy grins. Sips his herbal tea. Watches the water – morning sunlight captured in endless wells as the rain turns its surface into a great swathe of dimpled tin. He looks to the right. Hopes for a rainbow.

'What are you thinking about?'

He breathes in. Smells Roisin. Feels her hand snake across his tummy. Feels her head upon his forearm.

'Not thinking,' he says, as if the very notion might be considered a dirty habit. 'Just being.'

'No rainbow yet,' says Roisin. 'No beached whales.'

'I was half expecting a megalodon to waddle ashore,' says McAvoy.

'That's the baddy in *Transformers*,' says Lilah, helpfully, from the sofa. There is a thump as she falls backwards off the arm. 'I'm OK! Nobody panic.'

'I like the way you say "waddle",' confides Fin, trying to brush his hair in front of the mirror over the fireplace. It's thick and wavy and red. He tugs his sister's brush through his fringe then makes a face as his fringe grabs it and refuses to let go.

'Want any help, son?' asks McAvoy, sympathetically. He's no stranger to this particular problem.

'We should shave him,' says Lilah. 'Family time.'

Roisin grins at her daughter. She puts the palms of both hands around the warmth of her mug. Mimes a shudder as she stares at the rain. 'Still isn't slowing down.'

'We could send a dove,' suggests Fin. 'See if there's any dry land out there.'

'It's been worse than this,' says McAvoy. 'The defences will hold.'

'Austin's dad said the sea defences are a white elephant,' says Fin, trying to disentangle the brush. 'I'm not really sure what that means but it can't be good, can it?' He looks smart in his school uniform, neatly pressed blazer and dark trousers; white shirt gleaming, school tie neatly knotted at his throat. He's the double of his father, though McAvoy's long since gotten over the habit of wearing his old school tie. He looks like a bouncer preparing for a court appearance: three-piece navy-blue suit, cream shirt and a shimmery silk tie the colour of a pigeon's throat.

'It'll be murder getting across town,' adds Lilah, nosing her way between her parents and looking out at the falling rain. 'Seriously, Daddy, there's no point even trying.'

McAvoy makes a face at his daughter. She loves to tease him. Loves to act like everything is too much of an effort and that his diligence should be an object of scorn.

'You're not staying off,' says Roisin, knowingly. 'Get that out of your head, young lady. You've got eighty-eight per cent attendance – eighty-eight! Your brother had one half-day off and he had a temperature of one hundred and two!'

'I'm a lot cleverer than Fin,' says Lilah, simply. 'He can't even afford to go to the toilet during class. Every moment is crucial.'

'That's not very nice, Lilah,' says McAvoy – the closest he ever gets to admonishing his little girl. 'Say you're sorry.'

'Sorry,' says Lilah.

'Doesn't matter,' mumbles Fin.

'You can give me a dead arm, if you like,' says Lilah, kneeing her brother in the thigh.

'I'll bank it,' says Fin, and gives her a smile that lights her up.

At his side, Roisin drains her coffee and wipes the foam from her mouth with the back of her hand. She's wearing a velour jogging suit with the word JUICY picked out in sequins across the buttocks and breasts: garnet-and-gold necklaces jingling at her throat, black hair scraped back into a tight ponytail; false eyelashes and big hooped earrings. She'll pull her damp Ugg boots on her bare feet when she takes the kids to school. Will bask in the confused glances of the other mums and dads. They never know what to make of her; the Traveller who married a copper. Don't know whether to invite her to join the WhatsApp groups, or report her to the Neighbourhood Watch.

McAvoy feels Roisin's hand reach his. Feels her squeeze his fingers. 'You don't need to worry,' she whispers. 'He'd die before he let anybody so much as look at you funny.'

McAvoy feels a strange fluttering sensation in his chest. Turns from the window and finds his wife's gaze. 'I'm not worrying. I just wish he could give me a time . . .'

Roisin shrugs. There's nothing she can say. Her father has told her he'll be in touch sometime today. Whether that's in person or through an intermediary, she cannot say. McAvoy wonders how hard she is having to work not to offer to come with him, to keep him safe while he is a visitor to Papa Teague's world. She knows that to suggest it would hurt her husband's feelings. Also knows how welcome the offer would be.

McAvoy's phone buzzes in his pocket. It's a message from Andy – on his way. He takes the opportunity to skim through his various messaging apps. Hopes there will be something from Trish. From Helen Tremberg. Hopes maybe one of the Hawksmoors will have thrown him a bone. The only notification is from a news outlet informing him that there's still time to plan for next week's Blue Monday – statistically, the most miserable day of the year.

'Still trying to be mysterious, is she?' asks Roisin, a touch of steel in her voice. 'Probably expects you to come running. Don't let her off this time, Aector.'

'I'm sure we'll catch up later . . .'

'Yeah, on her schedule – not yours.'

'She's detective chief superintendent, Roisin . . .'

'And you're the best person ever,' chimes in Lilah, her mouth full, contributing from the kitchen in a spray of Rice Krispies.

'Oh Jesus, Mary and Joseph, will you look at this . . .'

Andy Daniells is driving his husband's expensive electric car – a sleek white Tesla that cuts through the standing water like a shark. He's driving absurdly slow, as if afraid that to put his foot down could cause a bow-wave capable of swamping the city. He's got his face close to the windscreen, peering out through a little window wiped into the condensation.

'Is he peddling?' asks Roisin, giggling. 'I've seen a mobility scooter go fecking faster . . .'

'Stefan is a bit precious about it,' says McAvoy, wincing. He rummages in his pockets, pulling out the blue overshoes he uses to step within the boundary of a crime scene.

'Stefan's a fecking prick,' says Roisin, giving Andy a big wave. 'I'll make you a hot chocolate before you go – if you get the chance, spill it on the leather.'

McAvoy steps away from the window to kiss his wife and children. Wraps his arms around them and feels their various limbs entangle around him; breathes in their mingled scents and flavours. Inhales them until he's full; until he feels safe; ready.

'You're doing a good job, Dad,' says Fin, quietly, in his ear. 'Don't let them tell you any different.'

McAvoy watches Lilah and Andy perform an elaborate game of death charades. From the comfort of the vehicle, he aims an imaginary bow and arrow. Lets it go with a 'wang'. In his grasp, Lilah shudders, clutches at her chest. Pirouettes. Falls inwards like a tower of burning sticks.

'Avenge me,' whispers Lilah, from the floor.

'Love you,' says McAvoy, and steps over his daughter, pulling his coat on. 'I'll give Grandad your love.'

Roisin wrinkles her nose. 'Call me when he's gone, my love,' says Roisin, and there's something in her gaze that gives him pause: a highness; a brightness. 'Don't . . . don't do anything dangerous.'

McAvoy kisses her. Tastes lip gloss, lipstick, cherry menthol vape. Tastes a trace of salt. When did she weep? He feels a sudden sourness in his gut; a strange twisting sensation, as if his innards were turning themselves into new shapes; his intestines a twist of cuneiform and treble clefs. He doesn't want to walk out the front door.

'Dangerous?' he asks, looking astounded at the very suggestion. 'As if I would even consider such a thing!'

'We'll see you at Hull Royal about sixish,' laughs Lilah, from the floor. 'Give Grandad my love.'

There's a honk from the parked Tesla. He knows he can't put it off any longer.

Out the door and into the rain: a blob of spilled blue ink amid the sodden, endless grey.

SIXTEEN

Forest Pines Hotel, Brigg, North Lincolnshire
9.16 a.m.

Pharaoh is very nearly running. She's moving down the long, lushly carpeted hallway at a speed that normally requires the Mercedes and a steep hill. Tries to tell herself to slow down; to get herself together: to be the person she's learned how to be. She can't stand this fluttery, disconnected feeling in her chest; the tingle in her fingertips, across her back.

She stops short at the end of the hall. Glances at a delicate lithograph – a hot-air balloon tethered against a pale blue sky, bonneted onlookers cheering at this feat of human ingenuity. Wonders when progress should have stopped. Whether a desire to halt progress automatically makes her a conservative. Shudders.

The door opens before she can knock. She pushes her damp hair back from her face. Slaps on a smile.

'Jesus, it's still coming down – had to park in the chairman's space, and if he doesn't like it he can take a three-wood and ram it . . .'

'Hello, Auntie Trish.'

Trish bites her lip. Looks down at the round face and blonde curls of Penelope Tremberg. She's wearing bunny pyjamas and holding a tatty woollen lamb in her left hand.

'Shouldn't you be at work?' says Trish, crouching down and giving the little girl a hug. She smells of sleep and orange juice.

'Euch, you're soaking,' laughs Penelope, pushing her away and squashing her head down into her neck.

'You look like a tortoise when you do that.'

'You look like a . . . like a . . .' she screws up her face in concentration, trying to find an insult that won't get her in trouble. 'You're a satsuma.'

Pharaoh grins. Follows her into the bedroom. It was a nice room before Penelope took over. Now it's littered with clothes, soft toys, colouring pads and discarded sweet wrappers. Pharaoh looks up to where the ceiling fan slowly revolves – a size six running trainer tucked onto its blade. Penelope follows her gaze.

'Mum wanted to hit the gym.'

'I'll be out in a second,' comes the voice from behind the bathroom door. 'Make yourself a tea if you want one.'

'I'll do it,' says Penelope, excitedly, and runs to the console table with its complex coffee machine and kettle. Begins rattling cups and saucers. Pharaoh makes a half-hearted attempt to stop her. She probably shouldn't be boiling the kettle. Then again, it's never too early to master a new skill.

'Just a splash of milk,' she says, making herself comfortable on the bed, booted feet dangling over the side. She feels the tiredness flooding her. Feels her arms and legs becoming rubbery. Feels the tingle in her lips and her feet. Wishes to God she could just close her eyes for a few minutes. She hasn't slept. Hasn't stopped since the link to Vicky's hidden camera went dead. She feels wired; jangly, even as sleep threatens to engulf her. Her head feels overfilled; painful and bloated with half-formed ideas and dark imaginings. She keeps trying to think like Tinman, to plot his intentions, but she's all too aware that she cannot find such filth and grime within herself. She cannot conceive of the life he has lived. He feels like some walking anachronism; a visitor from another time, another world, a guileful, skilful manipulator and crook, schooled and brutalised amid squalor and violence that she knows she cannot comprehend. He hadn't taken her calls when she'd rung him, frantic, in the moments after the line went dead. Hours went by before her phone buzzed in her hand – hours spent hammering out emails and backdating briefing notes; poring over the case files and cross-referencing against the original, shambolic investigation into Davey Hawksmoor's death. She'd had to fight to keep her thoughts from turning to McAvoy. She would have given anything to come clean – tell him what he's really doing, what she's used him for – the danger that she has failed to shield

Vicky from. She knows he would understand. Would offer her whatever help she needed. Would even say soft, shy words to make her feel better. She'd had to call herself a 'soft bitch' and down an inch of whiskey from the bottle before she got hold of herself.

'Oooh, you look like you're in a drying-out clinic!'

Pharaoh opens her eyes. Moves her sunglasses an inch down her nose and gives Helen Tremberg a bleary-eyed smile. Helen's looking good: tall and trim and athletic; brown hair tied back in a short ponytail to accentuate a roundish, pleasant face. She looks like she's spent her National Crime Agency salary well – soft flannel pyjamas and tasteful gold necklace serving to create an image of a photospread in a glossy magazine.

'Very *Town & Country*,' says Pharaoh, looking her up and down. 'You look like you've done a drive-by at Cath Kidston.'

'Sleep in those clothes, did you?' smiles Helen, gently moving Penelope away from the kettle. 'I can lend you something but I think they'd all be too long in the leg.'

'Missed ya,' says Pharaoh grinning, tiredly. It always does her good to see her old protégé. She's three rungs up in the NCA now, running her own team, marshalling operations with international reach. Pharaoh feels inordinately proud of the young Lincolnshire lass she plucked from uniform and brought to the elite new Serious and Organised Crime Unit within Humberside Police. She's done so well that questions have been asked about just who she might have in her pocket; which kingmaker is sponsoring her rapid rise through the ranks. Pharaoh never listens to gossip. Knows that her friend is simply a good and diligent copper.

'Still raining, I see,' says Helen, sitting down in the armchair by the window, curtains still drawn. 'Bridge still open?'

'Just about,' says Pharaoh. 'Almost took off midway over but I reckon willpower kept the tyres on the road.'

'Biblical, innit?'

'More to come, they say. Not just now . . . I mean like, the future. Extreme weather. More storms, harsher seas. I don't want to get all theological, but do you reckon this is Ragnarök?'

Helen laughs. 'Nah, I reckon things have always been shit.

People just used to be more accepting. At least people in the dark old days had the illusion of paradise. Now we just have . . . this. Weird, innit? People just believe in this one life, and yet they still choose to become an accountant and drive an Audi.'

Pharaoh takes her cigarette holder from her pocket. Catches Helen's disapproving look, and puts it back.

'I got your voice note,' says Helen, more quietly. She bends down to rummage in an open holdall. Pulls out a pink tablet and blue headphones. Hands them to Penelope and tells her to go snuggle with Auntie Trish. She grins as she does so and Pharaoh feels her heart slow a little as the curl cuddles up to her, attaches her headphones, and gives her entire attention to a cartoon about a blue dog.

'Strigoi,' she says, shaking her head, turning away to stare into the steam of the boiling kettle. 'You've been busy.'

'Gheorge can't authorise a raid on the sewers,' says Pharaoh, flatly. 'I didn't really expect him to. The sewers are a whole city and we don't know where she went in. Not to mention the fact that Tinman has made it plain he'll blow the place if any coppers try and come in again – take out himself and every one of his "children". Could be bravado but it means they can't go in without an awful lot of senior approval, and once you get past a certain level . . .' she winces, trying to remember how Gheorge had put it. 'The people in charge – it's not a question of whether they're corrupt, you can take that as a given. It's just a question of which of their paymasters you least want knowing about active investigations. He didn't even sound cynical – just said that's how it is. Best he can do is start asking questions, quietly – trying to find where the hell Vicky might be staying, how she got into the country, whether she's alone . . . Christ, Helen, what a mess.'

'Difficult situation to find yourself in, Trish,' says Helen, sympathetically. 'I mean, none of this stuff is in the handbook, is it? Keeping people safe from themselves seems to be harder than it used to be. Vicky got frightened, did a flit, buggered off to see her boyfriend in Romania and got in over her head. Whereabouts could you have interjected, as either a police officer or as a friend. She's a grown-up.'

Pharaoh makes a face. 'Well, you're obviously hungry. Did you really say "flit"?'

'Look, all I'm saying is . . .' she sighs, rubs her face with her hands. 'I dunno what I'm saying. Maybe . . . maybe I'm saying that even after all these years, you're still, like . . . you still just blow my mind, y'know? I mean, Vicky gives you this one little titbit, a snippet of something that might or might not matter, and from that . . . do you know how deep I've had to dig to get anything on this investigation? The amount of databases I had to request special permission to access just to make some kind of sense . . . sense of any of this.'

'I didn't expect you to come in person,' says Pharaoh. 'This little princess – what did she make of the mad dash through the night?'

'Loved it. Felt like an adventure.'

'And you didn't go to your dad's place?'

'Got a tenant, hasn't he? He's shacked up with his new lady love in Twickenham, neglecting all his granddad duties. Staying down south for at least another few months so he's rented out the bungalow. Didn't find out until I was on the doorstep with her majesty asleep on my lap and this skinny chap in Y-fronts comes out of the kitchen with a mug of Ovaltine . . . Sharp exit, four-star hotel and three hours of sleep. Still, better than a day in the office.'

'And you've got it?'

Helen smiles. 'The transcript? Vicky's original audio? Aye. I had Jamie isolate the background voice and run the whole thing through translation software. Tells a very compelling tale. Loose lips, for a gangster, hasn't he?'

'And that's official, is it? Tinman is serious? Not a cartoon? Not a clown? He's genuinely got clout?'

'Built a city under a city, Trish. Peopled it with vagrants, runaways and the kids nobody else wanted. Turned it into the beginnings of an empire. Got sidetracked with the theatrics of it all – so much so it's hard to tell the fact from the fable – but this is a man who's bled and scraped and fought every day of his life. He's not somebody you want to cross.'

'And Vicky's crossed him?'

Helen runs her tongue around the inside of her lip. 'If she's down there, he's not going to do anything rash. He likes publicity. For this man who exists in the shadows he's done a lot of interviews with journalists and film crews. Every time he gets interviewed it adds to his legend so if he's got a proper award-winning journalist down there in the dark with him, he'll use it to maximum advantage.'

'To what end, Helen? What's the endgame here?'

Helen pulls her phone out the back pocket of her pyjamas. Consults her notes. 'When he was arrested he had zero assets. No bank accounts. He's claimed in interviews that the police stole what he had spent his entire life building up. They didn't just raid his city, they rounded up his "children" and stole his life savings. Whether that was cash or jewels or pure heroin, he's never said, but I'm guessing that whatever is on his mind, money and revenge will have a lot to do with it.'

'And Strigoi?'

Helen takes a moment. Closes her eyes, as if debating with herself over the wisdom of her next act. Checks that her daughter is still otherwise engaged and notes for a moment the way the bright colours shift and swirl upon the child's skin; reflected blobs of pink and blue flickering, distorting; an ever-changing Rorschach.

'Here,' she says. 'Best if you listen for yourself . . .'

SEVENTEEN

Eastern Cemetery, Hedon Road, Hull
9.46 a.m.

'This is bloody horrible, sarge.'

'I know, Andy.'

'I mean, it's ridiculous, if you don't mind me saying.'

'I don't mind you saying. I didn't mind the last few times either.'

'Was that a tone in your voice, sarge? Was there a bit of an edge to that?'

McAvoy doesn't get the chance to reply. Daniells loses his footing and a great torrent of water sploshes down McAvoy's collar, soaking him to his already drenched boxer shorts. He tries not to let his annoyance control his face. Knows that there's nothing admirable about saying 'I told you so', even when it happens to be true. He'd been more than willing to carry the umbrella. Had been almost insistent that he, at six foot six, should either forego the offer of the purloined hotel brolly, or be the one to carry it over Andy, at five foot eight. Daniells had refused to acquiesce, insisting that the sarge, as an inspector, outranked him, DS Daniells, a mere sergeant. McAvoy sometimes wonders whether Daniells is deep undercover, masquerading as a genial twit.

'Grim, isn't it?' says Daniells, nodding towards the columbarium.

'I rather like it,' says McAvoy, wishing he were here by himself. He'd like to sit awhile among the urns and nameplates; the toppled arches and crumbling bricks, perhaps reading some Thomas or Yeats in the company of the quiet dead.

'Round here, I think,' says Daniells, drawing a loose circle with his wellington boot. A steady stream of brown water has turned the gravelled footpath into a fast-flowing brook. 'Here's where the flowers were. No grave. Odd place for them to be. Hadn't been blown there, hadn't been the weather for it. And you see, from here, if you glimpse where Davey was attacked, well . . .'

McAvoy steps into the space Daniells has vacated. 'You think somebody saw what was happening, dropped the flowers and ran?'

Daniells pulls at his lower lip. 'You said to look for anything, anything at all, that hadn't been done with sufficient diligence first time around. Anyway, I spotted it on one of the crime-scene shots. Managed to read the card through the cellophane. "For Mum, from Dee and the girls. Miss you every day. Sleep fight." Of course, that might be tight . . .'

'And you've found who Dee and the girls are?'

'Dee Cullen, now 44, living in a house on Trinity Grove in Hessle. Never gave a statement, never came forward. Worth a knock on the door, wouldn't you say?'

McAvoy tries to look encouraging. 'Excellent work, Andy.'

Daniells looks around, staring at the rain-darkened trees; the sodden grass; the headstones rising from the fetid water like drowned deckchairs. 'Damn funny place to come for a run, sarge,' he muses, as he has done numerous times on the short walk from the parking area. 'And taking a dachshund, that's almost animal cruelty.'

'Dog loved to run, according to Mae,' muses McAvoy. 'And Davey didn't. Little dog gave him an excuse to go slow, she reckoned. Was his usual routine. Dropped her at the hair salon, popped in to the post office for a bottle of water and a scratch card – you've seen the footage . . .'

'Next seen on recovered dashcam footage running over the bridge, eight minutes having gone by . . .'

'Footage recovered from the gates of HMP Hull allowing us to work out the speed of travel and to better locate the exact location at each moment on his journey . . .'

'And then in through the gates of the cemetery. Witness Leanne Shillito reports saying a hello and smiling at his dog as he passed her at nine thirty-four a.m. . . .'

'Found dead by one Chester Morris at two past ten a.m.,

having been alerted to a furious barking and a stray sausage dog running around, knocking over a vase of flowers he had just laid at his wife's grave . . .'

'And went rushing in there to see . . . well, he said it was just the back of somebody. Somebody dressed in dark clothes, clambering up the wall of the columbarium like a monkey and vanishing over the other side. Not seen on any camera footage.'

McAvoy glowers at the rain-lashed, pencil-grey assemblage of columns and grottos. 'And yet, they've always proceeded as if the only way this hard case could have been killed is if a group of people ambushed him. Why not just one person? Somebody who took him unawares?'

'I get the impression that the officer in charge was something of a fight fan, sarge,' says Daniells, diplomatically. 'He'd made some money on Davey over the years. And you saw how softly he went on Big Rab. Those interviews – they're like a chat between friends.'

McAvoy shivers. Tries not to show it. 'Lonely place to die,' he says, quietly. Thinks of the times and places he's faced his own demise; the times he's felt his heart beating for what he believes to be its last time; every cell of his being coalescing around the image of his wife, his children; willing himself to endure . . .

Daniells looks up at him. 'I'll give you a moment, sarge,' he says, seeing something in McAvoy's gaze which discomforts him. He mooches off, squelching off the path into the boggy grass before his boots find the gravel again. Ducks through the collapsed archway and into the peaceful, half-dark sorrow of this palace to the dead.

He leans against one of the walls. Reads a name upon a grave. Rights a fallen urn. Looks back into the main thorough-fare, hopeful McAvoy will be uncharacteristically swift in his introspection.

Ducks back behind the wall, rain striking hard against his pink cheeks.

Knocks something hard with his right foot, apologising instinctively. Bends down, fumbling in the surging water. He doesn't want to have kicked an urn, disrupted a vase of flowers; caused offence.

His hand closes around a large stone. He drops it back into the water, brushing his hands together.

Turns his head at the sound of a sudden shout, back the way he had come.

Doesn't even see the figure emerge from the darkness beyond the toppled brick walls. Doesn't know he's about to die until the arm is already about his throat, and the blood begins to bubble in his eyes.

EIGHTEEN

Audio transcript, ElIAR 338769
Transcribed from original recording by Vicky Dexter

Tinman: You think I don't know what you see when you look around me? Look at me – this mess of scars and chains and blades – this silly shiny silver man. I know what you see when you look at my children, sniffing, shooting, feet drenched in the muddy hot water, syringes and condoms bobbing like . . . like rubber fucking ducks.

You don't try and see through my eyes. You don't see a kingdom. A community. A system that works – where people obey the rules or they aren't welcome. A place where people can experience love and belonging. I am not just their father – I am the god of this infernal place.

I've been living in these sewers since I was a child. This was my cradle, my school. It was my first love, my home. Here, I learned to become what you see. I am the only one who succeeded in achieving something for the homeless. I turned darkness into light.

Under my rule, everyone has their own money, they have something to eat. They have all they need. Light, heating, understanding and parental advice.

People outside – they don't care. They turn their back. They don't see us – we are as rats to them.

That boy – Florin. He used drugs daily for ten years. He had no veins. Shot straight into his cock, his arteries. Gave himself gangrene! Stole. Sold himself. Threw dust in people's eyes at cash-machines then robbed them as they wept. The police would catch him, beat him. You know they use fibreglass sticks, yes? He was a half-made thing when he came to me, when he descended into my kingdom. Oh you know that kind of courage? To enter a hole with two to three thousand drug addicts who prick each other with syringes, and to inject from the start. Here, Florin, tell, tell . . .

Florin: He bought us food and treatments. Everything we needed. If he saw us barefoot, honest to god he'd buy us shoes. He would intervene if the police or some hoodlum picked on us. He would chase all the faggots that were coming to take the smaller kids away. We all called him Father.

Tinman: See! The programmes that the NGOs and the town hall came up with to integrate these poor creatures are useless. Everybody comes here and says 'oh, we tried to take them to some social centre or whatnot.' Take a stray dog that has lived all its life on the streets, put him in a cage and see what happens to him. That's what Hawksmoor found out, believe me. You see him, you tell him I haven't forgotten. I see him. See what he has now and the little of it he gives back to those who made him. We did each other kindnesses, once. Were friends. They'd be dead on the floor of Sighi Prison if not for me and mine. I wouldn't call in debts but . . . if one day I found I had been mistreated, if I'd been made a fool of . . . the Strigoi would rise, my friend. I swear it.

Interviewer: Strigoi? The vampire?

Tinman: No vampire – you don't know your history, my friend. Strigoi . . .

Interviewer: And you say you have control over such a beast?

Tinman: I treat him with a father's love. Unlike your archangel. The hero, yes? Big Rab – the rough diamond doing so much for those poor people. To steal our children, that was why he came. That was what he did! Took them from their mothers, their fathers, carried them home like turkeys for Christmas. Gave them to you poor childless Europeans to raise properly, safely, away from this . . . this pit. The hero. Shit! He lay down with monsters and became their master. A rich man, now. Rich on favours owed by the families he filled with our stolen children. But one came home. One came back from the fucking grave, you hear me! The grave! Rose as Strigoi! Strigoi! Undefeated, unbeatable,

un-fucking-stoppable! You see him fight, you witness the
demon. Rab knows that. Knows what I'll unleash if he fucks
with me. The Irishman too. If I find out he's fucked with
me . . . I know. Know about what you did to those children.
What you made them do. He'll take your teeth, monster.
De-fucking-fang the whole clan.

   Vicky: Sorry, sorry, I think I've got to set up now – do
you think we could have you just sitting back on the bed
like that, yes, perfect, and maybe a little more of the silver
stuff just spiking up your quiff, yes, fantastic . . . now . . .

Pharaoh breathes out, slowly. Opens her eyes and sees Helen
staring at her.
   'You've heard this already?'
   'On the drive up.'
   'So you've had time to think about it.'
   Helen stands up. Makes tea. Talks to Pharaoh in the mirror.
   'There's so little paperwork available on Hawksmoor's
arrests. We know he got pulled over endless times on his aid
trips and we know the prisons he spent time in . . .'
   'I've got the exact dates and places,' interjects Pharaoh.
'Gheorge came up trumps. Inside Gherla at the same time as
our Tinman, here. Tinman was arrested at the gates of the
prison – handing himself in on an outstanding warrant. Gherla
is hell on earth, Helen. And Tinman went straight in to general
population, so something's off from the start . . .'
   'He wanted to be inside at the same time as the Hawksmoors?'
   'Or somebody paid him to do it – either to protect him, kill
him or set up a conversation. We've no way of knowing. We
do know Davey Hawksmoor had to be treated at the infirmary.
Another inmate was also being treated for severe injuries.
Broken wrists, fractured cheekbone, crushed trachea. Real nasty
piece of work, according to Gheorge. Ruled the yard, if that
isn't too American a phrase for your delicate ears.'
   Helen closes one eye, looking for a moment as if she's trying
to remember a password. 'So . . . somebody goes for Davey
Hawksmoor, Hawksmoor half-kills him, gets released, comes
home . . . and a few years later this inmate comes to Hull and

kills him?' She wrinkles her nose, dissatisfied. 'That's not what you've got poor Aector running around on, is it?'

Pharaoh looks away. Polishes her sunglasses on the bedsheets and puts them back on. 'He's part of this, but . . . you know how he gets when he thinks we're doing something morally . . . compromising . . . I wanted to spare him that.'

'Come on, Trish, that's bollocks. You're using him like a— what are those things that aircrafts use to tempt missiles away?'

'Chaff grenades,' obliges Pharaoh.

'Yeah, you're doing that. You've got the Hawksmoors marshalling their energy against him so they don't know that you're tunnelling in from underneath.'

Pharaoh grimaces. 'Mixed imagery, Helen. Complex.'

'You've known about this Strigoi bloke from the off, haven't you?' says Helen, sharpening her gaze. 'Did Vicky really start this project on her own or were you pulling her strings from the beginning?' She puts her hands in her hair. 'I'd forgotten how bloody infuriating you are. You make me feel like Dr-bloody-Watson. Or who's that other one. Hastings. That's who I am. Captain-bloody-Hastings.'

Pharaoh laughs. Licks her lips. 'You know too, Helen.'

'The Irishman?' asks Helen, warily. 'I won't pretend that didn't tweak my interest.'

Pharaoh massages her fists, thinking hard. 'Rab would be a useful contact for a certain madman, don't you think? A madman who loves the fight game.'

They fall silent, considering the likelihood that Rab Hawksmoor could be connected to the head of an Irish crime family – a clan leader whose feud with a former underling caused the streets of Dublin to run red. 'Good front for some of their operations,' muses Pharaoh. 'Guns, drugs, people . . . all tucked safely away inside Rab's Red Cross vans. And this deal with Omnia – that would be a nice payday, don't you think?'

They hold one another's gaze. 'I was watching you when he mentioned the de-fanging. You didn't react.'

'Nor did you.'

'Where did you first hear it?'

Pharaoh sighs, feeling suddenly tired to her bones. 'Romanian woman. Irina. Firebombed out of the house she'd been placed in while her application for asylum was heard. Lost the only picture she had of her father. I was on scene – not long a det super. Shaz Archer took the statement, not that she had anything to tell. Just sat there, muttering to herself, and you remember Shaz – not exactly the maternal sort. I took over and we had a natter.'

'A natter in Romanian?'

'In English, knobhead. She'd worked in a hotel in Bucharest. Learned it from the guests. Some Italian too. Lovely lady, she was. Well, a girl I suppose. Twenty-two or twenty-three. Couldn't tell and I've no idea if the date of birth she gave was legit. She was just cheekbones and dark eyes, Helen – nothing on her, just skin stretched over a frame. Spent hours with her, just making her feel safe, like I was somebody she could trust. Watched her come to life before my eyes. Jesus, Helen, the life that girl had had. The things they'd done to her; the lies they'd told to get her there. She'd run away, you see. Servicing forty to fifty sweaty blokes a day, squalid little mobile home they had her in; her and the others . . .'

Helen pats the air, trying to slow her friend down. Pharaoh isn't even looking at her – staring into the past, into the brown eyes of a girl who thought she could trust her.

'It was the men who'd brought her over who firebombed the house, Helen. After she got away, after she handed herself in to the police, after we put her somewhere with other women, women from her own country – that was when they came for her. Burned them all out. Would have taken her with them if police hadn't been passing on a routine patrol.'

'And she told you about Strigoi?'

Pharaoh sips her tea. Swallows. Strokes Penelope's hair with her spare hand. 'She told me that Strigoi was who the bad men feared. Like, some sort of bogeyman for proper bastards – some monster who came out of the shadows. Dismantled him before their eyes.'

'Murdered?'

'Defeated. Killed in a straight one-on-one fight in some old asylum on the outskirts of Bucharest. The bad men – that's what she always called them – they had a man, an enforcer. Monster of a man. A beast. And this Strigoi, nobody had put any money on him, didn't know much about him except that he fought in the sewers, took care of business for some rich men – he destroyed their man. Osek. That was the bloody name I've been trying to think of. He killed Osek. That might chime with something our Romanian friends have in their organised crime intelligence files . . . you're looking at me like I've got something on my face.'

Helen is sitting back down, scratching at her head. She's taken a biscuit from the drawer and makes a small, involuntary noise of pleasure as she sinks her teeth into the sugary shortbread.

'The teeth,' says Helen, in a spray of crumbs. 'She told you about the teeth?'

Pharaoh nods, slowly. Regards her friend. 'How many bodies do they have him in the frame for?' she asks, quietly.

Helen picks her teeth. Eats what she finds there. Taps at her incisors. 'With that signature? Eight.'

Pharaoh whistles. 'And they're not all in Romania, are they?'

Helen shakes her head. 'Three in Romania. One in Hungary. Slovenia. Germany. A jiu-jitsu instructor in the Dordogne . . . drug dealer in Santander . . .'

'Canines pulled. Trachea crushed. Limbs snapped.'

'Dating back to 2014,' says Helen, quietly. She's breaking so many rules, here. Risking so much; too much. Can't seem to stop herself giving Pharaoh everything.

'Davey Hawksmoor's teeth weren't taken,' says Helen, at last.

'Davey Hawksmoor kept his teeth in a jar by the bed. And they weren't in his mouth when he was found.'

'Why now?' asks Helen. 'What's it got to do with the orphanage kids? What are you accusing Big Rab of being involved in? Because our human trafficking unit has given me chapter and verse on his every involvement and investigation and no suspicion has ever been backed up with evidence. On paper, they're totally clean. I admit, it's a hell of a front if he is involved in trafficking, but . . .' she stops herself. 'Tinman,' she says, quietly. 'Everything he lost, what was taken when he was arrested – he strikes me as the kind of man who might just hold a grudge. Just who he blames – that's what we need to work out. I can't piece together his link to the Hawksmoors, even if you take the aurolac into account and the fact they might have been in some of the same places at the same time. Really, it's Vicky he should be pissed off with, but you're not acting like you think she's currently dangling from her toenails while he has his fun.'

Pharaoh nods. Sips her tea. 'She's an asset, not a threat. He likes publicity. Knows how to craft his own legend. He's got better PR instincts than a Downing Street spin doctor.'

'And in the meantime, what? If you think this man is on his way here, or here already . . . what other targets could he have? And the bodies he's left – this trail of broken fighters, unsanctioned bouts, street fights – these men he's beaten and choked to death. They're what?'

Pharaoh stares down into her tea. She doesn't want it any more. Closes her eyes before she says what she believes.

'He's staying match fit, Helen. These fights, these bouts to the death that people put so much money on; that's so big and yet nobody ever really acknowledges . . . he's making money with each win, yeah. But what if he's just working his way up a ladder? What if there's somebody waiting for him who he doesn't think he'll be able to beat?'

'Wayne Hawksmoor? I mean, come on, Trish, he's a hard case but he's not about to step into the octagon and trouble Jon Jones, is he?'

'I don't know what any of that means,' says Pharaoh. 'Maybe he just likes it. Maybe he really likes fighting people, one-on-one, and only one person walking out alive. I mean, that's life at its purest, isn't it? You've had those moments, Helen – where you think you're going to die. You ever feel more alive than that? Ever felt more desperate for another breath? Maybe that's what this Strigoi feeds on. Lifeblood.'

Helen swallows. 'Are you going to tell McAvoy what he's really looking for?'

Pharaoh breathes out. Shakes her head. 'Not yet. If the worst happens, it'll only be me that knew in advance, and my pension's safe. I do at least have a viable reason to question Susie Hawksmoor. She is, after all, at risk. No time to waste with proper protocols and such. Not when there's an imminent threat to life. We can get her away from Rab and Wayne. Lay it on thick. I swear, she'll have to talk to us . . . no mother makes their peace with their son's murder.' She looks at Penelope, then at Helen. 'Do you think he's real? This insanity?'

Helen chews her cheek. 'What happened to Irina?'

Pharaoh looks away. 'They got her, in the end. Not here. Back home, after we sent her back to the little village where she came from. Killed her, burned her house down, killed her parents too.' She sniffs, refusing to let her emotions show on her face. 'Would be nice to feel like we were a country worth running to, don't you think? Just now and again?'

Helen lets the silence build. 'One other little thing,' she says, at last. 'You know how you asked us to keep tabs on Papa Teague . . .'

Pharaoh listens.

Knows, at once, what the silly sod has gone and done.

Smiles, slowly. 'Oh, Roisin,' she says, mostly to herself. 'You little diamond.'

NINETEEN

Mae wakes later than she used to. Doesn't bother setting an alarm anymore. Goes to bed when she's tired and wakes when she's had enough. She doesn't remember dreams. Hasn't for years. The anti-depressants she's been steadily increasing in dosage have a numbing effect on her inner world. Her memories feel as though they belong to somebody else; the pictures she sees all blurry, pointillist, fragile as a dandelion clock.

It takes her a few moments to find herself; to take full possession of the body she is always disappointed to find herself inhabiting. There is a painstaking stocktake of ailments, injuries, nagging concerns; the pain in her hip, numbness in her left shoulder; the building cluster headache across her scalp, kneading her skull with hard, gauntleted fingers.

She untangles herself from the twists of cotton blanket. The material is damp beneath her fingers, below her thigh, pooled in the wrinkled indentation beneath her. She makes a face, emits a little groan of distaste. Shuffles herself up the bed and lays her head back against the padded mauve headboard. Catches a whiff of herself: sweat and red wine, talcum powder; soap. Unpeels her nightie from her skin. Looks down at the space she still thinks of Davey's side of the bed. Allows herself a smile at a memory. By God they'd soaked some sheets together when they were young. She wonders, again, if he would still fancy her now. Whether his roving eye would have turned away from her completely as she weathered and shrank, as age carved wrinkles in her face and dragged her skin towards her knees. He'd been losing interest towards the end, she's accepted that much. She's spent years blaming the steroids – telling herself it was the illegal substances in his bloodstream that increased his aggression and killed his sex drive. She doesn't let herself glimpse at the alternative – that somebody else was taking care

of his needs. She doubts that McAvoy will find any answers
on that score. Davey was always good at covering his tracks.

For an instant, Mae's mind fills with a picture of the big,
amiable detective. She's surprised at the clarity of the picture,
so at odds with the smudged fragments she's usually able to
conjure. She's come to feel very fond of him during their brief
acquaintance, a feeling she would not describe as entirely
maternal in nature. She's always liked the bigger men.
Remembers that feeling of being cocooned, sheltered, within
Davey's embrace; his breath on her neck, arms like tarred rope
about her own slender shoulders; the weight of one bovine
thigh pressing her into the mattress. She puts her hand out and
rubs Davey's side of the bed. Misses him a little harder. Tells
herself to stop it. Feels the familiar flush of resentment.

'Don't go making me miss you, Davey . . . Don't you bloody
dare. I'm still angry. Don't go thinking I've mellowed.'

She shakes her head, amused by herself. Squints at the clock
on the bedside table. Realises she's missed the *Breakfast Show*.
She wonders whether Susie-bloody-Hawksmoor had anything
to say on the local news. She doesn't particularly like the feeling
of being talked about, observed, scrutinised. She doesn't have
much of a social circle but she's friendly enough with the people
in her village and her face is known at the Tesco in Beverley
and at some of the stalls on the Saturday market. She's not a
nobody. Not invisible. People will see her face and know that
she's the widow of the murdered fighter; the one who won't
leave things well alone. She supposes she'll just have to front
it out; put on her make-up and her best togs and carry herself
the way Davey taught her; the way she managed for all those
years as part of the family. Anybody who has anything to say
can damn well take their shot. Susie too, for that matter. She
sometimes finds herself trying to work out the exact moment
when things went to hell between herself and her mother-in-
law. They'd been close, once upon a time; Susie even telling
her she saw her as the daughter she never had. She knew her
son's faults better than anybody and was always there to give
him a talking to and a clip round the ear if she felt he wasn't
pulling his weight as a husband. They took theatre trips

together; a couple of city breaks to drink wine and abuse the credit cards. Even gave her a full-time salary for a blatantly part-time job in the office at the yard. Got on with Paula, Wayne's wife, and the accumulation of cousins, aunties and half-siblings that congregated for baptisms, weddings and funerals. Was a Hawksmoor woman all the way through. And now, slanging matches in the *Hull Daily Mail*! Not so much as a Christmas card this year. She can't help thinking they should be trying a little harder to keep her sweet. She knows things that could cause them a great deal of trouble, though to reveal them she would jeopardise the potential sale of the company and the whopping great payday that will bring for the board members. She wonders whether it makes her a bad person to be so unsure what to do for the best. Catches herself in the thought and gives herself a talking to.

'You're not a bad person, Mae – you've just . . . tried your best . . .'

She wrinkles her nose. Becomes aware of the silence beyond the half-open bedroom door. Her heart seems to fold in on itself as she permits herself to wonder whether it will be this morning that she enters the kitchen to find Kenny still and lifeless; whether, at long last, she can picture him reunited with his owner. Shakes her head, annoyed at herself, telling herself off the way she used to snap at the children.

'Don't be a soft sod, he's grand. He'll outlive us bloody all.'

Mae lets out a sigh that seems to start at the soles of her feet. She'd like a coffee. Would settle for a tea. There are moments when she misses the helpers; those thin, pale, dark-haired women for whom Susie and Rab had found a use; cleaning, cooking, polishing, every inch the Edwardian serving maid in their tracksuits and furry collars. Mae had never really questioned it. Susie and Rab helped the orphaned children of Romania and helped provide them with a safe place to stay and some money in their pockets if they ever made it across to England. They waited on them out of gratitude, she reasoned. Brought them their morning coffee and made their beds and laundered their clothes out of a perfectly reasonable devotion to their liberators.

Mae stops herself thinking about it. She's older, now. Wiser. Doesn't believe she was ever daft enough to be convinced by her own wishy-washy bullshit.

Seeking distraction, she picks up her phone. It's brand new, all bells and whistles, though she doesn't know how to use half of its endless features. Davey would have hated it. He thought mobile phone evolution peaked with picture messages: never missing an opportunity to send her something filthy, and amusing; his glasses artfully arranged on his wedding tackle; sometimes his false teeth brought in to the composition to add an air of menace.

She giggles, one hand to her mouth, feeling silly, girlish, naughty. Pats the other side of the bed again. Wonders whether Aector would take up more room or less than her husband. What Davey would do if she saw her making eyes at the big Scotsman. Couldn't ever resist a challenge, that was Davey's problem. Couldn't stand to lose face. Would take on a lion with his bare hands if somebody suggested it might just get the upper claw in a one-on-one. She tries to remember a time during their marriage when Davey wasn't nursing one grievance or building up another; his bruised body always healing for some straightener, some scrap, some high-stakes anything-goes brawl arranged for the entertainment of spectators and sadists. She never worried about him. Davey always won and on the occasions that he didn't, his dad was always able to spin a yarn that gave him a get-out clause. She lost count of the times he told her about some dirty trick employed by a victorious opponent; the soporific effects of the bottle of water he'd been handed on the way to the scrap. Nobody argued with him. Everybody maintained the narrative – Davey Hawksmoor was the man; unbeatable.

She feels the familiar thoughts begin to rise. Who could have taken him down without a fight? How many must there have been to have put him down without him even getting a few punches in? Wayne told her that he thought his brother was probably taken unawares, or that the evil bastards used the little dog as a hostage. She likes that story. Can imagine him giving up his life nobly in exchange for the promise that Kenny be let go. But she doesn't believe it. Not truly. She knows, deep down, who came for him. Thinks she knows why. She doesn't think McAvoy will get anywhere near the truth but she's made preparations in case he does. She's stockpiled enough co-codamol to contaminate the ground she's buried in.

'Come on, Mae, old girl. Out of bed and into the bath for you . . .'

Mae puts out her hand and uses the bedside table to push herself upright, twinges at her back, her calves; tingles in her fingers. She feels herself wobble slightly, one leg not co-operating, and her hand shifts, knocking against the water glass. She licks dry lips. Spots her spectacles on top of the paperback she'd been reading before she fell asleep; a book of translated poetry that McAvoy had given her on their second meeting. It contained some ruminations upon grief, he'd said, half-embarrassed, entirely sincere. It might help . . .

She puts her glasses on. Grabs the water. Raises it to her lips.

She jerks back as she feels something tough against her lip. Splashes herself. Looks into the glass and sucks in a deep, urgent breath; gasping, gulping.

The glass drops from her hand. Hits the bridge of her bare foot and bounces away, its contents splashing and spilling onto the patterned carpet.

Staring up; a gleaming semicircle; white headstones pushed into soft pink earth.

Falls backwards, hand at her throat, blood thudding in her temples, at her pulse, her chest.

Her dead husband's denture grins up at her, balefully, from the floor.

TWENTY

McAvoy raises the umbrella. Enjoys the sound of the raindrops hitting the material. Spoils it for himself by imagining beaks pecking at the fragile nylon. Gives himself a talking to.

He stands for a while in the little pocket of peace. Practises his breathing exercises. Slows his thoughts. His pulse. Pictures Davey Hawksmoor jogging along the drowned footpath, Kenny tucked into his coat. Sees shapes appear from behind the walls of the columbarium. Sees big men; bad men – men who've been lying in wait. Revenge? An abduction gone wrong? A warning? If somebody would just *talk* to him; if they'd just give him somewhere to start . . .

'You said you wouldn't and you did! You're a fucking pig!'

McAvoy isn't sure he hears the words at first. He's found a little bit of shelter at the edge of a stand of evergreens, staring out at well-tended groves, his back to the columbarium. He looks around, unsure of himself. Curses softly as he feels his phone begin to ring in his pocket. Fumbles with the umbrella and his sodden coat-tails as he tries to dig it out. Apologises, instinctively, as he sees it's Roisin calling.

'Hello, you,' he says, the umbrella tucked under his chin so that his voice sounds half-strangled. 'Sure I'm hearing things . . . weather's not picking up . . .'

'Aector, love, I've just had Daddy on the phone – says there's been a . . . well, a bit of a feck-up, like, and . . .'

McAvoy tries to rearrange the phone and umbrella and ends up tipping a chain of icy water down his collar. He ignores it. Tries to hear what Roisin is trying to tell him.

'Get off me! Get off!'

McAvoy stops still. Whips his head around to where the sudden shriek had emanated from.

'Ro . . . I've got to go, call you back . . .'

He isn't sure if he's hung up. Just drops the umbrella and shoves the phone in his pocket and runs, stumbling through the sodden grass, deeper into the copse.

'Stewie . . . you're hurting me . . . you're no . . . no!'

McAvoy sinks into a puddle up to his knee. Drags himself out, trying to grip his boots with his toes, falls forwards into a mulch of dead leaves and shovelled earth. Hauls himself up and darts for harder ground, pushing branches aside.

'Get off, Stewie!'

McAvoy stumbles into the clearing; a space between the rain-blackened trees. A man in a soaked grey hoodie has his hand around the neck of a thin young woman, her legs off the ground, feet kicking helplessly against the moss-slimed marble of a neglected tomb. She's batting at his hands, eyes round, desperately trying to continue her pleas for help, for mercy.

'Police! Stop!'

The man doesn't turn. Keeps pressing harder, his other hand now in her hair, pushing her back against the unforgiving stone.

McAvoy clears the space between them in three strides, grabbing the man's hand at the wrist and hauling backwards, wrenching it up behind his back and pulling him away. The woman falls to her knees as the man releases her hair, spit and tears and snot streaking her face. She's young. A teenager. He feels a sudden heat in his gut, a desire to keep twisting the man's arm, to hurt him, to make him beg . . .

McAvoy shakes the thoughts away. Comes back to himself, the static in his head suddenly clearing.

'Peeping-fucking-Tom, are ye? That's what gets you off, is it? Spying on a fella and his old lady getting their ride on, that it, big lad?'

The man has twisted in McAvoy's grasp and is delivering a torrent of words in a thick Donegal accent. McAvoy takes a moment to look at him properly. Black hair, brushed forwards, thick-set, muscle vest under his hoodie; firebird tattoos creeping up his neck to disappear into dark stubble. McAvoy feels the strength in him. Wonders how he's going to hold him still and get his cuffs out at the same time.

'Andy!' he shouts, feeling foolish as he tries to beat the noise of the rain.

'That your boyfriend, is it? He going to come have a wee fiddle with you, is he? Now you've got yourself a good horn on . . .'

From the floor, the girl begins to rise.

'Leave him,' she says, gasping. 'It's not, not what you thought . . .'

'Just sit still, miss. Help will be here in a moment.'

'Sweet Jesus but would you listen to him? Looks like a fucking grizzly bear and he's after calling for his boyfriend. Put me down yourself . . . try it, I fucking dare you . . .'

McAvoy looks around, hopeful of seeing Daniells emerging through the trees. He squints, unsure whether he's just seen something move; a shape in the hazy grey-green distance at the mouth of the columbarium.

'He wasn't hurting me, honest – he just got carried away . . .'

McAvoy feels his phone begin to buzz again. Wonders whether it would be frowned upon to knock the bloke out for a few while until he has time to catch his breath and answer Roisin.

'You must know lasses who like it rough,' says the woman, softening her gaze and putting one hand upon his chest. He notices her well-tended nails. Notices the size of the diamond in the cluster ring on her middle finger. He finds himself temporarily mute; inert.

'Your Roisin,' she says, making the soft *ssh* sound sibilant. She flickers her tongue, for effect. 'Loves it rough, doesn't she, Stewie? Loves the feel of being a little rag-doll, thrown around by the boys . . .'

In his grasp, the man called Stewie turns, sliding his wrist from the sodden cuff of the hoodie and lashing out with his elbow, aiming to strike upwards into McAvoy's jaw. He sees it as it comes. Manages to drag himself out of the haze. *His wife*, he thinks. They'd said Roisin!

McAvoy sidesteps the blow. Lets go of the empty sleeve and

hits Stewie behind the ear, feeling the stinging contact all the way to his elbow.

He turns back to the girl a moment too late. Doesn't see her step into his grasp until she already has the taser at his chest. Feels the stinging, searing heat as his body jerks, stretches, tendons elongating – bound in invisible fire.

She keeps the barbs in his belly. Pushes them past the skin, their sizzling spikes hissing as they cauterise the bubbling blood. She holds the trigger mechanism with index finger and thumb. Squeezes, hard, watching her own reflection in the eyes of the big police officer, biting into his own lip as the modified taser cooks him from the guts.

'Roz! Enough!'

McAvoy falls backwards. Behind his eyes: darkness, flame. Then the blessed kiss of oblivion.

TWENTY-ONE

'I don't like wearing them. It hurts my ears.'

'It's either that or Auntie Trish gets to choose the music.'

'That's like choosing between broccoli and cauliflower.'

'Could you please just do what I ask you? Just once?'

Penelope catches her mother's eye in the rearview mirror. Decides, on balance, that this isn't the hill she wants to die on. Pulls on her Sonic the Hedgehog earphones and settles herself in the car seat.

'What's wrong with my music?' asks Pharaoh, archly, from the passenger seat. She hates being in the passenger seat. Can't understand why the three of them couldn't crush into her convertible and instead had to slum it in this spacious BMW X90, with its heated leather seats and marked absence of rainwater in the footwells.

'Crisp factory,' says Helen, nodding to her right.

'That's what old people do,' mutters Pharaoh, huffing on the window and rubbing her cuff against the glass. If she squints through the spray on the windscreen she can almost make out the Humber Bridge – a few charcoal smudges puncturing the swirling, hissing grey.

'I just like pointing stuff out,' says Helen, checking her mirror and moving into the outside lane. They overtake the blue van that had been holding them up. Swing back into the inside lane – a feathery line of froth-flecked brown beginning to fill the windscreen. Pharaoh finds herself wondering how the Romans felt when they first laid eyes on the Humber. How many slaves they sacrificed to its sucking, sandbank-pocked depths before they decided nothing north of the river was worth the effort.

'That's you,' says Pharaoh, becoming aware of the buzzing.

'No, hang on, it's me . . .'

She pulls out her phone, surprised to see four missed calls from Roisin McAvoy. She's left voicemails too. Pharaoh feels her pulse points begin to tingle; a pain in her jaw, at the base of her tongue. Feels a slow, creeping dread beginning its familiar rise.

She jabs at the phone, trying to call back, head filling with all sorts of dark imaginings – all concerning the man they share.

'Trish, it's ringing . . .'

The screen lights up as Pharaoh tries again to call Roisin. She takes the call without glancing at the number, her fingers fumbling at the screen.

'Roisin, what's happened . . . is he hurt?'

'Slow down, lady. My English, it's not so good, yes? Not quite the tickety-boo.'

Pharaoh swallows, hard. Gathers herself. Gets her head together, watching a drip on the windscreen being chewed into endless iridescent drops by the gnashing teeth of the gale.

'She's OK, then?' says Pharaoh, breathing out, getting comfy in her seat. Everything else seems to disappear: chalk paintings on rain-lashed pavements. All she can think of is here, now: this man, who has her friend.

'I wouldn't touch a hair on her feet, I swear to you,' comes the voice, carrying a whisper of a smile. 'You scared me. Gave me fright. You are not a voyeur, I hope. That is the word, yes? For somebody who likes to watch?'

'How are we going to make things right?' asks Pharaoh, rummaging in her pockets for her cigarettes. She finds none. Takes off one of her bangles and starts squeezing it in her hand, the knuckles white, the pattern indenting her palm.

'Things are right already, Patricia. Am I saying that right? Patrisha, yes? I met a Patricia when I was in England, I think. Cleaned people's houses. Had a son, I think. Used to save her money for Saturday nights. How do you say it? Dry white wine is *drah whart wharn*, yes?' He laughs at his own inelegant Hull accent. 'A strange place, I think. I did not care for what I saw. I am happy here. Here where I am a father to my children; where I can help people. Vicky is going to tell my story, she has promised. She and I . . . I think we have an understanding. What happened to her friend, that was regrettable. I think he wanted to be the hero, you know? Put up the good fight? We had to hurt him quite a lot. But he is quiet now. Settled.'

'And Vicky?' asks Pharaoh, refusing to engage.

'Vicky has what she wants. She has the run of my kingdom. She has the world exclusive. She is, how you say it? A fly on the wall, yes? Recording it all. It will be worth money, this footage, some day. When all is over, people will want to understand.'

Pharaoh feels the wind buffet the car as they cruise onto the bridge; the entire structure seeming to shake as the gale screams in off the sea. She puts her palm over her ear. Jams her cheek to the phone.

'You like the celebrity, don't you, Tinman?' says Pharaoh, dripping contempt. 'Always looking for the angle. Always trying to be something from a comic book. Look at you, in your underground lair with your silly nickname and your silver hair; all your blades and chains. You're a drawing done by a teenage incel, mate.'

In the driving seat, Helen glances over. Pharaoh ignores the questions in her eyes.

'You're telling me Vicky is there of her own free will? That I should just leave things alone? That I should take your word for it?'

She hears a small, snuffling sound. Realises Tinman is huffing aurolac from a bag. 'She will call you, I swear. When she is done. I call myself as . . . courtesy. Your friend with the Bucharest Police. He kick some of my boys awake this morning – asking questions about English woman, have they seen, have they seen? They tell him nothing, of course, but they follow him. Hear him. He wasn't reporting back to any fucking superior officer. He called somebody else. Was it you?'

Pharaoh grinds her teeth. 'Like I'd tell you.'

'Vicky has told me a lot about you, Patrisha. This name of yours? Pharaoh? I see before, I think. It from Egypt, yes?'

'Great grandmother was a music hall performer – did an act called the Mummy and the Explorer. Ended up having her bandages unwrapped most nights, before the show and after, if you're asking. Adopted the name from the act not long before her husband threw himself under a train. All this useful to you, is it?'

'I am enjoying talking to you,' he says, and this time there's a real smile in his voice. 'You will stay away from *him*, yes? He would not hurt you for fun, but sometimes people get hurt around him.'

Pharaoh looks up as they pass through the toll booth, feeling the cool spray on her face as Helen winds down the window to pay the toll. She looks over to the brooding mass of the Country Park. Remembers blood spilled. Remembers meeting a big, shy Scotsman with a good brain and a soft heart, and deciding he belonged to her.

'What do you want me to tell Rob Hawksmoor?' asks Pharaoh. 'I'm going to see him now, as it goes. I think we've got lots to talk about. And I think, Tinman, that you might just be the man to make sure that all the bad people pay for what they've done. That's what you're about, isn't it? Helping your children? Why not help me catch the man who stole them away?'

Pharaoh knows it's a wild swing – that he might as well laugh in her face as confirm her fanciful suspicions.

'I don't like you talking about him that way,' says Tinman, quietly. 'Rob is . . . a good man. Decent man. Did a lot of good things. Sure he make mistakes, get greedy, turn a blind eye, bend some rules but fuck, who does not get things wrong from time to time? Rob and me, we understand each other, I think. He knows I would not stab him in the back – it is not our way. Not mine. Strigoi comes from the front, Patrisha. Goes straight for the throat. Rab . . . he does what he can in a difficult situation.'

'Give me the strength,' sighs Pharaoh, pointing Helen into the right-hand lane and accelerating damply into the leafy Victorian avenues of Hessle. 'You've unleashed this beast, have you? This Strigoi? Sent him to do your bidding? Revenge, is it? I wonder which of your children gave you up? Whether they were paid to tell the police where to find you, or if they gave you up only after they were face down and bloodied. Which fits better with your view of yourself, Tinman? I'd love to fucking know.'

She hears the anger, even as he tries to laugh. 'You have sharp tongue, Patrisha. Maybe get yourself cut, some day. Maybe cut right out.'

'What do you need from me?' she asks, letting her temper fully fill every overly enunciated vowel. 'Tell me what assurances you need to get a statement that's some actual bloody use.'

'I want you to be nice to me,' says Tinman, eventually. 'Talk to me as an equal. You are a detective chief superintendent, yes? This is very high! High for anybody but for woman? And I see from Google you are almost Roma! The dark hair, the curves, the big how you say . . .?'

'Don't you bloody do it, mate.'

'The eyes, yes? Perhaps you and me, we cousins, yes? I have many cousins. Many half cousins. I have left drops of blood from here to Ireland, Patrisha.'

'Ireland?' She attempts a Galway accent. 'Aye, but they're a grand bunch of lads, are they not? Love the craic? And the fighting. Love the fighting, so they do . . .'

'Don't let him die,' he says, suddenly, his whole demeanour changing. His voice thickens with emotion. Something like pain bleeds into his throat. 'That's what I want, Patrisha. Your friend, she is free to go, but she will stay. Her man – he is already trying to assist in the documentary. She understands now, you see. What they did. What was done to that poor fucking boy. He'll die before he stops. Do you know people like that? The dying rat that will keep fighting even as it watches its own heart stop. That is Strigoi. He is beyond my protection, Patrisha. But you – you can save him from himself. Don't let them kill him. He has to speak. If he lives, I will make sure he speaks to you. But you must not let him die, Patrisha. You promise me, you keep him safe.'

Pharaoh pushes her head back into the seat. Points to the right and watches Helen swing the 4x4 past the new houses and down towards the waterfront. Behind her, Penelope watches the torrent of filthy water thundering down towards the

submerged strip of grass by the water's edge. Sees her glance
in the mirror for her mum to tell her it's OK.

'Rab's old,' says Tinman. 'Fragile. Half-fucking-dead. Was
never the man he said he was, even in his prime. But that boy
– the tame fucking shark. He knows what he did. Knows this
reckoning had to fucking come. But you don't let Strigoi get
that far. You stop him.'

'Stop him before he's finished his work? I thought you sent
him? This would be so much fucking easier if you just told me
who he is and where to find him.'

'He's not mine to control any more,' says Tinman. 'He's
lost to me. To us. But he is not gone from our prayers.'

'Is he here, Tinman? This Strigoi, this man who won't stop
killing – is he here, on my patch? Here to finish what he started
with Davey Hawksmoor?'

Tinman swears in his own language. Spits. 'Started with
him? Ha! That was not the fucking start. Davey! Do not mourn
that fucking pig. He helped create the monster who killed him.
You think he found that funny, as the light went out in his
eyes? As Strigoi tugged his teeth from his gums. It has always
made me laugh to think of it.'

'And yet you were such good buddies in prison,' tries
Pharaoh. 'Watching each other's backs, keeping the Hawksmoors
safe. Even showed his appreciation by bringing his new friend
to England, showing him around, acting like king of the city
to impress his little Romanian street fighter. What happened,
Tinman? Seemed like you had a beautiful friendship . . .'

The line goes dead. Pharaoh grimaces. Jerks forwards in her
seat as Helen pulls the car to the kerb outside the little white-
painted cottage. Lace curtains twitch.

'Penelope, headphones! The lady I told you about – you
might remember her from when you were little – she's going
to watch you and . . .'

Pharaoh sees the front door open. Sees Roisin run through
the rain, all leopard print dressing gown and bare feet. Pharaoh
scowls, only to remember the missed calls, the voicemail . . .

The back door of the car is wrenched open and Roisin jumps
into the warmth. Her make-up is running down her face. She

was crying before she stepped into the downpour. Her eyes are seamed with red.

'Fuck, Roisin, what's happened . . .'

Roisin smears the heels of her hands across her cheeks. Manages a wet-eyed smile for Penelope, who's looking at her as if she's a mermaid that's jumped in through an open window.

'Daddy,' she says, and the word doesn't come out right. She sniffs. Tries again, nodding, meaning it. 'Daddy will fix it. He'll get him back.'

Pharaoh spins in the chair. Has to stop herself from reaching into the back and grabbing her by her stupid fucking polyester dressing gown.

'Get him back from where, Roisin?'

Roisin lowers her eyes.

'From Puttock.'

In the driving seat, Helen winces. She knows the name. Starts tapping away at her phone, logging into encrypted databases with her thumbprint. She looks at her daughter. Softens her face. 'Headphones, sweetie.'

'Daddy . . . he's here. He'll . . .' Roisin stops, her ringtone blaring out of her pocket, something incongruously upbeat by Shakira. 'Daddy, is he there . . . he hung up, like something was . . .'

Her face changes. Hardens. 'No, that's Andy . . . stop him, them . . . for feck's sake, stop them . . .'

TWENTY-TWO

Daniells feels himself dying. The darkness is wet cloth, gathered in great folds around him, binding him, wrapping him, pulling him deeper. He can't feel pain any more. Isn't sure if he's still fighting, still ramming his elbows back into the ribs of his attacker to push them back against the rocks of the columbarium; to stamp on their foot and run. There's a thudding sensation in his temple, a sensation of wetness at his mouth; gravel pin-pricking his knees, but it feels like it's happening to somebody else.

For an instant, the grip loosens. He sucks in a breath. Tastes blood. Feels the sudden cold rush of wind and rain as his senses flood with oxygen. Tries to turn, only for the figure behind him to tighten his grip, to squeeze – forcing his head forwards even as the arm about his neck closes his trachea. He opens his eyes. Sees the sodden pathway through a blurry haze of red. Tries again to force himself up. Can't seem to make his hands respond. Feels himself going limp; the darkness closing over him like a wave.

He barely makes out the sound. Doesn't register the exclamation of pain. Almost weeps as the pressure at his throat is suddenly released, sucking up great lungfuls of bloodied, spitty air, pinkish tears rolling down his dirty cheeks. He collapses on his stomach, face against the floor.

He makes out the sound of running boots. Angry voices. The thud and bang and crash of violence. He tries to make himself roll onto his back, to begin the slow climb back to his feet. Jerks as he feels strong arms lifting him up, patting at his dirty clothes, thumbing his cheeks to look into his eyes. Sees as if through a kaleidoscope, faces bobbing in and out of his line of sight. He makes out an unfamiliar face. Another, behind him. Two men. Takes another breath, hands patting his back, squeezing at his forearms.

'Be all right now, sir, so you will – just like putting petrol in a car. Fill her up, sir – big breaths now, big breaths . . .'

Daniells tries to slap away the hands that are tugging at him. Makes an attempt to speak and pain grips him; his mouth filling with the taste of wet metal.

'Take it easy, sir, take it easy, no rush, now . . .'

Daniells topples sideways, reaching out for the tumbledown wall, the nameplate by the niche long since obscured by the elements.

'No fecking sign.'

The man who has been tending to Daniells turns at the sound of the angry voice. Coughs. Spits. Daniells gets a proper look at him. Flat cap and skin like wet suede. Handsome, blue-eyed, craggy, stubbled jaw, dirty neck; a silk scarf tied at his throat and a workman's physique wrapped inside a donkey jacket soaked dark as molasses.

'Roisin . . .' manages Daniells, his voice little more than a croak. 'Roisin's dad . . .'

Papa Teague gives him a wink. Pats him on the back and turns back to the two men. One wears a camouflage coat and dirty jeans, his curly black hair dangling down wetly from a beanie hat, tiger-striping his pinched features. He proffers an umbrella. 'Floating like a paper boat, so it was.'

'Sarge . . .' says Daniells, starting forwards and feeling his legs give way. His senses seem to return in a flood. 'McAvoy,' he says, again, pressing his fingers to his throat. He takes the men in properly. Tries to make sense of what has happened and gives up when a wave of nausea rises up from his gut. He tastes dirt. Gags and has to reach out again for support. Only as Teague moves aside does he see the man lying on the floor behind him, both hands clasped to his brow, blood squeezing between his fingertips as if he were gripping a handful of cherries.

'Know him, do you?'

Teague aims a kick at the man's hands, forcing him to uncover his face for a moment. Daniells looks at him groggily. He's young. Not much more than a teenager. He looks strong, capable, but there's a plumpness to him, as if there was a toned sportsman hidden beneath an inch of fat.

'Dead!' he hisses, pressing his hands back to the ugly purple lump spreading across his forehead towards his short dark hair. 'You're all so fucking dead!'

'None of that now,' says Papa Teague, reproachfully. He kicks him in the ribs. Pulls him up by his wrists and forces him to meet his gaze.

'Your friends. They wouldn't have taken him, would they? Wouldn't have been that silly.'

Daniells screws up his eyes. Realises he should probably make some attempt at taking control of the situation. 'Don't . . . don't get yourself in trouble . . . I'll call it in.' He pats at his pockets, looking from Teague to his companions. His gaze lingers on the length of cord and leather that dangles from the wrist of Teague's second companion. He's young, wiry; dressed for the weather in a black anorak and combat trousers. There's a tattoo of a teardrop below his right eye. A silver hoop through the lobe of his left ear. He glances down at the cord, following Daniells' gaze.

'I'd say one hundred yards, eh boys? At least.'

'Sixty if you're lucky,' scoffs Teague, rubbing at his jaw and looking at Daniells as if trying to work something out. 'Boy's a decent shot with that thing. Wish we'd been filming that – would have been one to show our Valentine. Heck of a shot, boy, heck of a shot.'

Daniells feels the pieces line up. Realises he's been saved from a random attack by Roisin McAvoy's father. He starts attempting to tidy himself up, straighten himself up. Stops, short. 'McAvoy,' he says, pushing himself upright and making himself meet Teague's eyes.

Teague turns away from him and crouches back down beside the groaning, bleeding man. 'You've got some things to tell me, I shouldn't wonder. Question is, will you be after answering them without acting the maggot?'

'I don't even know what you're saying, you gypsy cunt!'

Daniells winces. Sees the other two men look down at their boots.

'Now that was a silly thing to go and say . . .' mutters Teague, almost regretfully. He pulls the scrabbling young man's hands away from his face. Sighs. Sticks his thumb into the open wound on his brow, pushing in. Worming in. Grabbing a finger and thumb of bleeding flesh, one knee across his throat.

'One tug, lad – one tug and it's not going to take you as long to wash your face, you hear me, boy? Shush now, shush, that's no way to conduct yourself, hush now . . . I just want to know where they've gone. And believe me, boy, you're going to tell me . . .'

Daniells tries to step forwards to stop the assault. Makes a half-hearted attempt to push between the other two men. They're respectful as they hold him back. Don't touch any of his sore places as they pin him to the rocky walls of the columbarium. He can't make himself watch. Lowers his head when he sees his attacker begin to drum his feet on the rocky path, Teague sitting above him, whispering into his ear.

'Don't,' pleads Daniells, throat closing up. He realises how cold he is. How wet and grimy. Realises there's blood on his chin.

Teague stands up. Takes the kerchief from around his neck and wipes his red hands. Behind him, the man curls into a foetal ball, whimpering as he clutches his face.

Daniells feels the men step away from him. Teague gives a friendly jerk of his head. He's got a cigarette between his teeth, blood on the filter tip. There's a rope burn around his neck, half hidden by thick dark hair and the two holy medals that twist together at his throat.

'Best you come along with me for now, sir,' says Teague, calmly. 'All this – it's a bit hard to write on a report, isn't it? I mean, people who aren't here, who didn't see this fecker try and kill you, they'd never believe you, would they? Fearghal with a slingshot? And your Aector – by Christ, I swear I was only trying to do the silly bollocks a favour. Been good to me, so he has.' He shakes his head. Looks to his two companions. 'I should tell her.'

The one called Fearghal winces. 'Jesus, she's gonna go fecking spare.'

Teague looks pained. Looks like a father who would rather

die than upset his daughter. 'Could always sort it – explain things to Aector, like – he might not even have to tell her . . .'

Daniells suddenly feels acutely aware of the absurdity of the situation. Sees himself, wet and beaten, tucked away from the wind in this old temple of brick, brass and ash, listening to the head of the Teague clan wipe his bloody fingers on his coat and try to find a way not to let Roisin find out that they arrived too late.

'I'm not going anywhere . . .' hisses Andy. 'I need to call this in – if somebody has him, we need . . .'

Teague steps closer. Daniells can feel the heat from the tip of his cigarette warming his cheek. He can't hold Teague's gaze. Isn't sure he knows anybody who could.

'Saved your life, boy. I'd say that means you owe me one. The alternative is Fearghal and Jonjo here carry you to the van with your legs kicking all the fecking way, but my girl speaks highly of you and that would be no way for us to begin a friendship.'

Daniells tries to think of something to say. His legs make the decision on what to do next. He finds himself running even before he's aware of having decided to.

Teague holds his coat. Pulls him back as if he were fitted with a handle.

'None of that now, boy,' says Teague, good-naturedly. 'Play your cards right, I'll tell you a story. It was one I had for the big man, but I reckon you'll enjoy it too.'

Daniells feels the two men take his arms. Watches Teague step back to the anguished figure on the path. Takes his wallet. Takes the phone from inside his white trainer sock.

Looks down at the man, almost kindly, before pocketing the items. Shakes his head.

'Backed the wrong horse, lad. Least you can tell your mates that Papa Teague gave you a scar, eh? Almost worth all this for the craic, don't you think?'

He opens the little burner phone and scrolls through the recent messages. Finds who he's looking for.

Types out a message: **Job done.**

A moment later it buzzes in his hand. A two-word message: **Good lad.**

Teague allows himself a smile. Pockets the phone. Reaches down, hauls the young man from the floor, holding him under the arm, allowing him to keep his palm pressed to the ugly wound.

'I think you'll be coming along too, lad.'

The young man doesn't try to fight. Just lets himself be steered down the sloshing path.

'Don't worry,' says Teague, gently, at his ear. 'He'll be dead before he knows you fucked up.'

Thinks: *And if Aector's hurt, God save you – his daughter's wrath will be Biblical.*

'You poor wee shite.'

TWENTY-THREE

McAvoy isn't fighting any more. He's bound in gaffer tape and tie-wraps, a musty balaclava dragged back to front over his face. He knows he's lying on his side, legs drawn up. Knows he's horribly, stupidly hot, his sodden clothes seeming to stick to his painful skin like wire wool. Knows he can't breathe properly – his face prickling, sweating, oozing through the sodden material.

'Woman called Mae rang, while you were having your little tantrum. Took a message, hope that's all right. Says Davey's teeth were in her water glass. That normal for you, is it? This sort of thing happen a lot in Humberside?'

McAvoy tries to change position, roll himself somehow upright. Strains, uselessly, against the bonds at his wrist, his ankles.

'I wouldn't, sweetcheeks. Any more exertions, I reckon that Scottish heart of yours is going to cook. I can almost see it – baked potato in a microwave.'

From somewhere nearby, McAvoy hears a hiss. Feels the heat increase. Sucks in a bitty breathe. Eucalyptus. Steam.

'Am I in a sauna?' he asks, through the balaclava.

There's a laugh. A sound of wet flesh slapping wet flesh. 'It's not a gameshow, son. No prizes for guessing in this round, I'm afraid. You're not here so we can play "guess where the fuck I am".'

'Sorry,' says McAvoy. He's trying to quell the rising panic in his gut. He's bound and masked, mummified in his wet clothes. 'I don't know what you want.'

There's another little snuffle of laughter. A foreign voice. Eastern European. Amused.

'He wants to know why you aren't shouting and pleading. He wonders if you fully understand.'

McAvoy feels heat rising from the wet floor. Realises he's lying on tiles; the puddle of water slowly turning to vapour.

'I did fight,' says McAvoy. He stops himself. 'Mae said Davey's teeth were in her water glass?'

'I'm not your secretary, lad. You've had a lot of missed calls from your wife. You'll be in the bad books when you get home.'

There's another burst of Romanian, the voice cold.

'You can go home, lad. Not much more than a mark or two on you and nowt a big lump like you can't take.'

'I want to help you,' says McAvoy, trying to keep the pleading note from his voice. 'We can talk. I can't think straight like this . . . I can barely breathe . . .'

McAvoy doesn't sense movement. Doesn't know he's in danger until a cold hand clamps around his fingers and twists. McAvoy feels the white fire of agony shoot all the way to his neck. Bites down on his lip, feeling the joints and tendons being twisted away from their moorings; the rigging in his hand beginning to fray, to tear . . .

'Now then, leave him be, lad, no need for that . . .'

McAvoy feels himself released – his hand a throbbing ball of fire and gristle.

'I don't know what you want!' he shouts. 'I was trying to help that young lady. I don't know who you think I am . . .'

'Aector McAvoy,' says the heavily accented voice at his ear. 'Detective Inspector. That's not bad, yes? Not a grunt, eh? Men work for you?'

'Men and women,' says McAvoy, unable to help himself.

There's a laugh from both men. 'Always wondered if you woke motherfuckers would die for political correctness.'

'I just meant . . .'

'Inspector, it really would be better to stop talking,' comes the voice from the seated man. There's another hiss – a fresh waft of heat.

'Terrible strain your heart's under, lad. Best thing all told is if you just shut your face for a bit and let the grown-ups talk to you, yes? Then we can all get on with our day. All I want to know is . . . where's Strigoi?'

McAvoy holds his breath, waiting for more. When nothing comes, he clears his throat, trying to get some strength into his voice, afraid his scorched trachea will produce nothing but steam. 'Who? Who are you talking about?'

For a beat, nobody speaks. McAvoy listens to the *drip drip drip* of the hot water as it falls beside him, around him, upon him. Feels the wool seem to engorge and tighten around his mouth and nose.

'The man you are looking for, who killed Davey Hawksmoor. Is he here?'

McAvoy feels as though he's submerged in a too-hot bath. Can feel the sweat oozing into his eyes; the heat in his nostrils and mouth.

'That's what you want?' McAvoy manages to half-shout the words, his rasping voice still managing to sound incredulous. 'Whoever you're protecting, they're not even in our sights! It's just a case review! No suspects first time, nothing new . . .'

'Strigoi,' says the Englishman, his tone insistent. 'Don't play the soft sod with me, lad. You had that sneaky rat Teague snuffling about in my dirty underwear! Gypsy bastard – thinks that a favour can be banked forever. Caught one of his thieving nephews in my old lock-up – fair shit his britches, little bastard. Fought his corner, mind. Rabid dog temper, the whole fucking lot of them. Bet your wife's like that, is she? Hot-blooded, ain't they . . .'

McAvoy strains against his bonds. Feels a slight give, the sweat on his arms managing to loosen some of the gaffer tape.

'Having a shite, are you, lad? Gone stiff as a board. Touched a nerve, did I? I tell you what, if you don't start being a bit helpful it'll be her that's wrapped up on the floor of my steam room and she won't be wearing her best clothes, I swear. I reckon I'll put her in something special. Ladylike. Something that suits her. Clear-heels and a muzzle, should do it.'

McAvoy can't stop himself. 'Don't. Don't talk about her. Tell me what you want. I don't know the name you said. I don't know who you work for.'

'Work for! By God you've got some front on you. I work for nobody, son. People work for me! And if Papa Teague thinks I'm about to turn a blind eye just because I owe him from way back . . . bollocks to that. You know. I know you fucking know!'

McAvoy feels the same bewilderment that usually floods him
when one of the women in his life ask him to explain why they
think they're cross with him. He knows that whatever comes
out of his mouth next is only going to make things worse.

The Eastern European man speaks again in his native tongue.
McAvoy tries to imprint the words on his memory, straining for
any snatch of something familiar. His mind races, even as the
heat rises and his throat threatens to close. What has Papa Teague
to do with anything? The man spoke as if they were familiars.
How could Papa Teague possibly be caught up with his investigation into Davey Hawksmoor's death? He tries to concentrate
on drawing pictures in his head – perfect Venn diagrams inter-
secting in all the ways that the Traveller boss and the Hawksmoors
could be connected. The image becomes too unwieldy. Papa
Teague has connections across Europe and beyond; bonds in
blood and money; handshake contracts and marriages of
convenience. Knows who he can call upon when troubles come,
and which of his friends are most likely to stab him in the back.

'Andy,' says McAvoy, the name rising unbidden. 'Did they
take Andy?'

There's silence in the room. The Eastern European speaks.
'When are you going to start worrying about yourself, Scotsman?
You know Strigoi killed Davey. You know why. You know about
that place. What Davey did to him. What the whole lot of them
did to him. He can have his revenge. What I need to know is
that I'm not going to get caught up in any of it.'

'Caught up in it? You've abducted a police officer!'

'Abducted's a strong word,' comes the voice, and something
in the tenor sounds strangely familiar, a blunting and elongating
of the *urr* sound. He knows the accent, if not the voice. 'You
tell me what a man's supposed to do, though, eh? Some thieving
Gypsy trying to get his hands on your footage, all to hand over
to some cop his daughter's gone and married – and fair play
on that, by the way, lad; got her mother's eyes and Beyonce's
arse, that one . . .'

McAvoy feels the bonds begin to give. Wonders how quickly
he can get the balaclava down, whether he can fight with his
legs tied, or whether he shouldn't just close his eyes, give in to

the gathering darkness. His heart is thudding, timpani in his chest. He can feel his pulse against the scratchy material of the balaclava.

'We don't even know it's the same man, do we? It was a fair fight, I said that then, I'll say it now. Davey took him down, the kid tapped, Davey didn't let go . . . three of my boys had to drag him off. Shouldn't have even got to that stage. Big Rab should have sorted things the moment it started getting out of hand.'

'I don't know . . . what you're talking about,' gasps McAvoy. 'All we know is that Davey got himself killed by person or persons unknown! Went out for a run, was attacked and beaten to death. I've got nothing. Nowhere! The Hawksmoors don't even want the case re-opening . . .' he trails off, suddenly realising what Roisin has done. She's gone to Daddy. She's asked for help for her feckless husband – asked him for knowledge that could only have come from his connections to the bare-knuckle and underground fight scene. And in trying to help his daughter, he's alerted somebody dangerous that the police are onto them. He wants to start explaining. Can't seem to find the words, his tongue lolling thick and swollen in his mouth.

'Call my boss . . .' he manages. 'Trish. She can work things out . . . none of this has to matter, we can talk, properly. I'll listen to what you have to say. If Davey was a friend of yours, you can help . . .'

McAvoy senses the movement this time. Knows what to expect. Knows how hard the man is going to twist his tendons this time. He jerks at the slipping bonds. Twists his wrists, his throbbing hands in agony as the tie-wraps cut into his skin, the nylon stretching, tighter, tighter . . .

He feels the bonds give. Rolls onto his back with both legs drawn back and thrusts out with his boots. Connects with something hard. Fleshy. Grabs at the sopping balaclava and wrenches it free, coughing spasmodically as the hot steam scorches his mouth, throat, lungs.

'Get up you daft bastard, he's going to . . .'

McAvoy looks towards the mound of flesh, a great wobbling tower of flab emerging through the steam like a mountain. Sees the other man trying to get to his feet, slipping on the tiles,

crashing down and banging his head on the terracotta. McAvoy
sees the ink upon his skin. The scars. The great ropy veins in
his thighs, biceps, chest. Drags himself to his feet, tugging at
the tape around his legs, pain lancing down his injured hand.
Looks at his mangled fingers and grabs at them instinctively,
tugging at the dislocated fingers until there's a sickening crunch.

'Dan, fuck's sake, hit him!'

McAvoy hits the man as he rises, throwing the punch with his
hip behind it, slipping as he connects, his coat whipping up wetly
in a spray of steam. He manages to keep his balance. Watches
the steam clear. The tattooed man is face down, blood pooling
at his head. McAvoy looks past him. Takes in the full vista of
the enormous man who huddles in the corner of the steam room;
a creature crafted out of discount tyres and wafer-thin ham.

'One shout from me and my lads will be in,' says the man,
licking glossy purple lips, the folds at his throat wobbling as
he pushes himself back against the wall. 'There's not just Dan.
You touch me, and I'll . . . I'll fucking . . .'

McAvoy turns away from him. Puts Dan in the recovery
position then hauls himself back upright. Takes off his coat
and rolls it up to place under the unconscious man's head.
Gives his attention back to the man who has brought him here.

Past him, to the closed glass door. Through the steam he
can make out what might be the edge of a pool; perhaps the
greenish blur of a potted plant.

'Where am I?' he asks, realising it's the thing that currently
matters most.

'Little place I've got the run of,' he says, his manner suddenly
talkative, garrulous; perhaps even an attempt at charm. 'Look,
all the theatrics, all that putting the wind up you – maybe it
was overkill, y'know, but look . . . do you really not know who
you're looking for? What was done to him?'

McAvoy glares into him. Tries to stuff down all the things
that he said about Roisin. Wonders whether it's possible to do
the right thing and still be a police officer.

'Let's find somewhere cooler,' he says, at last. 'And then you
can tell me whatever it is you think I already know.'

TWENTY-FOUR

Roisin leads them through the rain and back through the open front door. Pharaoh keeps her cigarette clamped between tight, bloodless lips; Helen shushing Penelope as she splashes in the puddles and giggles.

'Can't beat kids, can you?' mutters Pharaoh, growling. 'Read the room.'

Roisin pulls off her wet boots. Leaves footprints of her bare feet on the carpet as she crosses to the sofa and checks her phone.

'Nothing,' she says, mostly to herself. She stares at the room for a while, barely registering as Helen settles Penelope by the armchair and pulls out the box of Lilah's toys. Penelope gives a squeal. Pharaoh feels too tired to warn her of the dire consequences of putting her hands on Lilah's Rainbow Academy figures – she'll have to learn the hard way.

Pharaoh doesn't say anything for a while. Just stomps to the kitchen and starts making a pot of coffee. She knows where everything is. Knows how to put things away so as to cause Roisin maximum irritation. Pauses for a moment, her hands gripping the granite counter. She can feel the tears and the pain and the fear all building up behind the thinnest of membranes in her chest. Feels weakness in her knees; her own frailty searching for a way to be given voice. She can't let herself give in to it. Has to fix this. Fix everything. Make it right.

'Doesn't go there,' mutters Roisin, from the doorway. 'You know it doesn't go there.'

Pharaoh turns, ready to deliver a mouthful. Her anger deflates the moment she looks upon the bedraggled figure in the doorway. She looks smaller. Shrunken, somehow. Her hair hangs limply; her eyes seeming deeper set in her skull. She looks like a little girl in her mammy's pyjamas.

'You going to tell me what's happening, Roisin?' she asks, resisting the urge to give her a hug. 'Whatever it is, I'm sure he'll bumble his way through it.'

Roisin raises her head, a sudden flash of defiance in the set of her jaw. 'You've been keeping things from him, haven't you? I wouldn't be surprised if this is all some fecking scheme of yours – Christ knows you've got form for it. Like he hasn't bled enough for you. Like he isn't only still a fecking police officer because you'd be cross at him if he quit.'

Pharaoh's face twists, her cheeks flushing. 'We're talking about lying to Aector now, are we? What kind of fucking person gets their gangster daddy to solve their husband's investigations for him? As a present?'

'My daddy's not a gangster,' shouts Roisin, appalled. 'My daddy's a good man!'

'I've seen his record, love – the things he's been caught for and all the things he hasn't.' She stops, a little short of breath, wishing she hadn't thrown her cigarette into the sink. She looks past Roisin. Helen is standing behind her, looking uncomfortable and making half-hearted 'please shut up' gestures with her hands.

'I don't think this is helping anybody,' she says, as both women draw breath ready for another round. 'Trish, let's get a sense of what we're dealing with, yeah? You don't know Puttock – might be a good time to give you chapter and verse. I'm sure Roisin wouldn't mind telling us anything that might be helpful.'

Pharaoh turns away. Glares out through the window at the rain-logged little garden: a mobile home wedged incongruously across its width. Watches the rain cascade down its side.

'Go on then, smart-arse,' mutters Pharaoh, pouring the kettle into the cafetière, snatching her hand across her face lest a stray tear let her down. Her throat feels tight. She feels Roisin's accusations settle in the pit of her stomach. They sit there, sour, malevolent: a slow-working poison.

'Name came up in a briefing a couple of years back – not a name you forget quickly. Bit hard to tell the fact from the fiction – bit of a legend in his own ego but he's been around.

Real name is Kelvin Emerson but hasn't answered to that in a long time. He's connected, Trish. Knows the Irishman.'

Pharaoh hands Helen a coffee. Lets Roisin's stay in the pot.

'Just the headlines, Helen,' she says, teeth clenched. 'I've had just about enough of nicknames.'

Helen pulls out her phone. Moves her fingers quickly over the screen. Reads from a document that could be anything from a top-secret intelligence dossier to a Google search.

'Wrestler,' snaps Helen. 'Full-on Lycra and baby oil brigade. *World of Sport*. Played a dashing, razzle-dazzle tough guy. Never hit the heights but they loved him in the working men's clubs and the town halls. Fought for money before he found his niche. Took on the local hard case – anybody who could last two minutes in the ring with him would take home a cash prize, you know the kind of thing. Got his arse handed to him a couple of times and decided to move into promotions instead. His name's cropped up in connection with racketeering, illegal dog fights, illegal gambling. Had him in a few times but nothing's ever stuck. Couple of wits had given us snippets and he was on remand for nearly seven months when Worcester Police managed to charge him with criminal conspiracy, but star witness did a bunk. Hasn't been heard from since.'

'And this is who your daddy's upset?' asks Pharaoh. The enormity of it all is starting to flood her again. She thinks of Vicky. Of Tinman. Of the Romanian copper. It all feels so far away from the death of a trucker in a Hull cemetery.

'He and Daddy have done business together,' says Roisin, flicking her hair behind her ears and pouring herself a coffee. She pulls a crocheted blanket from the back of the armchair. Wraps it around herself. Warms her teary eyes on the steam from her drink. 'I asked him – said Aector was looking into the death of Davey Hawksmoor. He'd been a fighter. Not Daddy's scene – he's bare-knuckle, proper rules, bit of honour about the whole thing. Daddy said he knew a man who might have something useful. He called last night – said to let Aector know he'd come by. Next thing he's calling, saying one of his lads has fucked everything up, got himself caught breaking into Puttock's lock-up, told Puttock that he's Daddy's man – doing a favour for a copper. A copper! Said to warn Aector to watch his back until he got here . . .' she blinks back tears. 'Got here too late.'

'Any idea what your father was going to share with him?' asks Helen, putting a hand on her shoulder and giving a gentle squeeze. 'We've had intelligence in the past that suggests Puttock organised underground fights, proper scraps – blokes tearing the living hell out of one another. It stops when somebody can't go on.'

'Or somebody's dead,' says Pharaoh, glaring at Helen. 'You don't think this might be a little bit connected with the name I've been pouring in your ear since last night? Jesus, Helen.'

'What about Andy?' asks Helen, suddenly. 'Ro, you said his name. Where were they?'

Roisin holds up her phone, the screen blank except for the screensaver – a shot of her husband and kids standing proudly beside a snowman somewhere near the family croft beside Loch Ewe. Pharaoh looks away.

'Davey might have fought in one of his matches,' says Roisin. 'I know Daddy said he made his money in video nasties, but if I'm honest with you, I've never even really asked myself what they are.'

Pharaoh and Helen exchange a look. 'That was the phrase?'

Roisin nods. Sips her coffee. Stares into the mug as if divining fortunes in the froth.

'Try them again,' instructs Pharaoh. Helen rings Andy's mobile. Roisin tries her father. There's no answer from either. McAvoy's goes straight to voicemail.

'Of course, he could literally be stuck in a no-signal zone,' says Helen, tactfully. 'Weather like this, could be up to the dashboard in a puddle somewhere. All we know is that your dad's a bit worried about your husband, and it might be that we don't need to be worrying ourselves at all.'

Roisin gives Helen a grateful little smile. Wraps her fingers around the mug. 'She's a cracker, isn't she? Penelope. Aector will be glad to see her, when he's home.'

Pharaoh glares at the pair of them, contempt oozing like drool as they tell themselves pretty stories.

'Send me the file on this Puttock,' instructs Pharaoh. 'All you've got. Properties in his name, links to criminal associates, full work-up on his connections to the Hawksmoors. And to Papa Teague.'

'To Daddy? Trish, don't you fecking dare!'

Pharaoh realises she's barking out orders to somebody who no longer works for her. Hasn't in years. Didn't listen to her very much when she did.

'Trish, we need to do this properly. No more secrets. Call in the cavalry. There are two police officers missing.'

'Who might just be picnicking in a puddle,' snaps Pharaoh, lighting another cigarette. She offers one to Roisin. She takes it, shivering to the ends of her pink-and-white nails, studded with diamanté. Sucks in a lungful after lighting it from Pharaoh's own. There's a moment where they're almost nose to nose. Close enough to breathe one another in. Pharaoh catches the faintest trace of Aector's beard oil against the softness of Roisin's neck. Doesn't know whether to jerk away or press her face to it.

'You're ringing,' says Helen, and Pharaoh glares at her screen. Prays for it to be Aector. Hopes to Christ it's not Tinman. She isn't sure she's got the energy. She doesn't recognise the number but she knows the international code. Takes a punt.

'Gheorge,' she says, doing her best to sound unruffled. 'Not the best time, if I'm honest . . .'

The Romanian police officer interrupts her. He sounds urgent. Brisk.

'I've got a name for you,' he says. 'I don't know if I should give it to you – don't know if I want any part in this . . . if he's responsible for half the bodies that he's being linked to . . . if any of this is true . . .'

'Gheorge, mate, take a breath. What are you trying to tell me? We've got police officers missing, bit of an emergency . . .'

'Missing? Were they looking for Strigoi?'

'Jesus, Gheorge, if I hear the word Strigoi one more time, I swear . . .'

At the table, Roisin jerks her head up. 'Strigoi? You never said anything about that . . .' She starts to rise, the colour draining from her face. 'Does Daddy know? Did you— Is that what you were sending him up against? The fecking bogeyman?'

Pharaoh turns her back. Gives her attention to Gheorge.

'Give me everything,' she says.

Roisin sinks back to her chair. Helen stands behind her. Puts out a hand and Roisin shrugs it off. She glares at the table. Into her mug. Down at the floor. She holds her black Madonna pendant in her hand. Closes her eyes. Manifests her husband's nearness. Imagines him into her grasp.

Her words, a whispered prayer: '*Please keep him safe.*'

TWENTY-FIVE

A blue car, heading north, swinging right around the roundabout in a great wave of dirty water.

'Could surf on that,' mutters Teague, rolling a cigarette on his knee and using his elbow to nudge the car to the left. 'Mount Pleasant. What a name.'

'Sorry,' rasps Daniells, unsure what he's apologising for. He has a mad smile on his face, bloodshot eyes glazed with fear. 'I think it's from years ago . . .'

'Sex shop down there, isn't there?' he asks, nodding past the car showroom to the little sideroad at the edge of the industrial estate. 'You people. Shameless.'

In the passenger seat, Daniells finds himself staring at Teague's hands. There's a gold ring on every finger, his hands so multi-coloured with old tattoos that Daniells finds himself thinking of eggs boiled in leaves and onion skins; overlapping shapes leaving a découpage of lacework upon the skin. He shivers, resisting the urge to stroke his swollen throat.

'Where are we going?' croaks Daniells, his face a grimace that brings another pinkish tear to his eye.

'Ever the police officer, eh, boy,' says Teague, lighting his cigarette. 'Caravan park yonder. Know the boy who ran the security crew out of that one, so I did. By Christ but we had our pick! Grand lad, he was, God rest him.'

Daniells looks out through the dirty glass. There are few cars on the road. Hasn't seen many people. Isn't sure they'd be able to make it through the standing water outside the old cocoa factory if they weren't following the big pick-up truck. Teague's friends are in the vehicle in front – the man they hurt bound in the footwell, bleeding softly into the carpet. He gave up Puttock without much of a fight. Teague had spared Daniells the horror of it, walking him away while the thuds and kicks rang out. They'd found a garage off Mount Pleasant that suited their purposes. Daniells had tried to step into an area he figured might be covered by the city's half-decent CCTV. Hadn't gotten more than a few steps before Teague turned him around.

'What did he tell you?' asks Daniells. Then, weakly: 'He's my friend.'

Teague smiles, the cigarette pointing almost straight upwards. He gives him a little nod of respect. 'Wouldn't give it credence, would you? My daughter and a copper, still stone mad about each other they are. Drove me crazy with him, like he was a pop star or something. No Take That for my Roisin, no way – had to fall in love with the copper who helped her.' He stops talking, looking away, a tightness to his shoulders. 'Can't say he didn't earn our trust with that, boy. And he's never set a foot wrong – not with us, not with her. Harder for him than me, I reckon. I'm a Traveller whose daughter married some gorja detective. He's a copper who married a filthy fecking gypsy. And it's not like he's one of the boys, is it? Poor big bastard – to be that shy and take up that much room.'

'The people who took him – is it somebody trying to hurt him? He's put a lot of bad people away. There are so many people who would want him dead.'

'He has that, right enough,' mutters Teague. He shakes his head again. 'Must be a day for firsts, eh? Me, talking to a copper I don't know. Roisin's vouched for you. Told me a few tales, so she has.'

Daniells finds himself wondering just how much private information the sarge's wife has fed back to Daddy over the years. Feels a sudden stab of regret at thinking unkindly of a woman who's never shown him anything but kindness, and to whom his waistline owes its last two stone.

'Hawksmoor,' says Teague, blowing out smoke through his nostrils. 'Aector's trying to find out who did for Davey Hawksmoor, yeah?'

'And you know?'

Teague drums his fingers on the steering wheel, searching in the dash console for something that might serve as an ashtray. Daniells realises he doesn't know the car's interior. Hasn't driven it before.

'We've got nothing,' says Daniells, painfully. 'Dead ends all round. The original investigation – we hoped it was a case of leads not being followed up or not having the resources but it was thorough enough. They just had nothing to go on. Nobody came forward, nobody spoke.'

'And yet Trish asked the big man to take a look,' says Teague, a note of admiration in his voice. 'Funny that.'

He pulls the car into the centre of the road, spotting a lone pedestrian wading through the standing water. She's elderly, a vision in anorak, wellingtons and pull-along shopping trolley. 'I'd give her a lift but we're on a bit of a deadline, so we are. Least I can do is not soak the lassie.'

Daniells searches for something to say. Comes up empty.

'Let me do your thinking for you, Andy, how'd that be? So . . . you'll have it in mind that people were scared of the Hawksmoors, I'll bet. I know how you boys think. Put it down as some gangland thing, maybe. A reprisal for whatever dodgy shit the Hawksmoors get up to when the lights are out. Maybe something to do with what he's got involved in overseas? That close to it?'

'The gangland angle was a strong line of enquiry,' concedes Daniells. He sits forwards in his seat, opening the glove compartment. Spots a child's bobble hat and a rainbow water bottle. Can't resist. Glugs from the spout, the ice-cold liquid a balm on his wounded throat. Decides not to acknowledge the fact that it tastes of yesterday's Ribena.

'He's all right, Big Rab,' says Teague, taking one of the side roads towards the Bransholme estate. The buildings seem to thin out, the houses becoming more uniform – great soggy grassy areas setting the streets back from the hidden kerbs. 'Heart's in the right place. Just got himself in too deep; or at least, that's the story.'

'You know him?'

'Know his face. Know who he is.'

Daniells considers the options. 'From fighting,' he says, at last.

'Always been a lot of money to be made from seeing men fight, so. Where you find men, you'll find fighting. And where you find gypsy men, why, there you'll see warriors, boy.' He smiles at a memory. Rubs his hand across his jaw.

'I know a little about bare-knuckle,' says Daniells. 'What I've read. What Aector's told me in the past. Your son, Valentine. Had some bother . . .'

'Aye, boy'll be the death of me, so he will. Aector came through then, right enough. Christ how I hate the weight of it, these debts I can't pay back. Even this. Made it fecking worse, haven't I? Roisin'll skin me alive.'

'You were telling me about Davey. About Big Rab.'

Teague nods. 'Rab could fight. In the eighties, by God he was a mountain of a man. His da before him, so they say. And his da, well – he was Traveller, so I should imagine he was the one who put the fighting blood in him. Diddikoi, our Rab. Grandfather was a fierce tinker from St Mary's Chare.'

'I didn't know that. Don't know the name.'

'Came back into the fold when he was a teenager, so I'm told. Proved himself a hard bastard first time anybody asked him to prove his bollocks. Got to a bit of training, bit of sparring, put a beating on a lot of good men, if the stories Big Rab tells are the truth.'

'You sound very well informed . . .'

'I am well informed, Andy,' he says, taking his eyes off the road to glare bullet holes into Andy's damp chest. Looks away and smiles again, the moment over. 'Wanted to get it gift-wrapped for Aector, didn't I? Had to ask a few questions, refresh my memory. Anyway . . . feck it, I've lost me thread.'

'Rab could fight,' says Daniells, the taste of pennies in his mouth. 'You're saying Rab's got Aector? Big Rab Hawksmoor? He's too ill to even attend for interview. He's on oxygen. We haven't been able to get a word from him . . .'

'You don't listen, do you,' says Teague, frustration in his voice. 'I'm telling you Rab's all right. I'm saying he's got contacts and relationships with people I do a bit of business with. Might even have seen him at a party or two and by Christ I've seen him cheering his boys on from behind the haystacks while Davey were knocking the shite out of somebody who'd mouthed off that he could take either one of them down inside three rounds. Watched his boys take on a couple of lads I would have expected to wipe the floor with them. Only teenagers but both of them were terrors. Broken hands, teeth knocked out, fractured cheekbones – they wouldn't back down. I've a pal who watched the younger one take some Polish fecker's ear clean off his head.'

'In bare-knuckle?'

Teague winks. 'You're thinking of your Channel 5 documentaries, aren't ye, boy? By Big Fat Gypsy Bollocks, ain't ye? Big dresses and a room full of Shakiras. It's like judging the English on the basis of *Big Brother*, so it is. You see a glimpse of a few people who love being on the telly and you think you know a culture. Christ, boy – there are doors below doors below doors when it comes to fighting. Dungeons, should I say. You go deep enough into a sewer, you'll find somebody with blood all over his face and his hands behind his back fighting a sack of rats. And you'll find men putting money on who wins. There are fight clubs where there aren't any rules – where people straighten things out the way people have for centuries.'

'Mr Teague, I don't . . .'

'Real fight clubs, Andy. Fight clubs I don't let my kin go near. Fight clubs without any rules and nobody stops the fight. Two men walk in, one walks out. And the one who's standing there alive and bloody – he's just earned his sponsors pretty much whatever the feck they want. Two outfits arguing about territory? You don't want things to get out of hand? You pick somebody to represent. You lay down the terms. And you see if the other outfit has the balls to put their guy against yours.'

'That sounds . . . medieval,' says Daniells, swallowing painfully. 'I've been a copper seventeen years. If that were true we'd find bodies beaten to death most days of the week.'

'All taken care of in advance,' says Andy. 'Both fighters make sure there's a cover story if they don't come home. I've heard of lads whose wives still think they're off sunning themselves on a beach with some shapely Señorita when the truth is, they're long since ash on the wind. Tis an ugly world, Andy.'

Daniells sees the car ahead indicate to the left. They're

drifting past the bigger houses on the edges of Sutton. Wonders if they're going where he's beginning to think they are.

'Just tell me what any of this has to do with today,' says Daniells, his voice rushed. He feels like his brain is trying to eat itself.

'Rab's road to Damascus,' says Teague. 'Mercy dash to Romania after sobbing his heart out in front of the nine o'clock news – all those poor wee babbies in those hellish places. By Christ I'd have been there myself if the passport boys hadn't had a keen eye. Struck by a revelation, so he was. Go to Romania. Help them. Do what you can. And he did, the bold fecker. Him and his daddy were only a couple of lorries strong back then. Wouldn't know it now, would you? About to sell the whole fecking thing, though Rab'll be gone before he gets to enjoy it, so I'm told.'

Daniells starts gabbling, his hands clutching at an invisible ball. 'Mr Teague, who has McAvoy? Please, we can take a statement, you can give me all this background, but please just tell me who's got him.'

Teague waves a hand at him. Sets about rolling another cigarette as they roll to the kerb down the tenfoot near the Robin public house. Daniells knows where they are. Remembers parking in the self-same spot when Susie Hawksmoor had told them to stop digging through pains she couldn't bring herself to revisit. Remembers Rafe Cadogan, standing behind her, his hands gripping the back of the Queen Anne as if he were squeezing the life out of it, his eyes never leaving McAvoy's.

'There's a man I've done business with,' says Teague, thoughtfully. He's stepping beyond his own red lines – giving Daniells something that could have serious repercussions. 'A man who helped make the fights a bit more . . . lucrative. A promoter, you could call it. He and me . . . it's complicated, so I figured it wouldn't cause any upset if he never knew I gave my son-in-law a helping hand for Christmas. A lad I trust – he got wind that Puttock still had all the old footage from the fights.'

'They were recorded?'

'Long before camera phones this, sir. Lot of demand for

blood and guts out there. You think if they rebuilt the colos-
seums people would stay away? You could show two blokes
fighting to the death at seven p.m. on a Saturday night and I
swear you'd get twenty million viewers. Aye, people paid good
money for a copy. That's how Puttock started. Hawksmoor
lads were on the books. *Barbwyre Bouts* – that was what he
called it. Would have made a decent hashtag if we'd known
what any of that stuff was. Simple enough idea – two blokes
stripped to the waist, no ref, no fans, no noise. Two lads go
into a room and only one comes out. Filmed it on an old
camcorder and sold the tapes through his old contacts. I think
it made the Daily Shite when it emerged that people were
buying copies under the counter at newsagents, post offices
– even ice-cream men. Not that anything could be pinned on
Puttock. Made some serious money, from the bets as much as
anything else, same as when he was setting up the straighteners
for different firms and faces. Always negotiated a share of
whatever dispute was being settled.'

'And you wanted Aector to see a certain fight?'

'Bright spark, aren't you,' says Teague, finding the button
for the windows and easing them down. He lets the damp air
touch his face, eyes closed. 'Best laid plans aft gang agley, eh?'

'I'm lost, Mr Teague.'

Teague sighs, looking at Daniells with something akin to
pity. 'Look, it's simple enough . . . Puttock sent some men to
find out what Aector knows, because my man who got caught
– turncoat rat bastard that he is – told him what McAvoy was
looking into. So right now, Puttock might just be laying into
our big Scotsman trying to get him to spill his guts about
something he knows feck all about.'

'Oh,' says Daniells. It doesn't seem enough.

'Now,' says Teague, spinning one of his rings, 'the prick
who grabbed you – he's been quite forthcoming. Said he was
working with three people – came over from Doncaster in the
early hours. Working with somebody called Stewie, a lass he'd
never met before, and some Russian bastard who kept telling
him what to do. In the absence of anybody telling me where
I might find my son-in-law, I've got to go and ask Big Rab.'

'And why might Big Rab know?'

Teague grimaces, sick of not making himself understood. 'It was Rab who took Puttock's little scheme international, lad. How do you think they expanded the haulage business? Who do you think he's got himself in bed with? Saw an opportunity to help his children.'

'Davey and Wayne?'

Teague shakes his head at him. Makes to get out of the car. 'You'd best come along, I suppose. Better by my side than sat here like a wet sharpie. Dogs die in hot cars, right enough.'

Daniells feels as though there are scorpions in his head. Doesn't know whether to fight, run or just let himself be taken along for the ride.

'I'm a detective sergeant investigating the murder of their son,' says Daniells, desperately. 'You frogmarch me up to the door and I swear, things are going to deteriorate fast, and if I'm involved in Roisin's dad getting put away, I'm never going to be able to look the sarge in the face again!'

One foot in the car, one in the gurgling gutter, Teague laughs. 'We're all old pals, lad. They'll welcome us with open arms and they'll know better than to ask questions about why you're in our company. They'll have it sussed already. Wouldn't be surprised if they haven't made preparations for every eventuality. But it's that or Roisin, so I'd warn you to hurry your arse up.'

Daniells doesn't know what he's walking into. Doesn't know if he'll come out again or what bloody use he might be once he's inside the Hawksmoor compound, which starts a couple of hundred yards across the road and down a boggy track. It had been frosty the first morning he and the sarge had walked down its length. Thinks there might have been a robin and icy spider webs; a low winter sun rising above the smudgy line of paper-white fields. Fancies it's probably a river by now.

'I don't know what you want me to do,' says Daniells, hating the whine in his own voice.

Teague reaches into the back seat. Takes out a length of knobbly wood, a bulbous, polished knub at its tip. He tucks it inside his donkey jacket and gives Daniells a wink. 'Won't

come to it, lad, but if it does, I'll need a copper on my side
to tell them the truth. And everything I just told you – you
keep your mouth zipped, yes.'

'The fight you wanted to get for Aector – was it one of the
Hawksmoors? Who was he fighting? Is that why he was killed?'

Teague looks back one more time. 'Still don't want to say
it, do you? Still pretending you don't know who Rab's in debt
to?'

'Mr Teague, please . . .'

He rubs the shillelagh with his palm. Breathes out, slowly.
'That was the night he found out what had happened to one
of those blessed orphans he'd taken out of hell.'

'And that was?'

Teague shakes his head. A look of genuine pain seems to
grip his features. 'He'd picked up a demon,' says Teague, quietly.
'All those angels and he snatched the devil himself.'

TWENTY-SIX

Davenport Avenue, Hessle
3.10 p.m.

Pharaoh feels like she's driving a tractor. Can't get used to driving this high off the ground. Feels like a kid playing at grown-ups as she zips past the big Victorian houses; the neatly spaced trees. There's money here. She wonders if she suddenly fits in, here, behind the wheel of Helen's big 4x4: the voice of a Romanian detective bleeding out of the speakers above the hiss and glug of tyres upon the flooded road.

'Did what you suggested – thank you – but you must understand that the documentation from that time, it is unreliable. So many files were destroyed after Ceauşescu was killed. People were taking the chance for a fresh start, a new beginning. There were bonfires of documents. I've had to call in favours from people who haven't heard my voice in years, so if you need more than this it's going to take time . . .'

'Are you going to keep whittering on or get to the bloody point?' demands Pharaoh. She has a black cigarette sticking out of her mouth, unlit in deference to Penelope's lungs. She's starting to wonder whether it would be a step down the social ladder were she to chew it and spit her tobacco juice into a tippee-cup.

'You sound like my boss,' laughs Gheorge. 'My wife, too.'

'And you sound like every overstretched copper I've ever worked with,' says Pharaoh, a pain in her bicep as she turns right and down towards the little row of shops. She hasn't seen anybody else since she left Roisin's. The street lights throw out eerie halos of soft pixilated light; the rain illuminated in a succession of fuzzy orbs between the hitching posts of the tall trees. She thinks of a painting McAvoy had taken her to see

at the Ferens. Bites her cheek before the memory can churn
her guts.

'You are still afraid for your friend?' asks Gheorge, his voice
softening. 'None of my little birds have sung about an English
woman in the sewers, but they would only tell me if Tinman
had told them to. *Shit*, I swore I wouldn't let myself call him
that. It makes him seem something special, eh? He's a thug.
That is the word, yes? A drug dealer. A thief. Just because he
pays to patch you up after he's left you bleeding does not make
him a good person.'

'No such thing as a good person,' snaps Pharaoh. 'No such
thing as bad, neither. Now are you going to be useful or can
I get on with what I'm meant to be doing?'

Pharaoh realises she's holding the wheel too tight, her forearms aching with the strength of her grip. She tries to soften
her posture. Catches a glimpse of her own reflection in the
rearview mirror and snatches the cigarillo from her mouth.

'I've somewhere to be, Gheorge. Throw me a bone.'

She hears Gheorge give the laugh she is coming to rather
like, somewhere deep beneath the layers of stress and temper
that she is currently using as fuel. 'I have names for you,' he
says, sounding pleased with himself. 'Men with British pass-
ports who spent time in prison around the dates you gave me.
Your Robert Hawksmoor was no stranger to our cells. Eleven
separate spells in prison. Two convictions from a succession
of arrests and even then, the judges proved friendly. He's been
protected.'

'Protected by Tinman too,' mutters Pharaoh, squeezing the
big car down the narrow sideroad past the washed-out swing
park. She entertains the fantasy that Daniells and McAvoy will
already be here, that this is all a terrible misunderstanding that
she's going to roundly bollock them for. She's beginning to
suspect that things might have spiralled well out of her control.

'Constantin Barbu,' says Gheorge, correcting her. 'Record
going back to 1985, when he gave his age as eleven years old.
No address. Picked up for attacking a shopkeeper with a broken
bottle. From there, hard to say how much of what he tells
reporters is true and how much is pure fantasy. His life, it is . . .

brutal. Violence. Drugs. Profiteering. Protection. He could be a rich man pretending to be a sewer rat or he could be a complete nobody pretending to be a king. We know he used to fight with the Roma.'

'Roma? Sorry, you'll have to forgive my ignorance . . .'

'Gypsies,' says Gheorge, flatly. 'We have many gypsies in our country. Some people, they think gypsies are lazy, dishonest, that they take more than they give. They have suffered for this prejudice. People do not want the Roma near their homes – they push them to the margins – that is right, yes? – make them live as peasants. Any crime that the police cannot solve – find a Roma and people will sleep easy again.'

'And Constantin is Roma?'

'Why you think he wears the silver paint; the contact lenses; better to be known as a gangster in a kingdom of rats and shit than some thrown-away gypsy.'

Pharaoh spots a little parking space ahead. There's a long line of terraced houses, smaller than the ones back on the grander avenues but still solid and inviting; long front gardens and the occasional trampoline; net curtains and sympathetic double glazing. Takes a deep breath before she begins the lumbering process of reversing into the gap. Has to stifle a gasp as the car takes over, dashboard flashing, moving her into the space as if being controlled remotely. She sits with her hands up, afraid to touch anything. Wonders when she became obsolete.

'I'm going to have to skedaddle in a second, Gheorge . . .'

'Skedaddle?'

'Headlines, please, Gheorge.'

'He was arrested on a murder charge in 1997. A fight, held in Giurcani – so close to the border it's almost Moldova. Organised by one of the clan leaders. A dispute, settled the way such men have settled things for thousands of years. A man by the name of Daniel Anghelescu. A dangerous man. Vicious. He was a thug for one of our crime families. Built like a bear. Body found dumped on waste ground outside Iaşi. Constantin was arrested at the hospital being treated for injuries that would have killed some people. Broken knuckles, dislocated joints, cracked jawbone . . . told police nothing. Didn't speak. Took whatever was dished out in the interview room and never broke. Impressed a lot of people – not least when he walked out of prison with the Englishmen he'd kept safe from men who would have torn their throats out.'

'I'm starting to get the picture,' says Trish, glaring through the damp windscreen. She squints at the white car parked three vehicles away, up towards the top of the incline. It's blocking somebody's gate. Sits at the very top of the shingly parking area in a manner that blocks in three smaller vehicles. She feels a flash of familiarity, a sense that she knows this sumptuous, too-big Porsche Cayenne.

'What you are thinking – it is possible?' says Gheorge, seri-ously. 'Constantin is a dangerous man. We have no record of him leaving the country other than an application for an Irish work visa in 2009. If he came to England with Rab Hawksmoor . . . he must have made his own way.'

Pharaoh glances at her notepad on the passenger seat. Dee Cullen lives at number fourteen. Andy Daniells had accessed the Police National Computer on seven separate occasions in the last twenty-four hours. He'd searched twice for Dee Cullen. Pharaoh had spent a hellish half hour speaking to the civilian staff at Gordon Street, trying to build up a picture of what Andy had been looking into, in the hope that it might give a location where they were heading. Roisin's phone has gone cold. Helen is up to her neck in databases and intelligence reports, trying to turn a mess of suspicions and rumours into something approximating a working theory. Pharaoh can't sit and do nothing. Can't listen to Roisin chewing the diamanté off her nails and isn't sure it would look good in any future public inquiry if she gave in to Penelope's demands that she stop worrying, and give her a pony ride.

'Did he have his teeth?' asks Pharaoh, distractedly. Another call is beeping through. She feels her heart slam against her rib cage. Feels her temples buzz with static.

'Swallowed some,' says Gheorge. 'No sign of them being pulled out. I've sent out some quiet calls to other forces, any signs of similar injuries, similar victims. They're dribbling in,

Trish. That is right, yes? Dribbling? Stories of fights between clans. Of this man. Perhaps Tinman had an apprentice, yes? We hear stories. Places where vicious young boys are taken; taught to hate, to kill without mercy. Who can know if such stories have truth? I will keep you . . .'

'Strigoi,' says Pharaoh, under her breath. 'I keep hearing this name. Your king of the sewers – he wants me to know about this unstoppable killer . . . name I first heard a long time ago.'

'Strigoi . . . a vampire, yes? That is what we call them. A bedtime story for naughty children.'

Pharaoh frowns at the phone. 'Don't get coy, Gheorge. You're telling me you don't sit around drinking schnapps and sharing war stories and wondering whether there really is somebody out there killing men who think they're untouchable?'

This time, Gheorge doesn't laugh. When he speaks, there's some gravel to his tone. Pharaoh suddenly wonders who else might be listening. 'There are people you might want to speak to, Trish. Maybe . . . maybe you and I should talk properly. See whether we can trust one another, eh?'

Pharaoh chews her cheek. Decides to risk a name. 'You know somebody who might answer to the name of The Irishman?'

Gheorge breathes out, slowly. 'I think somebody else is buzzing through,' says Gheorge, the sound of paper burning as he sucks a half-inch off a cigarette. 'I hope you find your friend. I hope we get the chance to talk again.'

'And I hope you buy yourself something pretty with your pay-off,' growls Pharaoh, ending the call and taking the other as she steps from the car and into the whirling, patchy wind. She grimaces. Ducks into her coat and tries to light her cigar-illo, half-crushed in her palm. 'Go on, Helen.'

'Connections between Puttock and Hawksmoor going back years,' says Helen, without preamble. 'I'm getting a whole world of subreddit posts from real fight fans, naming Puttock – Kelvin Emerson – as a promoter, fixer; footage of somebody with his build being interviewed in silhouette for a documentary on the underground fight scene – he's a piece of work. Questioned by police in relation to the murder of Brody.'

'Of the Quinlans, you mean?' asks Pharaoh, with a grunt of congratulation as she sucks in a lungful of smoke. 'Dublin Quinlans?'

'Self-same. Brody was Eamon Quinlan's son. Mad bastard, if you'll forgive the precis from the psychiatric reports. When the turf wars were kicking off a few years back, Brody killed one of the rival faction's main enforcers, Mouse Tansley. Came to Manchester to lie low . . . found later to have been staying in a property registered to Puttock. Little place just off Saddleworth Moor. Kept a "no comment" defence. Brody's body is still being discovered. A new piece bobs up from time to time.'

'Chalked down to a gangland reprisal?' asks Pharaoh.

'Just another victim of the turf war,' agrees Helen. 'If Davey Hawksmoor made an enemy of either one of the warring factions we might get an answer, but we'll never get a name.'

'No, but we'll get Aector and Andy back. After that, nothing else matters.'

Helen doesn't speak for a while. Pharaoh can hear the tension as she breathes. 'Getting too big for you, is it?' she asks, hoping to poke her protégé into doing the wrong thing for the right reasons. 'There's a career case to be made here, Helen.'

'Don't tell me that matters to you,' she snaps. 'Don't tell me you haven't been playing us all for fools since the first moment Vicky told you about her contact in Bucharest.'

Pharaoh breathes out a slow lungful of grey. Hears the rattle that precedes a cough and bites it back. 'Make all this make sense for me, Helen. You're the one with the big budgets.'

She hears Helen take a slurp of something hot. Hears her wince. When she speaks again, she sounds like her usual self. She's made up her mind. 'I've got calls in to a few useful friends who can brief me on the likelihood of Tinman's story having any basis in fact. Should have a call back from the Home Office inside the hour with a list of all the British citizens held in Romanian jails between 1990 and 2010. It'll be a whopper but I've got a software package that can whittle it down. Then we really need to start making things official, Trish. We don't know whether Andy and Aector are missing or in danger or just getting coffee in a no-signal zone, and I'm starting to get twitchy about how any of this is going to look, and . . .'

'Thanks, Helen,' says Pharaoh, ending the call. She glares into the wind. Prepares to trudge up the little incline towards the house with the uPVC tulips in the front door. Stops herself when movement ahead snatches her attention. Over the top of a high, wind-tossed hedge, a large umbrella is gliding incongruously down what she presumes to be a garden path. The door to number fourteen is open. Dee has visitors.

Pharaoh hurries back towards the car, climbing inside and slipping down the leather seats, angling herself so she can see out through the big windscreen without being spotted from outside. She buzzes the windows down a couple of inches. Watches as the umbrella emerges from the little footpath at the end of the garden. Pharaoh gets a good look at two men, one holding the big black umbrella over the head of the other. The man who holds it is thickset, balding; a face like a hessian sack full of potatoes and blades. There's a thick silver necklace around his black roll-neck; the collar of his Harrington bomber jacket touching his cauliflowered ears. The man beside him wears a tailored grey suit over a blue silk shirt, his elegant black shoes seeming to glide as he steps nimbly between the puddles in the rutted road. He's handsome. Well groomed, the lines in his short hair precise; the edges of his goatee immaculate. He's got a half-smile on his face. Pharaoh watches them climb into the Cayenne. Watches as they talk for a moment, the big man at the wheel. Settles herself lower as the vehicle reverses back down the hill. She scribbles the reg on the pad on the passenger seat. Closes her eyes in concentration. She knows the man in the expensive suit. She gives a grunt of triumph as she places him; a photograph in McAvoy's briefing document. One of the executives at Hawksmoor Freight and Logistics. Cadogan, she remembers. Rafe Cadogan.

She glances back up at the house. Her pulse quickens. Rafe Cadogan paying a home visit to the same woman Andy was checking out? She tries to rearrange the map in her mind to make room for what she's learned. Feels a migraine coming on.

She climbs from the car and walks briskly up the slope, down the little footpath and opens the gate into the garden of number fourteen. She sees toys in the garden; a pink bicycle on its side; outdoor dumbbells half sunk in a sodden flower bed. Gives a copper's knock.

It takes a while for the shape to appear in the frosting of the glass door. Through the opaque glass, she looks oddly sinister: an inky outline that ripples as it moves. The door opens slowly. A face appears in the space. Black hair, pale skin, pinched features. She's skin and bone beneath the layers of dark materials that are draped about her; shawls and blankets, giving her the appearance of oil-slick birds.

'Dee Cullen? I'm Trish Pharaoh. A police officer. I need to talk to you about—'

The woman in the doorway staggers back as if shot, the folds of her gowns opening to reveal a knotted hand clutching a polished stick; a brace around her knee. She manages to find her balance, gasping for breath. Winces in pain. She tries to speak and her thin lips seem to burst, blood running from her mouth to smear her chin, to drip at her neck. She raises her hands. Spits. Starts to sob, snot popping in her nostrils as she stares at the bloody white objects upon her palm.

Pharaoh steps forwards, puts her arms around her trembling, stick-thin shoulders. Looks at what she holds.

Canines. Incisors. A molar, root like a mandrake.

Amid the blood, they form a crooked smile.

TWENTY-SEVEN

McAvoy almost falls as he stumbles from the baking heat of the sauna into the sudden cool. Wipes the sweat from his eyes with his sopping coat before turning back to the glass door and offering an arm for Puttock as he hobbles, painfully, through the opening. Mounds of flesh puddle at his ankles, knees, elbows, wrists, his head appearing to sink into his neck. He grunts as he moves.

McAvoy takes hold of him by his greasy forearm, pulling him into the cold air of the long, cool space. McAvoy glances around. He's standing a few feet from the lip of a swimming pool. Elegant pictures of botanical sketches look down from the greenish walls. Leather-leaved plants sit in pot-bellied containers along both walls. The windows are covered by shutters, the light emerging from tastefully hidden downlighters set into the wall. There's a little seating area a few steps away: a trio of sun loungers and a coffee table set with a jug of orange juice and a tray of pastries.

'This your place?' asks McAvoy, glancing over Puttock's shoulder at where his man still lays on the wet tiled floor. 'Where am I?'

Puttock wheezes as he moves in painfully slow increments towards the chairs. 'Friend of a friend,' he gasps. 'You're not far from home. You and . . . we can sort this, eh? Have you back in the bosom of your family before the day's out, yeah?' He looks at McAvoy with an air of resignation. He looks tired. Done in. Looks borderline comical as he drags his colossal frame to the plastic seats and drops down onto the chair. McAvoy takes off his coat. Snatches up a towel from the mound behind the door and throws it to Puttock, who covers himself with a nod of thanks.

'My phone,' says McAvoy. 'People will be worrying.'

Puttock looks pained. 'I think Stewie took umbrage. Wouldn't expect to be seeing that again.'

McAvoy glares at him. Takes a moment, his head swirling, new pains starting to make themselves known in his joints. He rubs at the little indentations where the taser prongs punctured his skin.

'I'm going to go and find a phone,' he says, at last. 'I'm going to ask you not to run.'

Puttock gives an unexpected burst of laughter, his colossal frame wobbling as the strange, girlish titter emerges from his puckered mouth. 'Run! Fuck's sake, lad, only way I could beat you in a race is if we were both on our sides and it was downhill.' He reaches forwards, hand trembling, and manages to pour himself a glass of orange juice. He gulps it greedily, the sticky fluid running down his chin, dripping onto his stomach and chest. McAvoy spots a water dispenser hidden behind a pot plant. Splashes cold water on his face and gulps down three cupfuls of icy relief.

'Could have gone better, this,' says Puttock, flopping back in the seat. 'Own fault, of course. Didn't put two and two together, did I? Not the first thing you think, is it – copper and a gypsy. Bet that's cost you dear, eh? When I see Teague, we may have to have a little chat. Could have just asked, couldn't he? Didn't need to go rummaging around in my precious things.'

McAvoy stands still, looking down the length of the pool room. Smells chlorine. Menthol. Sweat. There's a wooden door at the far end. He could walk out, find a phone, call for backup. Could secure convictions against Puttock and his right-hand man just for what they've done to him. But he can't help but let his thoughts turn to Davey Hawksmoor.

Wearily, McAvoy sits down on the neighbouring chair. His wet clothes stick to his skin. He feels shivery. Aches down to his marrow.

'Sensible, lad. Glad to see you're thinking with the right side of your brain. All that silliness – roughing you up and whatnot – you know it's just part of the dance, don't you? Just the way things have to be done. No hard feelings, eh?'

'Davey Hawksmoor,' says McAvoy, without emotion. 'Who killed him?'

Puttock looks surprised by the question. 'You're asking me? You're the copper, lad.'

'But you know.'

Puttock shrugs. Finishes his drink and flops back against the headrest. Gives his full attention to McAvoy, piggy eyes seeming to look right through him. 'Lot of people have claimed the credit for it, if that's the word. Lot of fighters have had a few too many drinks and let their mouths run away with them. Wayne was a decent scrapper. Hard. Had a nasty streak to him. Wouldn't quit. He'd suffer dislocations and breaks rather than tap. Would have taken somebody remarkable to put him down and keep him down. But then, the Hawksmoors have always been good at making powerful enemies out of powerful friends.'

McAvoy watches dirty water drip from the end of his tie as he sits forwards on the chair and gives Puttock his full attention. 'I don't know you. I don't know anything about you. I'm here because I got involved in something at the cemetery . . . whatever it is you're protecting, whatever you're afraid we all know about you . . . we don't. I can't make promises but if you help me, maybe we can reach an accommodation.'

'An accommodation,' says Puttock, quietly, licking his lips. 'Funny bugger, aren't you? Not like any police officer I've put a hurt on in the past.' He lets out a pained sigh. Nods towards the little coffee table. 'Top drawer,' he says, and McAvoy leans forwards, opening the drawer and looking inside. There's an old video cassette in a clear plastic container: an identification code written on the label in a neat hand.

'Teague's lad told our Stewie that he'd been sent for that,' explains Puttock. 'You can imagine, can't you? Kept that to myself for a long time. Felt a little aggrieved, if I'm honest. Gave my word nobody would see that. Would have kept it too.' He looks at McAvoy with something like an encouraging smile. 'We could talk, I'm sure. Reach an accommodation.'

'I'm all ears, Mr Puttock,' says McAvoy, softly. 'You can talk to me.'

Something changes in Puttock's expression as he considers
his options. 'Not as fit as I used to be, as you can see. Not
sure I need to be thinking about where I'm going to grow old
but I sure as shit don't want it to be in prison. Not that I'd
get a chance to serve my time. I share this with you, I'm as
good as dead.' He lowers his voice, suddenly conspiratorial.
'He's here, you know. Whispers are that he came in on a cargo
ship that docked at Immingham. You think Rab's got a smile
on that face of his? Oh lad, what I wouldn't give to have my
camcorder rolling when he gets his hands on him.'

'On Rab?' asks McAvoy, struggling to keep up.

'Rab? Lord, you really don't know anything do you? Christ,
Rab's all that's held his leash these years. Looks at Rab like
he's the Almighty. No, if he's here it's because somebody's done
wrong. Somebody needs putting right.'

McAvoy runs his hands through his sodden hair. A noise
from the sauna catches his attention. Puttock's man is dragging
himself, painfully, into the cooler air. McAvoy looks back to
Puttock. Spreads his hands. 'I'm going to find a phone,' he
says. 'And then your world is going to feel very different. You
look like you're afraid of somebody.' He looks at the tape.
'What's on this? What did he want me to see?'

Puttock gives a pissed-off look at his henchman as he tries
to pull himself to his feet.

'Big Rab's got a soft heart. Not much brains but a good
heart. You know the stories, read the papers – thinks of himself
as a proper modern-day outlaw. Dark Angel, isn't it? But he
were sincere about his causes. Done more good than bad in
his day. Just wasn't made for what he saw over there. Couldn't
walk away after what he'd seen.'

'And what had he seen?'

'Hell, lad. A place they called the Dying Room. You saw the
footage when the world found out about those places. The
suffering. All those poor little buggers with their dark eyes and
grasping hands, silent in the dark. Rab wanted to take aid to
the places it was needed most. Didn't do things the way the
charities usually do. Didn't go through the proper channels.
Very good at making friends is Rab. Heard about a place high

up in the mountains. Transylvania, if you'll credit it. Found his way to this foul-looking Soviet breeze-block palace. Told them he was there to help. To provide aid. Food, toys, clothes, care. Treated him like a messiah. Gave him the grand tour . . . and that's when he saw. This room where they put the kids who they'd decided weren't going to get better.'

'He abducted a child,' says McAvoy, narrowing his eyes as he tries to recall the dates and details from Hawksmoor's file.

'He *rescued* a child,' says Puttock, his face hardening. 'Two, if you believe the stories. Snatched up the first two babbies he could lay his hands on and walked out the door. Didn't have a plan, didn't have a destination – just had this little lad in a piss-soaked nappy hiding under his coat. Got back in his lorry and drove away.'

McAvoy waits for more. Glances back at the half-conscious man. Listens as the rain thunders against the glass. He wishes he had a pen and paper. His head is full of jagged words and angry consonants, names half-remembered from the briefing document and sodden case files.

'Dreghet orphanage,' he says. 'The worst of them all.'

'Wouldn't have got himself to that forsaken place if he hadn't had a couple of lads watching his back. And one of them, well, he tidied up after Rab, like. Made sure they got home. And Rab – he's been in his pocket ever since.'

'He brought the children back to England?' asks McAvoy.

'Brought one back. T'other didn't make it. They had to drug them, see. Poor little lass, her body weren't strong enough. Broke Rab's heart. He's been trying to make amends ever since.'

McAvoy wipes the sweat from his face. Feels a tongue of sickness licking at the inside of his throat. 'And the other?'

'Story goes, he brought him home. Not a hard job for a trucker if he's serious about what he's doing. Brought the little bugger back and told his missus what he'd done. Said he couldn't do anything else. Swore his boys to secrecy and said that he was their cousin – little lad with dark eyes and no words, and limbs that had been twisted up by illness, by neglect. Rab did what he could for him. Even got in a doctor to help with his disabilities.'

'He lived with the family?'

'Near enough. Rab had a place built for him. Safe. Secure. Comfortable. Kept him there and visited daily. Taught him English, read to him, played with him. You can understand why Davey and Wayne got jealous. They couldn't even admit he existed, even when their dad was making the papers for all these mercy dashes; for getting arrested in Romania. They . . . picked on him, I suppose. When he was gone. Davey would go and spend time with him and he'd always be bleeding by the time he left him. Nasty streak to him, like I said. And the lad . . . the things he'd seen, the world he'd lived in – he was damaged. Not well. He had nightmares. Couldn't control himself. Used to wake up screeching. One day Davey went too far. Pulled the kid's teeth. Vampire teeth. Said it was the only way to stop him becoming a monster.'

McAvoy looks down, feeling sick. 'And Rab permitted this?'

'No, he didn't,' says Puttock, flatly. 'He was disgusted. Appalled with what his son had done. God knows Rab had tried to get him to understand what he was doing. Even started taking the boys with him on his aid runs. They got a taste for it too, but if Rab was thinking that Davey would soften once he witnessed the work they were doing . . . no. No, Davey always had a head for business and opportunity. Even as a teenager he wasn't scared of anybody. Ended up getting in trouble with some Roma and the fight led to police being called. Rab's whole party were thrown in some awful Romanian prison. It was Davey who got them through it. Made friends with this absolute headcase, pit fighter covered in scars who got himself arrested just so he could keep the Englishmen safe from attack. Did his job, too. Walked out with them. Made his way to England, as arranged, as promised. Started to fight for Rab. For me. Vicious, he was. Utterly vicious.'

'The child,' says McAvoy. 'The child Rab stole, and hid away, and let his son abuse. What happened to him?'

'He got himself an ally in Davey's new friend. Got himself a teacher, too. Somebody who spoke the language and knew what he'd been through. Taught him to channel all that hate and make some money for Rab and his friends. Everything on the up and up. Hawksmoors started getting bigger, Davey started lining his pockets. Started having some decent fights, all arranged by yours truly. Started taking himself very seriously.'

'The child,' continues McAvoy.

'That child was a fucking monster,' says the fat man, his expression changing. 'What he'd seen, what had been done to him – what Davey did when his dad wasn't watching. Didn't take much effort for his new teacher to unleash his viciousness. It was Davey who saw what he could do. Him and his Romanian pal – they started teaching him to fight. He was an apt pupil.'

'The video shows one of his fights?'

'The video shows Davey Hawksmoor fighting an Irishman. Big lad. Right-hand man to Grant Molloy . . .'

'The Molloys who went to war with the Quinlans? Irish turf war?'

'Self-same. Few pals of mine wanted to intercede. It was getting too big. Too many bodies. Too many innocent bystanders. Everybody felt a one-on-one would stop the bloodshed. Davey was on the undercard.'

'An undercard?'

'You don't think like a showman, do you? Davey fought one of their soldiers. Hard fight, but he won it. Molloys didn't like that. Didn't agree. It all broke down. Rab didn't want to be there in the first place – him and the Quinlans had history of their own. It all fell apart.'

'And the child?'

'Child wasn't a child any more by that point. Child was a trained killer. That little dead-eyed boy who Rab used to read to – Davey and his mate turned him into something dangerous. Davey was convinced he could be unstoppable in the backyard fights – even tracked me down to show me what his lad could do. Brought a couple of my lads with me, met them as agreed. And they brought out this wiry, dead-eyed teenager in a hoodie, limping as he walked, holding hands with Davey like he was a mascot at the football. Felt farcical. Whole thing felt like a waste of my time. Then I saw him fight. Put two of my lads in the hospital without ever seeming to raise his pulse rate.

Just out and out viciousness. Didn't let go when you tapped. Didn't stop when you were beaten. He'd been trained the way people used to be – the fight's over when the other person's dead.'

McAvoy closes his eyes. 'You started arranging fights for him?'

'Tried to. Rab put a stop to it. Furious, he was. Sent his Romanian pal back to Bucharest. Davey was off the rails by then. Every trip to Romania to do good, he'd find a way to line his pocket. Wasn't long before he got felt up by some serious people. They saw the opportunities. Haulage firm with a legit reason to be in and out of Romania whenever they saw fit? Trafficker's dream.'

'And Rab knew about this?'

Puttock shrugs. 'Rab can convince himself of anything – even that the people he's in bed with are doing some good in the world. Even now, it's all about legacy for him. They treat him like a king in the parts of Romania where he's delivered aid. Got plans for a big school now, last I heard. That's what he's got lined up when the sale goes through. I reckon Rafe will let him have it. He's taken everything else.'

'I still don't—'

There's a sudden shout from the end of the pool room: agitated voices just beyond the glass. Puttock turns his head just as the lights go dark – the whole room pitched into an absolute blackness.

McAvoy starts to stand. Hears a woman's voice, shrieking. Hears a man sobbing in pain – his guttural whimpers suddenly cut off with a sound like a branch breaking clean in two.

Puttock starts to rise. Can't summon the strength.

There's a splash somewhere nearby – Puttock's man blundering wildly into the pool.

McAvoy moves silently. Takes the video from the drawer and tucks it into the waist of his trousers. Snatches up his coat. Moves past Puttock, noiseless as he darts along the wall towards the hazy outline of light that marks the door.

'Wasn't me who did Davey, lad. I'm just the promoter. Just catering to the market . . .'

He hears a door slide open. Hears the sounds of struggle. Of violence.

Hears a gunshot, a popped-cork noise followed by a sudden damp, gurgling exhalation.

McAvoy stares back into the darkness. Makes out a shape. Wiry. Black. Motionless.

He hears another shot. Something whistles past his head and embeds in the door frame.

Runs for the door.

TWENTY-EIGHT

'It's coming apart, love.'

'No, lass – just keep the faith.'

'Faith was beaten out of me long since, Rab.'

'Aye, well. I've still got enough fight for the pair of us.'

Rab makes sure not to glance into the mirror behind his wife. Doesn't want to see the truth of himself – to stare at the ruination inflicted by age and injury; of carrying secrets until they ruptured his blood vessels and turned to pus in his gut. He wonders when he last felt able to truly consider his own likeness. Since Davey, he supposes, sourly. Just like everything else. There was a before and an after: everything balanced on the pivot point of one senseless death.

'Immingham Docks,' says Susie, quietly. She's leaning against the open door to the red-roofed outbuilding, half in and half out of his sacred space. She doesn't want to step inside. Doesn't want to come into the dry in case she sees something that makes a lie of what she has told herself all these years.

'I know, love. You think I don't know? How do you think he got here, eh? Who do you think he's coming for?'

Rab turns away as he throws the words, unable to witness the effect they'll have on her. She doesn't deserve this. Not at her age. Not after what she's been through. Not because of him. He wants to cross the few paces between them. Wants to hold her and put his head against hers – promise her that he can make things right. But she's always seen right through him. He knows she'll make him falter. And he can't falter now. Can't.

He realises he's breathing heavily. Rubs a hand across his forehead and feels the grease on his palm. He looks back to the pictures on the wall. They shimmer like scales: a multitude of faces smiling down at him, gap-toothed, dirt-faced, snot-lipped. His children. His family. He's taken a polaroid of every child he's helped to a better life. The school in Transylvania will carry his name but it's this that he considers his legacy. The pictures are a stained-glass window in this cool, dark church. Sometimes he feels the need to kneel. To genuflect. Other times it is he who feels as God – he who sees a congregation of adoring, grateful faces. Since Davey's death he has focused on his failures. On the kids he couldn't help. The kids he left behind. The ones he steered onto the wrong path. He glances at the very first picture; the pale, gaunt face; the knotty limbs; the great lumpen birthmark across his cheek and neck. Hears himself recite the same old lies. Who else would have taken him, eh? Who'd adopt a kid like that through the proper channels? Who would leave anybody in a place like that?

He closes his eyes, weary of the weight of it. Sees himself again, blood on his boots, two wriggling, sopping children under his coat. Remembers the look on Paddy Quinlan's face as he clattered down the crumbling steps and threw himself into the van. He hadn't had time to plan. Just grabbed the little buggers out of sheer mercy. He shudders to think how messy it had been that first time. Feels a flush of pride as he thinks upon how good at it he got. How many kids were given new lives thanks in part to the mistakes he made the first time.

'He can't forgive you, Rab. If he's here, he's coming for you. For us.'

Rab turns from the wall of faces. Considers his wife. Feels a pang of disloyalty as he realises just how old she looks. There's the whiff of the grave about her now, clear as the scent of her perfume. All that money he's spent on products; lotions and potions and the latest anti-ageing serums – and this is what he gets? He bites down, angry at himself. He's always had a spiteful side to him but he's got better at keeping his nastier impulses to himself.

'Whatever anybody thinks, he's had a life because of me. He'd have died in that place.'

He hears his wife breathe out, a tired, rattly exhalation. 'Jesus, Rab, it's me. Nobody's listening. You know what you did. What I let happen. You know what he was . . .'

'Leave it!' barks Rab, lashing out at empty air and rounding on her, colour rising in his cheeks. 'Haven't we prospered? All that we have, all that we've done – it's all from that decision. That one day. And you can't tell me that the good hasn't outweighed the bad. All those children, thriving, living good lives . . .'

'Not knowing who they are, not knowing their life is a lie!'

'Don't turn it on me just because you couldn't be a mother to him. Any kindness from you and he'd have been a different boy. But you couldn't stand the sight of him any more than Davey could!'

Susie's face twists, anger contorting her features. 'You dare put that on me! You bring home a half-mangled baby, hardly breathing . . .'

'We had to drug him for the journey home!'

'And you tell me that we're going to look after him – that we'll just tell people he's a nephew or a friend or something . . . that you'll get him fixed up . . .'

'Good as my word, wasn't I? You know how many risks I took for him. He does too!'

'You threw him to the wolves, Rab! Once the shine had worn off, once you realised what you'd done . . . don't tell me you could bring yourself to look at him either. Christ, Quinlan got the good end of the bargain, didn't he? Talk about betting on black . . .'

Rab doesn't get the chance to respond. He hears a shout from the main house, just as his phone starts to vibrate in his pocket. His pulse begins to quicken. Wonders if this is it. Whether today is the day he'll find out if he's a liberator or a trafficker.

He hears footsteps splashing across the yard. Vic. Marin.

'Men on the lane,' shouts Marin, accent thick as the day they dragged him off the lorry. 'Four of them. Freddie has gone to stop them. Mr Hawksmoor, you come . . .'

Rab takes a moment to run through the possibilities. Feels the phone buzz against his thigh. It's Freddie. He answers the phone. 'You all right, lad? Who's come to say hello, then?'

'Freddie can't come to the phone right now,' says Papa Teague, jauntily, in his ear. 'He's got a boot on his throat.'

Big Rab doesn't recognise the voice, but he knows the accent well enough to deduce who's jumped his man. He tells himself this is all part of it – that he's a man with a masterplan and that he foresaw this eventuality. That he's a wartime general who sees the entirety of the war instead of the blood and screams of the battlefield.

'I won't say your name – never know who's listening.'

He hears Teague give a little laugh. 'We'll be having this conversation directly. Me and my boys could do with a wee chat. Friend of mine – got himself into a bit of barney with somebody who might have been acting on your say-so. Could do with you putting my mind at ease, as it were. Would hate to think a mutual friend is acting the maggot. Could upset a lot of people if so.'

Rab looks at his wife. At the two men in the doorway, the rain hanging behind them; pitted tarmac and standing water at their feet. *It looks like a picture*, he thinks. Looks like it's been framed perfectly.

'I took a call from that mutual friend not more'n an hour ago,' says Rab, wheezily. 'Way I heard it, you made this happen. You should have asked me for the footage. We could have made a night of it – watched it together . . .'

As Rab speaks he hears a shout from the yard. He moves quickly to the door and peers out, back towards the house. Four of them, dragging a fifth. He squints – unsure what to make of the rounder figure in the dirty blue suit and raincoat who limps after them, holding his side as if suffering from a stitch.

'Told you we'd be along,' says Teague, in his ear. 'By Christ this is a nice gaff you've got. Love the way you've got it laid out. Hard to get close to you. Hard for people to see how much you're worth . . .'

Rab steps into the rain, Wayne's two associates either side of him. He tries to walk like a young man, back straight, head high.

'Feels like a gunfight,' shouts Teague, from across the yard. 'I'll be Wyatt Earp, eh? Now, shall we get the kettle on? Thrash it out, eh? His wife's anxious to see him and I'm anxious to

feck off out of everybody's business. None of this matters a
jot to me, Rab. Just the copper.'

Rab grits his teeth. 'I never knew, Giuseppe. Not that he
was kin to you. Not until now. Could have saved himself a
hurting if he'd said you and he were connected.'

'Be a cold day in hell afore he even admitted he knew the
spelling of my name,' laughs Teague, pulling up the collar of
his coat. 'Keeps his own counsel, does Aector. Would trust him
to go to the grave afore he broke a vow. But you should have
done your homework, Rab. Looks to me like it's all coming
down around you.'

Rab sees Dan reach into his coat pocket. Watches as he pulls
out a lock knife. He glances at Rab, waiting permission.

'Could get dramatic all this, Giuseppe,' shouts Rab. 'Too
old for brawling in the muck and the rain. I'll get the kettle
on, like you say. See if we can't—'

Rab doesn't get the chance to finish his thought. He's interrupted by the sound of a muffled shot: a series of pops that
echo on the damp, grey air. He doesn't see the quiet man slot
the stone in the slingshot. Just watches Dan drop beside him,
a hole like a gunshot in the centre of his brow. Marin runs
towards the intruders. Papa Teague kicks dirty water towards
him, scoping up grit and dirt with his boot. Marin yells as his
face is filled with tiny projectiles. Doesn't even get his hands
up before Papa Teague steps forwards and headbutts him in
the side of the face. Marin slumps backwards, legs buckling.

The man in the blue suit starts forwards, grabbing Teague
by the arm. Starts to shout that he can't let him do this, has
to stop this, he's arresting him on suspicion of . . .

Rab stands still, the rain soaking through his clothes. Turns
towards the door to the place where so many memories are
buried. Realises he's still holding his phone in his hand. That
it's pinging against his palm. That somebody is trying to warn
him . . .

Another shot, closer now. He looks to Susie. Looks to the
floor of the old barn.

He hadn't wanted it to come to this. Not here, at the last.
Not when he's got the chance to . . .

'Rab!'

Susie's shout cuts into the buzz of static. He moves back towards her, following her gaze as she stares at the wall beneath his collage of rescued infants. Hears the *thud, thud, thud* of a great weight hurling itself against the wall.

Only has a moment to throw up his arms and wrap himself around Susie before the wall gives way in a great avalanche of bricks and dust and plaster.

There's a moment of silence. A moment when he works it out.

Looks down at the shape as it begins to rise, shedding dust, debris, stretching out, pulling himself to his feet . . .

A voice at his ear, thick with pride.

'Feck me, Aector . . .'

Then the brown eyes are staring into his, tears streaking the dust and grime and blood on his cheeks.

'Rab Hawksmoor,' wheezes McAvoy, rubbing his neck. 'You are under arrest.'

TWENTY-NINE

Helen stares through the kitchen window into the little backyard. She fancies the rain might be easing off. Wonders if she should send out a dove.

'Is Roisin still sad?' asks Penelope, at the kitchen table. She's using Lilah's colours and card, drawing swirls of red and orange, yellow and cerise. She never draws straight lines. Could lose herself in infinite loops and spirals.

Helen manages an encouraging smile for her daughter. Fills the kettle as she talks – her insides already glugging with tea but her hands desperate for activity.

'Ro is a very brave lady,' says Helen, squatting down by the table and ignoring the double clicks in her knees. 'We're just sorting out some grown-up problems. Everything is going to be fine.'

Penelope returns to her colouring, her left fist full of different coloured pens. She moves them in whorls and helixes across the page, making little humming sounds to herself as she does so. Helen feels the hot stab of guilt. Wonders how long her little girl will be immune to the consequences of her mother's work. Sees her, twenty years down the road, sitting in a psychiatrist's office and telling some judgemental cow what Mummy exposed her to. For an instant she allows herself to consider a worst-case scenario – the phone ringing, the doorbell buzzing, some red-eyed constable breaking the terrible news that Aector isn't coming home. She finds her eyes prickling with tears, a hotness at her throat. Flashes Penelope a smile as she returns to the workbench and starts making Roisin another coffee. She watches her through the window, walking back and forth from one side of the yard to the other, hair lank, soaked to the skin, cigarette held in a shaking hand as she talks urgently into the phone she presses to her head. She's talking to her mammy. Begging her to make things right. To bring him safely home.

'Sod this,' mutters Helen, feeling her temper begin to rise. She's beginning to feel surplus to requirements. Beginning to feel like a spare part. She couldn't go with Trish because Roisin was in no fit state to watch Penelope. She's a high flier in the National Crime Agency and so far all she has contributed is hot beverages and platitudes.

'Was that a swear?' asks Penelope, suspiciously.

'Yes, it bloody was,' says Helen, looking at her phone and cursing the absence of notifications. She's tired of waiting for people to return her calls. She's requested urgent call backs from two intelligence analysts and a team leader from Organised Crime. She's rung Pharaoh's tame copper in Bucharest, only to find herself repeatedly directed to voicemail.

'Do you mind?' asks Helen, picking up a piece of paper from the table and selecting a purple felt tip. 'Thanks.'

She leans over the counter, staring at the blank page. Closes her eyes and lets out a long, slow exhalation. Starts to sketch something out, the nib of the pen squeaking in the silence.

For a time there is just the sound of the dripping rain and the scratch of nib upon paper.

'OK, then,' she mutters, when she's done. She looks down at the scribbled timeline. It's barely legible but it serves as a framework, a Christmas tree she can decorate with her thoughts.

'That's good,' says Penelope, dragging her chair across and climbing onto it so she can see what Mummy has been doing.

'Thanks, sweetie,' smiles Helen.

'What is it?'

Helen stretches, cat-like, a sudden sense of tension in her joints. Behind her daughter she can see a canvas mounted on the white wall. Aector, embarrassed, barefoot in yoga pants and a singlet, arms around his smiling wife, both children giving crazy grins as the image captures them mid leap. They're arranged against a white background, Roisin all glitz and make-up; something unashamedly alluring about the way she gazes into the camera. She thinks upon Aector. Fights down the fear and sorrow that threatens to pull her down.

'Just getting some ideas in a row,' says Helen, giving Penelope a squeeze. 'You want to know?'

Penelope nods. Looks at the times, dates, names and places like a scholar poring over an ancient text.

'So . . . this man here,' she says, pointing to Rab's name. 'A long time ago, he went to a place where people were being mean to children. He saw how awful it was for them so he decided he would take toys and clothes and books and things for them so they had something to smile about.'

'Like Santa?' asks Penelope. 'He sounds nice.'

Helen gives her an encouraging nod. 'Now, some people wanted to stop him doing that. They thought he should mind his own business. But this man decided not to listen and he kept going to dangerous places, trying to help.'

'That's good,' says Penelope.

'These names here – they're his children. Davey and Wayne. When they were a bit older he took them with him. He used to take all sorts of people with him – not always very nice people but they wanted to do some good. And because he didn't do things the way they'd always been done, the police over there kept stopping him. Arresting him. Putting him in prison.'

'For helping children?' asks Penelope.

Helen sighs. 'Some people think he might have taken some children from the bad places.'

'That's good,' says Penelope.

Helen shakes her head. 'No, it's not. It's against the law. Those children had mummies and daddies . . .'

'Where were they?' asks Penelope, looking puzzled.

Helen feels the energy drain out of her. She can't think of a way to explain to her daughter that an evil dictator named Ceauşescu outlawed contraception and forced families to have more children than they could afford. Can't find the words to tell her that in communist Romania, the state told mothers that placing their surplus children in government-run institutions was the best thing they could do to help their country prosper. For a moment she sees again the TV reports she remembers from childhood. All those silent cradles; all those naked, malnourished children staring blank-eyed through the rusty bars of cages. She wonders if she could have left a child

there. Whether she mightn't have done what Rab did and tried
to at least save who he could.

'That's a funny name,' says Penelope, pointing at the under-
lined word next to Rab's.

'Eagle eyes,' says Helen, stroking her hair. 'It says Quinlan.
He's a very bad person, Pen. He's in prison so you don't have
to worry yourself, but for a long time he made so much money
from being bad that he was as powerful as . . . as . . .'

'A king?' suggests Penelope.

'Exactly. He was like a king. But a king who made his soldiers
do really, really nasty things to people he didn't like.'

'Like what, Mummy?'

Helen decides that she's probably on the verge of doing
irreparable harm to her daughter's psyche. Gives her a cuddle
and a kiss on the head and tells her to go and draw a really
funny-looking caterpillar in greens and blues. Penelope loses
interest in the Quinlans and skips back to the table, seemingly
unaffected by her brief descent into the world of human trafficking and organised crime.

'Quinlan,' she breathes, shaking her head. Even incarcerated
he's got more power and money than the governments and
legal systems which squabble over him like vultures pecking at
a carcass. He's serving his time in Ireland but prosecutors all
over the world want their piece of him. Last Helen heard, he
wasn't letting it get to him. Sees the whole thing as a temporary
setback that will all be fixed in the fullness of time. He's only
in prison until he decides to leave.

'You're ringing . . .'

Helen snatches at her phone, noting the international dial-
ling code. Takes a breath before pressing it to her ear.

'Helen Tremberg . . .'

'Ah yes, my name is Gheorge – you are Trish's friend, yes?
A police officer?'

Helen leans against the counter. 'I emailed you. Texted. Left
a message. Sorry – probably came across as a bit over the top.
Bit of an emergency here, Gheorge. Is now a good time to
talk?'

She hears Gheorge laugh, a pleasant enough sound followed

by the crackle and burn of a cigarette being smoked next to the receiver. 'Emergency? When is it not, eh? Trish is OK? She is an interesting woman. She gave me a telling off. I'm not sure I deserved it. She is OK, yes?'

'Can't really go into it Gheorge,' says Helen, switching to the efficient, slightly distracted tone of voice she always uses at work. 'Trying to juggle a fair few plates here so if there's something new, you can tell me, I'll feed back to Trish.'

'I was hoping to tell her myself,' says Gheorge, ruefully. 'I think she's going to be pleased. I don't know why, but I find myself needing her to tell me I've done a good job. Is that normal?'

Helen gives a bark of laughter. 'You and everybody else, Gheorge. She's just got that way about her. She said you were working back through prison records, calling in some favours – I'll make sure she knows you saved the day if it's useful.'

'Fine,' grumbles Gheorge, a little disappointed. 'You have a pen?'

Helen picks up the felt-tip. Flips the piece of paper. Starts to write as Gheorge tells her what he's discovered. Only stops when he says a name they both recognise.

'And you're sure?' asks Helen, pen poised over the page. 'Quinlan?'

'Arrested alongside Rab, Wayne and David Hawksmoor. Some bad sorts from the Emerald Isle that my friends in Organised Crime will be salivating over.'

Helen glances up. Roisin's off the phone, sitting on the front step of the caravan that blocks off the entire bottom half of the garden. She's chewing at her nails, another cigarette burning down to ash in her trembling hand. She allows herself to think of Roisin without Aector. Thinks of Fin. Lilah. Sees graves and flowers and an empty chair. Wonders if she could have stopped this.

'Terrific,' says Helen, trying to keep the tremble out of her voice. 'Can you just say those dates again?' She scribbles on the white page. 'And this is when Tinman was inside with them?'

'Looks like he got himself arrested just to be on the inside while they were there. Whether that was to do them harm or watch their back, it will be an interesting question to ask.'

'And you're going to ask him?'

Gheorge laughs. 'I've clambered around in those sewers enough for a lifetime. But I have some friends – little birds who chatter in my ear. Your friend Vicky – she is safe. Her fool of a lover too. Tinman only cares about notoriety. Reputation. Headlines. He's terrified of people forgetting who he is. She's going to tell his story. His and Strigoi's.'

'You really believe in Strigoi?'

'The man or the monster?' asks Gheorge, a smile in his voice.

'The man. This dangerous monster who's on his way to take revenge for whatever wrong was done to him? You think there's even the slightest chance he's real?'

'He's real,' says Gheorge, without pause. 'Those friends of mine I've been asking questions of – they've been trickling back in. Rumours and unsubstantiated claims, mostly, but there's enough similarity between the stories to convince me that there is a very dangerous person hurting bad men. Monsters, you might say. Taking their teeth when he's done.'

Helen looks at her daughter and decides that she can't have this conversation within earshot. Moves to the back door and steps into the damp air of the backyard. Roisin doesn't even look up.

'Teeth,' she asks.

'Tudor Lupatescu,' says Gheorge. 'Biggest, nastiest piece of work in the local fight club. Real bastard. Body found down the little tourist street just off the main square. Beaten to death – cause of death, repeated blunt-force trauma. Teeth pulled with pliers. He was connected to an organised crime family, so it's been put down as a gang killing. But the similarities, well – let's say this path from Romania to your beautiful part of the world, there are bodies dropped like litter. All men with criminal records – all following the appearance at the gym of a stranger with a birthmark. Big – face and neck.'

'And nobody's been looking for this man until now?'

'We're all looking for him now, Helen. But I don't think he's here anymore. I think he's your problem.'

'And he's coming for Rab Hawksmoor?'

'I don't know, Helen. Perhaps killing his son wasn't enough for him.'

'And why did he go for his son in the first place?' asks Helen, mind racing.

'I don't know,' says Gheorge. 'Was he a bad man? A bully? A monster? They seem to be his type.'

'A friend of mine might have got caught up in all this,' says Helen, quietly. 'A good man. His family wants him home. Trish has . . .' she stops herself, about to accuse her old boss of playing a game with potentially lethal consequences. She sees Roisin's head jerk up. Sees her drag herself up and splash through the standing water.

'Is it Aector? Have you heard? Is he . . . is he?'

'I'm sorry, Gheorge, can I get back to you when I've digested all of this? I need to get my thoughts in a row . . . tell Trish . . .'

'Of course,' says Gheorge. 'I'll keep digging. I think your Vicky will be calling home soon. Maybe Trish will be gentle with her – we wouldn't have all this if she hadn't started things.'

Helen ends the call before she says something indiscreet. Vicky started this, did she? Helen doubts even Trish can maintain that illusion all the way to court. Vicky was just another pawn. Trish had her sights on the big prize from the very beginning. Vicky just gave her a way in.

'Aector? Daddy?'

Helen shakes her head. 'No news, Ro. But you know Aector. You know your dad too. This is just a Monday for the pair of them.'

Roisin manages a smile, even as the tears spill down her cheeks. 'I didn't mean to get him into trouble. I just thought Daddy could help. He was over the moon, so he was. Said if he could help Aector and get a bit of payback for Sawney, that was a good day's work.'

'Sawney?' asks Helen, trying to keep up.

'Friend of Daddy's. Shot outside his house when the two families were fighting in Dublin. Daddy always had a soft spot for him. I don't know how helping Aector makes things better for Sawney – I just wanted to get him something nice.'

Helen puts her arm around her friend. Holds her close as she pulls out her phone and pulls up the NCA database.

Mutters, as she types: 'Next year, just get book tokens.'

THIRTY

Pharaoh sits on the varnished hardwood floor, her back to the front door, holding the sobbing, bloodied woman like a child. She can feel her whole body trembling; the vibrations strong enough to make her molars chatter against one another. She's having to fight the urge to mother her. Would like to wipe her brow, her nose, her eyes; to cup her face and hold her gaze and gently tell her that whatever the problem is, she'll make it go away. It's taking a colossal effort of will to simply let her cry herself out. She can't make sense of how they got here; what sequence of decisions and consequences led to this place, this now: numb-bummed on the dusty wood, embracing a stranger as she weeps.

Pharaoh surveys the room. Drinks in the details. Two big, bold Lempicka prints on the main wall; a Diego Rivera on the chimney breast. The sofa is mid-range; a russet tone, dotted here and there with spillages and smears. There's a bookshelf in the nook beside the chimney breast. She can make out a few leather-bound classics, some charity-shop pulp fiction. If she squints, she can make out some of the titles on the bottom shelf. Recognises the spine of one bulky tome she keeps a copy of in her own desk drawer: *Practical Homicide Investigation*. It's pressed up against a box file and a collection of lurid true-crime books. She recognises the words 'cartel'. Sees 'Quinlan'. Keeps her face impassive as she lets her gaze hoover up the rest of the small, cosy room. White walls, patterned curtains; a TV that looks like it may be about to fall off the glass stand. A bouquet of white roses sits abandoned in the dying light that bleeds in through the bay window. Pharaoh thinks of gravestones. Thinks of accident scenes.

'The man who hurt you,' says Pharaoh, quietly. 'I know his name. I think I know what he is. Walked past my car as he left. Smiling like he'd done a good day's work.'

She feels the woman stiffen. Feels her start to sit up. Pharaoh puts a little extra pressure into her embrace. Holds her fast.

'Those flowers are from him, I presume. Likes to give a little sugar with his salt, does he?'

'Please,' she hears, the words muffled by her hands. 'Please don't make it worse.'

'Worse, love? He just pulled your teeth out. Or made his mate do it. What was it, eh? An extra warning? Or are you so deep in his pocket he gets to do this when he likes? Men like him – you want him out there in the world? Free to do what he does? Talk to me, love. We can make things right. Put him and the people he works for inside . . .'

Jerkily, rising as if falling, the woman struggles from Pharaoh's grip. Turns to her, smearing a bloodied hand across her cheek, sniffing back tears, snot. Her words distorted, the sound whistling gloopily through the gaps in her teeth, the swollen chasms in her gums. 'I can't . . . can't talk to the police – it's been too long. I've been theirs ever since they found me. I've . . . I've . . . they own me! You have to leave. If they see you . . .'

Pharaoh sucks her teeth. Lets her scorn show.

'I'm a detective chief superintendent, love,' says Pharaoh, cocking her head, wiping the tears off her dress. 'Head of CID. Been about a bit. As coppers go, it's hard to get much higher without having to start wearing a uniform. I wouldn't talk to me either. But I'm also a lass called Trish. I've got four daughters. A dead husband who may have been my one true love and who may have been a violent crook. Now, I swear to you, you can tell Trish anything you want. You don't have to tell the police anything.'

The woman staggers a little as she hauls herself up. She's delicate to the point of brittle, her movements suggesting a skeleton crafted from fine china. She raises a tissue to her mouth. Dabs at the ugly gaps in her swollen gums. Her face crumples as a fresh wave of tears start to come.

'Let it come, love,' says Pharaoh, not taking her eyes off hers. 'This one's an implant, as it goes,' she adds, tapping one of her incisors. 'Original was punched out. Fair chance I swallowed it, which is one of those mistakes that can really come back and bite you in the arse.'

The woman's face contorts as something like a smile emerges from the bloodied lips. 'He did it on purpose,' she says, her voice barely audible, the effort of talking seeming to pain her afresh. 'Held me down. Used pliers. He was so angry.'

'Cadogan?' asks Pharaoh, warily.

The woman nods, lowering her eyes. 'I'm Dee,' she whispers. 'I . . . I made a . . . this isn't me. This isn't my world. I'm not . . . not meant for this . . .'

Pharaoh grimaces as she starts to pull herself up, smoothing down her damp clothes. She crosses to where the flowers lay. Picks them up and reads the card. Turns back to Dee.

'He brought you flowers and then went for you when they weren't enough, eh? His mate too?'

Dee leans on the back of the sofa. 'I shouldn't have . . . I made him cross. I saw the articles . . . all the stories in the paper about the buyout, what the company will be worth . . . I wondered if it would have a . . .' she peters out, looking ashamed of herself.

'Whether there might be a bonus payment,' says Pharaoh, tactfully.

'I think I said trickle-down effect,' says Dee, breathily, pressing the back of her hand to a ripening bruise upon her cheek. 'I do work for them. For him.'

'The Hawksmoors?'

'For Rafe,' she nods. 'Admin. Letters. Typing up reports, sending things to clients and translators and stuff . . .'

'You're employed by the company?'

She looks pained. Looks like everything she's built her world from is starting to crumble. 'No, it's more sort of a freelance arrangement.'

'A freelance arrangement that started after you saw something, is that correct, Dee?'

Dee half slides into the armchair. Swallows something foul-tasting. Sits forwards, hair hanging like pondweed.

'You saw something at the cemetery,' says Pharaoh. 'Ten years ago. Scared you so much you dropped your flowers . . .'

Dee makes little fists. Shudders as a tremble takes hold of her. 'I didn't see anything! Nothing that would matter to anybody. I said that then and I'll say it now. But Rafe said I should be compensated for the trauma – that he could set it up so I received a stipend; could put me down as a consultant on the books.'

'How much, Dee?'

She lowers her eyes. Rubs her thumb around her bloodied mouth. 'Works out around 20k a year . . .'

'And you thought maybe it might go up when the deal goes through?'

Dee nods. 'I didn't know he was coming. I haven't been well. Not for a long time. I just asked whether the company might be able to contribute – there are gadgets that can help; that take away the pain for a little while . . .'

'Neurological pain?' asks Pharaoh, running an appraising eye over her. 'Stabbing pains and sudden bouts of dizziness? Brain sending messages to your extremities telling them they're under attack with razor wire when in fact you're just lying in your bed happy as a pig in shit? Aye, I've got a friend, suffers the same. They say it's a trauma response.' She gives a little shrug, raising the roses to her nose and taking in a deep whiff of the heady scent. She rubs the petals between finger and thumb. Wonders how much Rafe Cadogan spent on his little gesture. Whether he handed them over before or after he took pliers to her teeth.

'He didn't want to hear it,' sniffs Dee. 'He turned up unexpectedly – him and Dragan both. Just knocked on the door and handed me these flowers and said they needed to talk to me and I was just gabbling and it came out and he . . . him and Dragan too – it was like they were waiting for something. On edge, like. Rafe doesn't get flustered. He always knows what he's doing. But it just came out of him – went for me in the middle of me gabbling on about nothing much at all . . . I don't know why he did it other than I was talking about money. But when he was up close to me, when his fingers were around my jaw, he wasn't talking to me then. His nose was touching mine. I could smell this nasty chemical smell from his mouth. I swear when he looked into my eyes it was like he was talking to somebody else. I was just somebody to take it out on. Dragan had to drag him off me. I've never seen him like that. Never thought he could do something like this.'

Pharaoh fumbles in her pockets and finds a halfway-clean hankie. Passes it to Dee who dabs it against her swollen lip; the bloodied tissue falling to the floor.

'What did you see, Dee? Why has Rafe been paying you off for the past ten years?'

Dee's face folds into a mask of pure anguish. She pulls at her hair. Picks at the skin around her nails.

'Davey Hawksmoor,' says Pharaoh. 'You were there when he died.'

'No,' says Dee, shaking her head. 'I didn't see that. Not then. I was tending my mam's grave. He ran past and I did a double-take because there was something inside his hoodie and it looked weird – that's why my mind took a picture of it.'

'His wife's dog,' says Pharaoh.

Dee nods. 'Saw him for a couple of seconds. Maybe ten minutes later I heard a shout – the kind of noise people make when they've been fouled in football. It was none of my business but it was just one of those odd things, so I took a few paces towards the columbarium. That must have been when I dropped the flowers.'

'You saw Davey's body?'

Dee shakes her head. 'No. I just saw a man. He wasn't big or broad or tall. Just average size. And he was walking away. Limping, actually. Quite a bad limp. I told this to Rafe the first day he called – him and Big Rab. They wanted to know what I'd seen. Showed me pictures. Kept asking me all these questions I couldn't answer. Then they offered me the job, like it was normal; like that's the kind of thing that happens every day . . .'

'Rab's son had died,' says Pharaoh. 'He was looking for blood. You gave him something he needed and got your reward for it. Are you still in touch?'

Dee shakes her head. 'Just Rafe. He calls sometimes. Texts in the middle of the night now and again. I don't know what he wants from me – whether he thinks I saw something and is waiting for me to crack. I didn't know what they were capable of, what they're into, who they're all hooked up with. The "job" I do for them – I see things. Some of the paperwork I have to take care of . . . they're not good people. Not the way I thought.'

Pharaoh chews on her lower lip. Turns to stare at the long, green lawn. 'Kids at school?' she asks.

'With their dad,' replies Dee, holding her stomach as if gripped by a hunger pain. 'I— I— am I in trouble? What I've done . . .' she raises her head suddenly, a flash of defiance adding colour to her pale, gaunt features. 'He pulled them out of the gums! It felt like my head was caving in. I felt like the whole of the inside of my face was about to fall in on itself. And he's just staring into my eyes, asking me how I like it, whether I remember, whether I think I'm somebody special . . . after that it was just him and Dragan shouting at each other in Romanian and . . . then you were here.'

Pharaoh feels her phone buzz in her pocket. Ignores it. Glances again at the bookshelf. 'You've done your research, then,' she says, one corner of her mouth twitching in the slightest hint of a smile.

'I don't want to be involved in anything,' sniffs Dee. 'I didn't want to see that man. I didn't ask them to come here. Didn't ask them for money. Didn't ask Rafe to treat me like a charity case. I mean, they saw me and knew what it would take. Knew my price the second they looked at me. And when I asked if it was going to go up – even after all the years I've proven I can keep quiet – he just became this monster. Became somebody else entirely.'

Pharaoh lets the words soak in. Tries not to look too closely at the thoughts and images that are spraying a great kaleido-scope of colour inside her mind. Doesn't want to attach the wrong neurons together. Doesn't want to spoil the picture by looking too closely. Lets her mind work it out in the background – her forebrain focused on the ringing phone, on the sniffing woman, on the box of crime books linking her paymasters to some of the most vicious bastards in organised criminal history.

'I'll take you to hospital,' says Pharaoh. 'Or I can get somebody else to, if you've seen enough of me. I'll make sure there
are people there to keep you safe.'

Dee gives a little burst of laughter; spit popping pinkly at
her lips. 'Safe? He pulled my teeth out in the living room! Took
pliers to me. All the fear went out of him the second he saw
the blood – the moment he realised how much power he had
over me. It was like . . . like there were two people behind the
same mask.'

'I need a statement,' says Pharaoh. 'All of it. From Davey to
the present day. I've got an officer you'll love. Giant of a bloke
but always looks like he's mourning the death of a puppy.
You'll love him. Silly sod's off the reservation at present, but I
think all roads are soon going to lead to the same
destination.'

Dee starts waving her hands, wringing at the hankie,
plucking at the material of her clothes. She keeps shaking her
head. 'I can't,' she says. 'I can't . . .'

Pharaoh crosses to her and puts an arm around her shoulders. Tilts her face and looks down into her dark, tear-glazed
eyes.

'The words Rafe and Dragan exchanged,' she says. 'I need
to know everything you remember. Every syllable. Every
sound . . .'

'He whispered a word as he hurt me,' whispers Dee, her lip
trembling as she allows the memory to take hold. She folds in
on herself, the tears flowing like blood. 'Whispered words I
didn't understand but . . . he called me Strigoi.'

THIRTY-ONE

McAvoy dreams.

Drifts.

Tumbles back into the moment when he believed, truly, that the darkness was going to claim him, swallow him whole . . .

He hurls himself forwards as the bullet buries itself in the door frame: wood and glass erupting in a torrent of tiny splinters. His greasy hand slips as he fumbles for the handle, the darkness behind him suddenly full of angry shouts; yells of violence; pain.

Voice nearby, singsong, playful. 'I can see you, copper. Can see what you're doing . . .'

McAvoy puts his shoulder to the door. Clatters into a cold, drafty space. A little light bleeds in from a grainy window halfway up the near wall. He can see tiled stairs leading up. A linoleum hallway stretches away into the distance; a blue light glaring in the half dark. He starts to take the stairs, hauling himself up four steps at a time, hand slipping on the banister.

'Not built for speed, are you, big man? Come on back – make your last few breaths mean something, eh?'

McAvoy glances back. A tall figure in a black jacket stands in the doorway, night-vision goggles giving him a bug-like appearance. He's holding a silver handgun at his side.

'Easier if you just accept this is happening. Alternative is a bullet in your arse. And if you make me run, I swear, I'll have my lads skin you and wear you like a fucking wetsuit . . .'

McAvoy reaches the top of the stairs. Throws himself forwards. Hears the discharge of the handgun, ungodly loud in the echoing space. Feels something tug at his coat – the recording tumbling out of his belt as he tumbles forwards. There's a sickening thud as he cracks his jaw on the tiled floor; a grotesque pain as he bites halfway through his tongue. He

falls onto his side, raising his hand as he snatches a glance
back down the stairs. Sees the man in the night-vision goggles
raise the weapon, left hand closing around the right, finger on
the trigger.

'Never even knew what you were involved in, did you, soft
lad? Think you could bring down the fucking Quinlans on
your own? Don't you go worrying about your lass now – we'll
take care of her . . .'

McAvoy rolls to his left, snatching up the cassette. He
flings it without aiming; a pitiful, final act of desperation.
Watches it smash into the wall by his killer's head. Sees the
smile. Knows it. Knows who's about to kill him.

There's a sound from inside the pool room. Smashing glass.
A scream that fills McAvoy's mind with images of hell.

Rafe Cadogan turns back. Snatches off the night-vision
goggles just as the darkness about him becomes flesh.

McAvoy hauls himself to his feet. Lurches down the half-
dark corridor, braced for the shot that will put a hole in him
front to back. Looks back. Sees Cadogan on his back, an arm
around his throat, another twisted around his arm. Hears the
crack of bones, the tearing of tendons; the screech as limbs
detach from their moorings.

McAvoy puts his shoulder to the door at the end of the hall.
Tumbles into a room that seems utterly at odds with the
violence from which he flees. It's round: not a single straight
line within its cosy confines. There's a burgundy chesterfield
sofa in the centre of the floor: a zebra-striped rug covering
grey concrete. A laptop computer sits atop a glass coffee table:
a globe half open to reveal bottles of expensive spirits. There's
a projector positioned beside the sofa, casting images onto a
pull-down screen that hangs from a hook in the ceiling.

McAvoy stops. Sees.

On the screen, a woman with chocolate-coloured eyes: black
hair falling elegantly to her shoulders; a crucifix disappearing
into her silky white blouse. She's sitting at a table. Beside her,
a child. They're studying the pages of a colourful book, heads
almost touching. Behind them, a row of neat bookshelves, an
oil painting of some sunlight-gilded saint.

McAvoy turns as the figure emerges from behind the metal storage cabinet to his right. Recognises Wayne Hawksmoor. Has just a moment to lift his arms – to see the big man's face twist in fury – and then he's on his back, blood running down his chin; his attacker raining down blows, trying to lock his arms against his legs; the weight of him on his chest, his throat.

McAvoy feels an arm clamp about his throat. Feels the hiss of blood in his ears, his nose, his eyes. Throws up his elbows to try and create a moment's separation, gasping down a desperate lungful of precious air. Pushes up with what's left of his strength, the man on his back clinging to his throat, spittle and blood flecking his face. McAvoy reaches back, taking a handful of skin, of hair; his thumb slipping into a nostril, fingers squelching grotesquely into the warm wetness of his attacker's eye.

Throws himself backwards into the glass coffee table. A burst of sticky wetness at his neck, the gurgled cry as a shard of gleaming glass cuts deep into his attacker's belly, his backside, his thighs.

McAvoy rolls to his side, hands bloodied, gasping for air. Looks down at the bleeding figure who wriggles in the maelstrom of glass.

On the screen, woman and child continue undisturbed. They smile as they play. He wonders whether they are victims. Whether they have been rescued by the Hawksmoors, or trafficked. Whether this is the life they want, or one that has been forced upon them.

McAvoy pulls himself upright, not sure which is his blood, which is Wayne's.

The rug slips to the right as his boots scrabble for purchase. There's a hinge set into the floor, two metal loops set a few feet apart. He hears feet on the stairs. Hears shouts. A sudden explosion from somewhere below.

He tugs at the loops. Feels the floor begin to give.

Looks up to see a man with a great blistered birthmark covering one side of his face: padlocks and chains at his neck, his ankles, his throat. Sees him smile: two perfect golden canines winking in the light.

The strange man looks at the woman on the screen. Seems to falter for a moment.

McAvoy hauls up the hatch.

There's a ladder below. He throws himself forwards, clattering down the metal rungs. He lands on bare boards. Cracked stone. Puts his shoulder to the plasterboard. Puts his fist to it, the pain surging up his arm and rattling his teeth. He hisses in pain. Throws another punch, the ground giving way as he hurls himself forwards. Raises his arms as the floor rushes towards him.

And then he is smashing on down through plaster and brick, timber and dust, through feathers and dirt and rain . . .

Rab Hawksmoor, looking down at him. Papa Teague, cradling his head. Andy Daniells tussling with a muddied, bloodied figure he can't place.

The words, from nowhere. 'Rab Hawksmoor, you are under arrest . . .'

And then nothing but the kiss of the dark.

THIRTY-TWO

Three days later
Clough Road Police Station, Hull
10.02 a.m.

P haraoh sips her black coffee. It's already cold. Tastes of the cigarette she stubbed out in it twenty minutes ago. Grimaces as she swallows, throat tight, jaw aching. She's been grinding her teeth in her sleep again. Holding herself steady in meetings, debriefings, inter-agency Zoom calls. It's taken its toll.

'I can make you a fresh one . . .'

Pharaoh shakes her head. 'Don't worry. I haven't tasted anything less spicy than a king prawn bhuna since I hit forty. Honest, Frank – I've been known to eat the coasters at dinner parties. Shouldn't make them look so much like crackers, should they?'

Behind his desk, Assistant Chief Constable Frank Koza gives a tight smile. He hasn't worked with Trish for very long. Heard the stories before he arrived at Humberside Police and seems rather pleased to find that they only hinted at the reality of the woman who sits across his polished walnut desk. He hasn't felt intimidated by anybody in a long while. She has the ability to make him feel like a teenage boy caught rummaging in the knicker drawer of his best mate's mum.

'It's a success, Frank,' she says, tiredly. She's slouching in the swivel chair, sunglasses on her head, leather jacket draped across her middle. 'He's not broken yet, but he's bending. There's a quality to the "no comment" that speaks volumes.'

Koza still looks troubled. He's a decent officer, not far off his thirty years. Transferred over from Lancashire a couple of years back, enticed by the promise that it's never dull in Hull. He's already regretting the decision. Hadn't considered that the language barrier would be a problem. Wonders whether he can buy something online that might help him flatten his vowels. He has the look of a farmer: red cheeks, greying black hair swept back from a broad, wind-chapped face. He always looks uncomfortable to Pharaoh – always seems like he wants to step out of his uniform and go climb into some greasy overalls; climb into the guts of a tractor and start tinkering.

'That's the goal, is it?' asks Koza, carefully. 'A confession?'

Pharaoh shrugs. Wrinkles her nose. She's been spinning her senior officers like plates on a pole ever since she first moved to CID. She always gets what she wants. This time, she isn't quite sure what that is.

'What we want is for him to see that we're his only option,' says Pharaoh, cautiously. 'He's old. He doesn't want to spend his dotage on remand – not with prosecutors in Romania already starting extradition proceedings. His whole life has been about redressing the balance, settling the scales, as it were. We give him the chance to do that. Put a bad, bad man away forever and there's hope for your soul.'

'We're discussing souls now?' asks Koza, looking sceptical. 'I don't deal in imponderables, Trish.'

'You're in the wrong job, then,' snaps Pharaoh. She looks away before she can glare a hole in him. Looks out from the second-floor window into the pale, washed-out sunlight. It hasn't rained since Monday. Hull looks wrung out; scrubbed to the bone.

'And Wayne?' asks Koza, not taking the bait.

'We'll have questions when he wakes up. Depends what his dad gives us when he breaks.'

'The mum's still saying nothing?'

'She's been keeping their secrets for nigh-on fifty years, Frank. Doesn't do her any good to break the habits of a lifetime.'

'So it's the daughter-in-law we have to thank, is it?' asks Koza, pulling the file closer towards himself and leafing through the bundle of statements. 'Your Aector – seems as good with the little old ladies as he is with the psychopath killing machines.'

Pharaoh gives a grunt of laughter. Treats Frank to a smile.

'Came forward as soon as she heard about what happened at the compound. Gave us everything she knew. Loved Davey but he wasn't as good as his dad at keeping family secrets. Told her shortly after they met – the mercy missions, the chases across the Carpathians, the kids Daddy brought home. I don't know if Davey was a bad lad all the way through but he was a jealous sod. Always vying for Daddy's attention. And Daddy, well – he just wanted to do the right thing, whatever that might have been. Got into bed with the wrong people. Ended up making a monster.'

Koza nods. Turns the pages. Looks at her over the top of the folder.

'NCA are jolly pleased,' he says, without emotion. 'Quinlans are about as big as it gets. They've been bulletproof for years. If they can nail any of the top tier they'll take the opportunity, even if it's for something they did thirty years ago a long way from home.'

Pharaoh feels the urge to pull herself from the chair and to cross to the window – to stare down into the car park. McAvoy's down there somewhere, hobbled and bloodied and looking like a bull that's survived the abattoir. She's promised him a talk. He has things he wants to get off his chest. Things he needs to say. She'll let him say at least some of them, if only so he can report back to Roisin that he's stuck up for himself. She wonders whether he's memorised every single word of Roisin's vitriol-laden speech, or if he'll permit himself room to improvise.

'There are some gaps in this report that one could drive a harvester through,' says Koza, looking pained. 'Your friend Vicky. This statement from her contacts in Bucharest – if she backs away from testifying, she could make a case for entrapment. Reading between the lines, it could be said that you manipulated her into placing herself in grave danger.'

Pharaoh doesn't reply. Lets the tension build for a while.

'Trish?'

'Don't read between the lines, then, Frank. Just read what's in front of you.'

Koza looks down before the smile can show on his face.

'Not exactly textbook, is it? Procedurally speaking?'

'When the criminals start following a playbook, I'll start doing the same,' snaps Pharaoh, putting her hands on the arms of the chair. She's had enough of this. She's picking Vicky up from Humberside Airport early this afternoon. She's got hours of footage for her to watch; endless interviews with Tinman and the children in his kingdom beneath the streets. He's promised to give Gheorge a full written statement confirming that the child he knew as Dorin Hawksmoor was stolen from a Romanian orphanage in April 1991. That he was trafficked to England and raised as Rab's own. That Dorin was too dangerous, too scarred, to be able to live anything approximating a normal life. That Rab confined him to a grain silo packed with toys and treats and television; tried to make his existence better than the one from which he had been snatched. He hadn't reckoned with his son's dark side. Hadn't reckoned on Davey sneaking in to torment and tease the twisted, dark-eyed child with the knotted limbs and the crimson birthmark. Hadn't imagined that Davey would drag his brother in to his nightly visits to the silo; the two of them filling his nights with pain, suffering; seeing how far they could push him before he let out the demon that lived inside him; the monster that had attacked their mother when she tried to bathe him; that killed the little girl that Rab also had grabbed that day in '91.

'And Cadogan,' says Koza, looking up. 'His father is Quinlan's armourer?'

'And more besides,' says Pharaoh. 'He took care of everything in Dreghet. When Rab told him what had happened – the staff member ending up dead, the two kids in his care – Cadogan went to work. Made everything better. Rab knows where her body is. All he has to do now is tell us. And he will. He'll tell us everything. What choice is there? We can put Quinlan away. Cadogan senior . . .'

'And Rafe?'

Pharaoh gives a huff of laughter. Sees again the devastation in the private leisure spa that Davey and his dad had built years before. Sees Rafe Cadogan's body, teeth pulled, eyes striped with blood, windpipe crushed flat. Two of his men dead in the pool. Puttock spitting blood, dragging himself towards the door, glass digging holes in his stomach. Puttock's given Pharaoh everything he knows. Is willing to make up a whole load more if it gets him the protective custody that might just buy him a few extra days.

'And there's no sign of the perpetrator? This Strigoi?'

'No sign he exists at all, sir – other than the bodies. A lot of bodies. Davey woke up the monster within him right enough. But it was Rab and his Irish friends that did the damage to him. Made him fight. Made him kill. Sold him to Quinlan, who put him to work. All those fights, all those men he put down and kept down. Quinlan probably put him up against Davey for his own amusement. I've seen the fight, sir. Even when he had him down, Strigoi couldn't kill him. Kept looking at Rab like he was his father. Like he was a Roman emperor preparing to give the thumbs up or the thumbs down. Rab couldn't do it. And Davey, well . . . he knew how to fight too. When Rab stepped in . . . Jesus, to have been a fly on the wall. Rab told Quinlan his man was dead. Made sure to tell everybody else the same. Dumped Strigoi back where he found him. Kicked him out the back of a wagon on a dirt road in Transylvania. He went looking for the one man who'd been kind to him. Tinman.'

'And this vendetta against the Hawksmoors? Why now?'

Pharaoh grinds her teeth. 'It was never a vendetta against the Hawksmoors, Frank. It was an act of service to Rab.'

'I don't follow, Trish . . .'

Pharaoh closes her eyes. Counts backwards from five. Makes it to four.

'When Rab found out from Tinman that the lad had found him, that he was still alive . . . from that point on, Rab's life became about trying to stay useful to the Irishman. And having an unstoppable killer at your beck and call makes for good currency. So does having a route across Eastern Europe. A charity. A haulage company. Do you know how many guns, drugs and people he's helped the Quinlans bring out of Eastern Europe? Every aid convoy, every visit to some poor orphanage, he brought back what Quinlan and Cadogan needed. This deal with Omnia, it opens up a whole new world of opportunity for them; puts their outfit into the top tier of cartels.'

'You didn't answer the question, Trish . . .'

'Davey was Strigoi's reward. Everybody he killed, he was thinking of the boy who beat him, hurt him, pulled his teeth out; made him fear the dark. Strigoi may have killed a lot of people but it was only ever about Davey. Whether or not Rab gave the OK, I doubt we'll ever know. But Strigoi got his revenge. He'll come back for the other brother, I'm sure.'

'I'm sorry . . .'

'Wayne did some terrible things to him when he was small. Lived his life in fear ever since Davey died. He needed somebody stronger than him, somebody who would protect him. Buddied up to Cadogan, even while he was telling his dad that he couldn't abide him, that he wanted to get them out of the deal they'd been forced into keeping ever since Dreghet. Once Strigoi learned that Wayne was going behind his dad's back . . . it was always going to end as it did.'

'Your contact with Bucharest Police . . . they're looking for him?'

'Aye,' says Pharaoh, drily. 'I'm sure it'll be a piece of cake.'

Koza sucks his teeth. Drums his fingers on the desk. 'So we know who did it, but we haven't got him in custody. We know that the Hawksmoors were trafficking drugs, guns and people, but that they were only doing it because the Quinlan outfit had the goods on them about what happened in Dreghet. We know that Tinman kept them safe in prison and he was rewarded with a spot at the table – a place to call home and a job keeping the kid he nabbed from killing anybody they didn't want him to. We know there was a falling out and Tinman got sent home and that the poor little sod he taught to fight grew up to become a monster.' He pauses, breathing hard, trying to keep a sense of it all. 'We know that Puttock used to run fights-to-the-death for the benefit of paying punters. We also know that Quinlan is going to be out of prison very soon unless we find enough to keep him where he is. And there's a good chance he's going to feel very, very poorly towards the people who've blown the Omnia deal and failed to stop the murder of the heir to his throne.'

Pharaoh nods. 'The Teagues have gone to ground, sir. Don't worry on that score.'

'I'm more worried about your McAvoy,' says Koza, quietly. 'Quinlan doesn't forgive. Doesn't forget. Your name isn't the one that's going to be associated with any of this. It's Aector and Andy that were in the firing line.'

Pharaoh glares at him. Raises her eyebrows and her sunglasses drop onto the bridge of her nose. 'That be all, sir?'

'Actually, I . . .'

'That's what I thought,' says Pharaoh, pulling herself out of the chair and heading for the door. She leaves her coffee cup on the desk. Wonders if it would be career suicide to go back and piss in it.

She hears him call her name as she slams the door. Doesn't look back. She already knows what's coming. Knows that McAvoy is a dead man unless she can do the one thing she always thought she was incapable of.

He's there when she steps out through the double doors and into the pale light of the morning. Big and broken, awkward and shy. For a moment, she wants to tell him everything. What she knew, when she knew it. Knows that she won't. She'll go to her grave with her secrets. Just has to hope that it's later rather than sooner.

'All OK?' he asks, concern in his eyes. 'Not in any bother?'

Pharaoh shakes her head. Shrugs. Resists the urge to hug him.

'There was something you wanted to say to me,' she says, climbing into the driver's seat and watching him wince his way into the little convertible at her side.

'It can wait,' he says.

'You're sure?'

McAvoy nods. Settles back in his chair as Pharaoh guns the engine and reverses out of the parking space; the last of the puddles turning to dirty spray around the tyres.

'You think he's gone?' asks McAvoy, quietly. 'You think he's on our side, or theirs?'

Pharaoh reaches across. Can't help but put her hand on his cheek; his beard thick against her clammy palm.

'Sometimes, Aector, I really don't know what to do with you.'

McAvoy opens his eyes. Stares into the mirrored lenses of Trish's sunglasses and sees himself. Sees the ruination that being a police officer has wrought.

'I don't think I want to do this anymore, Trish,' he says, softly. 'I don't think I can . . .'

She doesn't have to reply. Her pocket starts to buzz. She snatches at the phone and sees the number. Feels a curious mixture of exhilaration and dread.

'Mr Quinlan,' she says, reaching into the glove compartment and finding cigarettes and lighter. 'To what do I owe the pleasure?'

Beside her, she senses McAvoy twitch. She blows him a kiss. Don't worry, it says – this was always part of the plan.

She doesn't smile as she hears the sounds of suffering, as the man in the prison cell screams in agony, sobbing, desperate, throat full of blood.

Pharaoh listens. Glances at McAvoy and suffers a moment's disquiet. Wonders if, this time, she's pushed him too far. Whether she's crossed one of those godawful 'boundary' things she keeps reading about.

Turns away. She can put him back together later.

Listens, as Strigoi fulfils his duties to Big Rab, holding the phone to the dying man's ear as he squeezes the air out of him; as he pops the pulled, bloodied canines into a new collecting tin.

She drives on, into the light of the day.

Thinks: *I'll see you in Hull.*